# The death of an Irish Lover

# The death of an Irish Lover

*A Peter McGarr Mystery*

BARTHOLOMEW GILL

WILLIAM MORROW
*An Imprint of* HarperCollins*Publishers*

This is a work of fiction. Names, characters, places and incidents either are the product of the author's imagination or are used fictitiously. Any resemblance to actual events, locales, organizations, or persons, living or dead, is entirely coincidental and beyond the intent of either the author or the publisher.

WILLIAM MORROW
An Imprint of HarperCollins*Publishers*
10 East 53rd Street
New York, New York 10022-5299

Copyright © 2000 by Mark McGarrity
Interior design by Kellan Peck
ISBN: 0-380-97797-4

Library of Congress Cataloging in Publication Data:

Gill, Bartholomew, 1943–
The death of an Irish lover: a Peter McGarr mystery / Bartholomew Gill.—
1st ed.
p. cm.
1. McGarr, Peter (Fictitious character)—Fiction. 2. Police—Ireland—Fiction.
3. Ireland—Fiction. I. Title.
PS3563.A296 D434 2000
813'.54—dc21                                                                           99-58663

First William Morrow Printing: April 2000

Printed in the U.S.A.

FIRST EDITION

RRD   10  9  8  7  6  5  4  3  2  1

www.harpercollins.com

# Notes

Leixleap is a composite fictional town
based on several Shannon River communities
in the Midlands of Ireland.

# Part One

1

# Peter McGarr

Pulling his car onto the shoulder of the dual carriageway, McGarr peered down into the valley of the Shannon.

Below him stretched a vista that had remained unchanged at least since Ireland had been cleared of its forests in the seventeenth century—a patchwork of green fields, iridescent under a pale sun and bounded by a web of gray-stone walls.

The pattern stretched in every direction as far as the eye could see, dotted here and there with bright bits of black-and-white cattle that were feeding on the last green grass of the year before being confined to barn or haggard the winter long.

It was fully autumn now, and the smoke of kitchen fires could be seen rising from farmhouse chimneys into the chill air. Down in one low field, a hopeful farmer was disking the land to plant winter wheat in spite of recent snow. A cloud of crows wheeled in the lee of his tractor, diving for the grubs and worms that the bright blades were turning up.

The Shannon itself divided the idyllic scene, as in many ways it did the country, east from west. A wide and sinuous strip of silver, the river had overflowed its banks in places, rushing to the sea. But on a high bluff in a bend of the confluence lay the town that had summoned McGarr. Because of the report of two deaths. "Murdered together in bed," the caller had told him.

Called Leixleap (literally, "Salmon Jump"), it was a collection of no more than three dozen houses around the spires of two churches and a bridge over the river. The ruins of a sixteenth-century castle occupied the highest ground, and there was even the outline of a motte—an ancient earthen fort—from pre-Christian days when the river had been the main thoroughfare of the Irish Midlands.

Lined with narrow vintage dwellings, Leixleap's old main street traced the river with tour and fishing boats tied along a diked wall. There was even a riverside park—courtesy of an EU grant, McGarr would bet—jutting out into the stream. At the bridge, the old cobbled street formed a T with a newer road that was lined with shops that were busy on this, a Saturday.

"It's there you'll find me," the voice had said to McGarr on the phone. "Mine is the biggest, prettiest, and surely the most valuable edifice in town. And it's that that bothers me, Peter."

Sitting in his office in Dublin Castle, where he had been completing paperwork of a quiet Saturday afternoon, McGarr had waited.

Finally, the man had added, "It was done, I'm sure, to finish me. And it will, without your help. You're my only hope."

McGarr had turned in his chair and looked out the grimy window into Dame Street, which was choked with shoppers and traffic, now as Christmas approached. The . . . hubris of the man is what he remembered of Tim Tallon, who had been a schoolyard bully.

Son of a powerful and wealthy judge, he had thumped and punished every smaller boy at the prestigious Christian Brothers Academy in Synge Street. Until he stole from one, who had the courage to tell. And the good brothers had promptly expelled the hulking lad.

That one had been McGarr, a much younger scholarship student who found Tallon waiting for him after school when McGarr set off for his working-class home in Inchicore. Across Dublin the larger boy had gone at McGarr repeatedly, with the fight broken up mercifully by a publican on one corner, a butcher on another.

That man had whispered in McGarr's ear before releasing him, "Now, Red—I'll give you a running start. If you don't think you can get clear, you're to lay for him with something solid. Go for the knees. Then, stay out of reach."

Good advice and well taken. In an alley off Davit Street, McGarr had surprised Tallon with a length of lumber—a low blow to the side of one knee. And then, nipping in with short, sharp punches, he had drubbed the larger, slower boy, until yet another charitable adult had finally intervened. On Tallon's behalf.

At home that evening, McGarr's father—smoking a pipe in his easy chair in their diminutive sitting room—had glanced over his newspaper, taking in McGarr's broken nose and black eyes, his torn and bloody school-uniform jacket and trousers, and finally his bruised and scraped knuckles. "Something to say?" he had asked.

McGarr had not.

"Are you 'right, lad?"

McGarr had nodded.

"And you'll find the money for new gear?" he asked, there being eight others at the time in the family.

Again McGarr had nodded.

"So—is there anything that needs attending?" He meant, at school.

McGarr shook his head.

Regarding him, his father had smiled, which was a sign of approbation from the unassuming good man who very well understood what growing up in Dublin could be like. "Go in to your mother now. Maybe she can patch that nose."

McGarr had neither seen nor heard from Tim Tallon until the phone call now some forty years later. And with what? Only the report of a double murder, if Tallon could be believed.

"Sure, Peter—we've been following you and your career in the papers and on the telly for . . . how long has it been? Decades. And when we found them dead only a minute or two ago after the maid opened the door to make up the room, well then I says to meself, says I, I'll call Peter. He's an old friend and mighty. He'll handle this thing the way it should be handled. Hush-hush, like.

"Tell you true, we've scrimped and scraped, worked and saved to build this business and—Christ—something like this could ruin us surely. You know how things go."

McGarr did indeed, if there were in fact two naked corpses lying in the bed, as Tallon had reported. Chief Superintendent of the Central Detective Unit of the Garda Siochana, the Irish Police, McGarr was the country's chief homicide cop, head of what the newspapers called the "Murder Squad." And there was no way Tallon's wish could be met ultimately; sooner or later tragedy of that sort would have to be made public, with the media making the most of it.

But in the near while, at least, McGarr would see for himself. "And you've told this to nobody else?"

"Nary a soul."

"The local guard."

"The sergeant? Janie, I wouldn't think of it. He's a bastard, that one. A regular town crier, if you know what I mean. He'd have it on every tongue in no time, and only I'd be the loser. It's why I called you, Peter. Tell me you're coming

down, tell me you can keep this quiet. I'm beside myself
with worry."

McGarr said he would be there.

"In, like . . . a patrol car?"

"I'll drive my own, if you prefer." McGarr's modus ope-
randi was to accommodate people whenever he could. Often
their wishes were revealing.

"I'd like that, I would. And no need to park in the street.
Pull right through the arch that joins the buildings—you can't
miss it—and park 'round back. I'll be waiting. When do you
think you'll be getting here?"

"Presently."

Slipping the receiver into its yoke, McGarr decided that
Tim Tallon had changed little from their schoolyard days. No
mention had he made of who had been killed—their names,
their families—only how the deaths would affect him personally. And his pocket.

McGarr reached for his hat.

2

Tim Tallon

Before pulling through the archway, McGarr stopped his car and glanced up. THE LEIXLEAP INN, a large painted sign proclaimed.

It pictured wigged and powdered gentry debouching from a gilded coach before which hounds and footmen milled. Girded by a bib apron and with lackeys in train, the proprietor could be seen approaching the coach, golden brimming flagons in hand.

A fire blazed beyond the open door of the inn, and a long table groaned with provender. In the street a rural idyll was being played out, mainly by handsome swains, busty lasses, and towheaded children. Of course, there was a blacksmith present, shoeing a horse.

That had been the ideal . . . when? Perhaps in the eighteenth century, but more probably never.

And yet the reality at the end of the twentieth was little different, at least in regard to the building, which was really two large gray-stone structures that shared one roofline. They were joined in the middle by an archway. What looked like a pub stood to the left and the inn proper to the right.

With large and rounded Georgian windows and a patterned slate roof in three colors—salmon, teal, and gray—the twin buildings were surely handsome. And each had two fronts, McGarr discovered when he drove through the arch into a wide fan-shaped courtyard that was the car park of the inn.

When first constructed, the complex had faced the river, not the street, and the remains of a formal garden led down to a stone wharf where a rather large speedboat was docked.

Outbuildings, once stables, lined the cobblestone courtyard, which was packed with cars. McGarr parked his Mini Cooper in the last slot remaining and got out.

A short stocky man in his mid-fifties McGarr had a long face and an aquiline nose that was bent to one side. His eyes were gray, and the hair that could be seen tufting from under a twill cap was red and curly.

McGarr's overcoat was twill as well. And with a brown knit tie on a patterned beige dress shirt, neatly pressed brown trousers, and shell cordovan brogues, he looked rather more like a successful countryman than a confirmed Dubliner and the nation's top criminal detective.

Locking the car, he turned toward the building.

"Is that a toy car?" a young voice asked. He had not noticed the girl who was sitting in the sun against a wall. She was pointing to his low-slung and boxy Cooper, which was something of an antique, although well preserved.

Combining a powerful engine with catlike cornering, the hybrid design was perhaps the ideal vehicle for the narrow city laneways and winding country roads of Ireland.

"No more than what you're holding is a toy," he said jocularly. "Where'd you get that? Does your mammy call you on it?"

With both hands the girl was grasping a beeper, as though attempting to divine its secret with a prayer. There was a pause before she looked back up at McGarr, hopefully it seemed. "Do you think she can?"

"Certainly, if arrangements are made."

No more than seven or eight, the girl lowered her tangle of blond curls to the device. "What arrangements? When? Could you do it?"

It was then they heard a door open, and a gruff voice bellowed, "Out! Get out! How many times do I tell you this isn't a play yard. If your father's in the bar, go to him now. If he's not, get yourself home. I'll not have you begging from my guests."

Jumping up, the girl said, "I wasn't begging," and scampered across the cobblestones toward the archway.

"Bloody imp. No mother at home, her father and uncle up in the pub. I suppose you can't expect more from her. But I'll not have her here under foot or tire."

Big as a boy, Tim Tallon had become a large man with a span of shoulders and narrow hips. But he had acquired a sizable paunch, and—both pigeon-toed and bowlegged—his gait seemed less of a stride than a sideways shamble, belly first.

Unlike McGarr, who was nearly bald beneath the cap, Tallon had kept a thick shock of dark hair that was only now graying along the sides, and his face was handsome in a pugged way, apart from a double chin.

McGarr took in the rest of Tallon, as he approached:

Beneath a pricey Barbour fishing jacket, the man was wearing a Prussian blue shirt and puce-colored knit tie. Casually, the top button was left undone. Blue jeans and a pair of leather half-Wellies—polished to a mirror sheen—completed his garb. And in all he looked sportingly stylish and very much the proprietor of the hostelry behind him.

Tallon held out his hand. "Good to see yeh, lad, although we get a glimpse of you from time to time."

With his other hand Tallon also seized McGarr's shoulder.

"They don't make 'em big in Inchicore, do they? Only tough. What's it been like all these years, Peter, kickin' arse and takin' names?"

Which, McGarr supposed, was a rhetorical question, the . . . humor aside. Freeing his hand, McGarr asked, "You mentioned two bodies. Are they about for the viewing?"

Tallon's features glowered. "Of course. A horrible matter. An outrage and a tragedy. They're up over the pub. This way."

Yet the large man turned toward the doorway he had come out of, the one that led up a graceful flight of Georgian stairs to what was obviously the inn, explaining, "Now, Peter—I want you to do me a favor for old time's sake, and indulge me a wee moment, please. You've got to see what I have here, before we go over to them. Just so you know."

In gilded script across the pale blue Georgian door was written, *"Mon vere n'est pas grand, mais je bois dans mon vere,"* or, "My glass is not large, but I drink from my glass."

Before joining the Garda nearly a score of years earlier, McGarr—like so many of his generation—could not find work in Ireland and had been forced to seek employment abroad, first with Criminal Justice in Paris and later for Interpol, mainly in Marseilles. And he was fond of things French. "De Musset, isn't it?" he asked, pointing to the inscription.

"What? Oh, that—it's something Sylvie put up for the all the French and Belgians we get. Makes 'em feel at home. She's one of them herself—Belgian I mean. They're all right, I guess." Tallon lowered his voice. "For frogs."

Opening the door, he led McGarr into a vast and well-proportioned hall filled with furniture. McGarr counted four settees, twelve chairs and a table, two screens and some potted palms. The quality of everything bespoke money, and plenty of it.

Pausing before a pair of rosewood coffered doors, Tallon

slid them open dramatically and swept McGarr into a drawing room that was also overfurnished with heavily draped windows and another mass of velvet chairs. The walls were hanging with as many paintings and pictures as the plaster could support, McGarr judged. The bar, while small, was comprehensively stocked nearly to the tall ceiling.

"Will you take something, Peter?"

McGarr only glanced at Tallon.

Next came two conservatories and a vast and elegant dining room with the very same groaning board that was pictured on the sign out front. But real. And it held every manner of roast meat, fowl and fish, along with other gourmet preparations, Tallon assured McGarr. Three cooks in high hats were attending a good crowd of maybe thirty.

"Transient trade?" McGarr asked to assess the success of Tallon's operation.

"No. Never. We only accept nonguests by reservation at least a week in advance. But, may I say, we have *plenty* of those."

And said with all humility, thought McGarr.

"My head chef studied with Dionne Lucas," Tallon continued, chin now raised. "And I've got the best ghillie on the river. These chaps here"—Tallon spread his arms—"are mainly French and German and from the Low Countries. They're mad for pike. And, of course . . ." He paused briefly. "The eel are running."

McGarr turned to the taller man. "Why?"

"Why what—the eels?"

"Why are you showing me this? Where are the bodies?"

"Like I said on the phone—I'm showing you this, so you'll know."

McGarr studied the man's face, which was, like his own, lined and creased in middle age. Whether from outdoor sport—as Tallon's clothes suggested—or some health problem, the man's color was high. Yet his muddled dark eyes held McGarr's gaze. "So I'll know exactly what?"

"What I have on the table. The ante. What I can lose here."

Curious now, McGarr asked, "Why do you think you'll lose anything at all?"

Tallon's eyes shied, darting toward the tables and back. "You know how people are, Peter—well-off people, people like these who can fly over here and fish for a couple of weeks on a lark. And think nothing of it. The people who can afford this place.

"It was different when Syl and meself started out six years ago. But now? There're scads of other more modern resort hotels with every convenience, not an old refurbished place, like this, in the middle of a cow town. Any hint . . ."

Tallon broke off. Again his eyes surveyed the guests before returning to McGarr's. "You don't know what it's cost me and Syl to do up this place—piped heat, new plumbing, double-glazed windows. The bloody roof?

"The whole thing had to be restructured and the patterned slates cut by hand. It took three effing years! We've got our last farthing wrapped up in this place, every last one. This thing could ruin us altogether, it could."

McGarr had heard pleas for discretion and confidentiality in the past, but seldom before he had actually viewed the corpse and crime scene. He pointed to the door. "Please."

And yet as they climbed a galleried stairwell with a great mounted prize pike at the top, Tallon wore on about how the house had been the fishing retreat of the Dukes of Leinster and how Syl—his wife, McGarr supposed—had come upon it as a ruin, after he had retired from the Tourist Board after twenty-five years, and she had sold the family business in Belgium.

Tallon even stopped twice at bedrooms that maids were

cleaning, "So you can see the details, how Syl has insisted that everything be just so."

Which was overdone, McGarr could see without having to step in. Like the old saw about nature, the Tallons appeared to abhor vacant space. Even the archway joining the two buildings was filled with furniture, paintings, a bronze of Pan. Or was it a gelded Bacchus sans horns? Other accoutrements of what McGarr thought of disparagingly as "gracious living" were sprinkled about with the abandon of a television program about privileged domesticity.

Tallon had to use keys to open the two stout doors at either end of the archway. And once into the pub side of the double buildings, the questionable elegance ceased.

3

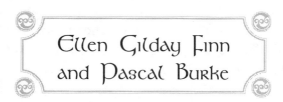

# Ellen Gilday Finn
# and Pascal Burke

The quarters in the pub half of the double-sided building seemed almost Spartan in contrast.

There were no tables, no paintings, not even a framed print on the walls. Only three chairs positioned between the four rooms that lay on either side of the hall. Tall, straight-backed, and mute, they stood resolute, rather like a ghostly jury, McGarr imagined.

Tallon stopped before room 5 and fanned through the ring of keys that was attached to his belt by a snap cord. "These rooms are taken on a B&B basis by commercial travelers, lorry drivers, and anglers who either can't afford the inn or aren't interested in much more than the sport and the pub. It's right below us.

"At night, the chatter and noise come straight up through the floor, which is why, I suppose"—he twisted a key in the lock and pushed open the door—"nobody heard it. Or if they did, no thought was given to the possibility." He stood back and let McGarr enter first.

The bed, which stood rather like an island between two

windows in the center of the room, was high with a tall foot-board. McGarr had to walk around to get a clear view.

There, with a sheet half over them, lay a naked man and woman, she on top of him, her head on his chest, her right hand still clasped in his left. A bullet—something powerful, like a 9mm—had been fired through her temple. And . . .

McGarr moved closer to examine the man. Blood had flowed down the side of his large chest and pooled in the depression that the weight of their bodies made in the mattress. And . . . the bullet had passed into his chest, McGarr speculated, since there appeared to be no visible mark on him and her head was directly over his heart.

She was a young woman. A natural blond. Diminutive, with a pixyish look made all the more apparent by a rather short if stylishly feminine cut to her hair and eyes that were startlingly blue, even in death.

Like some blonds, her skin appeared smooth and translu-cent. But it was also evident that she had either trained regu-larly or taken part in some vigorous sport. Her back was taut and well muscled.

The wound was clean, dark, and the size of a 10 P coin, any blood having flowed in the direction of the bullet. And with her mouth slightly open in what looked almost like the first movement of a smile, the expression on her dead face was jarring. It seemed almost . . . ecstatic.

Scarcely twenty-five, McGarr guessed. There was a tattoo of a butterfly at the base of her spine. She was wearing a cheap electronic watch with a plastic band and simple gold earrings to match the wedding band on her ring finger. And her nails had been enameled the light blue color of her eyes.

McGarr studied the man.

Who looked to be twice her age. Fifty, say, but sturdily constructed. Hirsute to say the least, he had a great mass of steely gray hair on his head, face, chest, and even his arms. A farmer's tan gave him a rather Latin look. With dark eyes and large even teeth, he had been a handsome older man.

Who, like she, had been caught so unawares by their murderer that his only concession to death appeared to be the slackness of his jaw. McGarr reached down and drew the sheet off them.

Even his legs—which were between hers—were crossed at the ankles, as though to suggest that the activity that they had been engaged in had been leisurely, at least for him. Or that it had been her duty or opportunity to . . . entertain him, given her position, straddling him.

He was wearing a condom, and his penis—hugely engorged in death—lolled between their thighs.

"Husband and wife?" McGarr asked.

Tallon piped scorn for the possibility. "No chance. Look at them. He could have been her grandfather. And maybe he was, for all we know."

When he chuckled, McGarr turned his head to him.

Tallon raised a hand. "Please don't take that wrong, Peter. It's just that he was obviously as guilty as she in that." He jabbed a finger at the corpses. "And don't I know her poor husband, who's a local lad. She'd been making a cuckold of him with this man, off but mainly on—if you know what I mean—for nine months now.

"And can I let you in on another little secret?"

McGarr only continued to regard Tallon, who seemed suddenly animated. On his curious legs, the tall man moved to the closet and with a finger pushed wide the closet door that had been open a crack. "They were two of your own."

He turned to McGarr, his eyes glittering, a thin smile on his lips.

There hung neatly on hangers were two groups of clothes, one obviously male and the other female: uniform outdoor jackets in two different colors, durable shirts and weather-resistant trousers, a pair of half-rubberized ankle boots for him and full farmer's Wellies for her. Their undergarments were neatly folded on an upper shelf.

What struck McGarr was the order of everything, as though these two had not thrown off their vestments and made urgent—could it have been?—love. No. They had calmly, dispassionately arranged their clothes before climbing into bed together. Young fetching woman and late middle-aged man.

Why? Because . . . they had done so before, he supposed. There was not even a bottle of wine or a bit of whiskey in sight to loosen inhibitions or provide relief in case the congruence proved uncomfortable. What they had been having here had been arranged and pursued with method. "Two of my own in what regard?"

"Why, in regard to your occupation," Tallon announced with near glee. With the tips of his fingers, he pulled back the placket of the woman's jacket to reveal, first, what looked like an official police photo ID that had been clipped to an inner pocket.

"Eel police," Tallon explained.

"I beg your pardon."

"The Guards—your Guards—who're assigned to catch poachers on the river. The ones that are snatching up all the eels. There's big money in that."

McGarr had heard or read of the operation, which was teamed with the Shannon River Fisheries Board. But even though the enforcement officers could issue arrest warrants and were allowed to carry guns to defend themselves from the thugs that the highly profitable activity attracted, they were employees of the Fisheries Board, not the Garda Siochana. And yet they were, after a fashion, cops. Dead cops.

McGarr glanced over at the pair, who were still locked in an embrace. "Names?"

"His is Burke, Pascal Burke. He was in charge of the eel-policing operation and had just returned from Dublin, where he lived, after a fortnight up there. It was how he worked, two weeks up there, two down here.

"She's Ellen Finn, who would come down on his first day back and give him the big welcome that you see there."

Tallon paused to shake his head. "Whoever shot them must have used Burke's shooter, which is missing. Or, at least, it's not in his holster." He opened the larger jacket to reveal the holster hanging there. It was empty. "But hers is still where it should be."

Tallon opened the smaller foul-weather jacket; a kidney holster had been strapped over a hanger in a way that could support the weight of a 9mm weapon. From it protruded the distinctive butt grip of a Glock.

"You looked for it," McGarr said. "You went through their clothes. And her purse." He pointed to the large leather handbag that lay on the carpet between the closet and the bed, much of its contents spilled out.

"Me? No, Peter, this mess here is not me. It's how I found the place, with the door of the closet nearly closed. I figure this—whoever murdered them managed to slip into the room or was here before they arrived, and while they were busy doing whatever, got hold of his gun there in the closet and moved to the bed without being heard. Then, the bastard whacked the both of them. Bingo. One shot through her head and into his heart."

There was a kind of awe in that.

"And, mind, Peter—I'm not trying to do your job for you. It's just—"

"But you went into her purse." McGarr's voice did not rise up in question but rather fell, as though affirming a fact. He nodded before adding, "You searched the room for her weapon?"

"No, Janie—I wouldn't think of it. It's just that I knew she carried a gun and was good with it. Didn't she shoot out the tires of a poacher's van recently and run them in. It was in all the papers.

"But I swear, Peter, as God is my judge, I only glanced into the thing and said to Syl, there's no way it could be in there. Ask her, she'll tell you.

"In fact, the first glimpse I got of them I thought of you. Call Peter, says I to meself. He's an old friend, he'll know what to do, how to go about this quietly. Isn't he the chief of the murder cops? The best. Hasn't he made a career out of this class of thing? He'll know how to keep the lid on.

"Syl agreed. 'Call Peter,' she insisted, 'he's known you all your life, he'll be discreet.' "

"Where is she now?"

"Who?"

"Your wife."

"Resting. This thing has done her in, so it has."

"Could you get her?"

There was a pause. "I think I could. Why?"

"Was it she who discovered them?"

"No, the maid did."

"Then, I'd like to see her, too."

"I'm afraid she's gone home. This whole thing—"

"Well then . . . ?" McGarr's hand came up with the fingers splayed, as though to suggest that could Tallon not provide him with the maid, then he was powerless to keep . . . what was the phrase? The lid on. "It's your choice."

"Of course. I'll get you the both of them. It might take some doing with the maid. But my wife will be here immediately."

When Tallon left the room, McGarr did two things: He used the cell phone in his jacket pocket to contact his office. Reporting the double murder he requested a medical examiner to certify the deaths, a team from the Technical Squad to go over the room and seal any evidence, and an ambulance to transport the corpses to Dublin for postmortem exams.

In no way would McGarr compromise his office where a double murder of two law officers was concerned, "old friend" or not. And Tallon's fixation with publicizing the matter, which was inevitable, rather interested him.

If most of Tallon's guests in the inn half of the hostelry were foreign fishermen or even Irish fishermen, how much would the report of any crime that happened over the pub, which was physically—and seemed to be treated by Tallon— as a separate operation, matter to them? McGarr himself was a longtime fisherman, and what concerned him was the availability of fish, a good meal, and a better bed at day's end.

"Connect me to the Leixleap barracks, please." When the sergeant answered, McGarr asked him to come to the room. "I need your help."

"Can I ask what it's about, Chief Superintendent?"

"How soon can you get here?"

"In a wink. The inn is just around the corner."

"I'll be expecting you." McGarr rang off.

Moving out into the hall, McGarr carried two of the chairs from the hall into the room and placed them together at the side of the bed.

# 4

# Sylvie Zeebruge

"Know them?" McGarr asked the Garda sergeant when he arrived. An older man with a scrupulously shaven face and a neat blue Garda uniform, Declan Riley looked more like a bank guard than the commander of the local barracks. He nodded.

"Well?"

From the hall they heard a door open.

Riley dipped his head to one side to mean "quite well"; his face was grave, his eyes somber. "Pascal Burke is his name. Another sergeant, like meself, and her boss." He shook his head, plainly disturbed at what he was seeing.

"A bachelor Burke was. And very much the Dubliner." Riley's eyes rose to McGarr, who was another. "That's to say—"

McGarr waved Riley off, knowing what he meant: city man among country folk.

"He always seemed to have the readies to splash around," Riley continued. "Drank. And ate well, usually across the way on the other side of the inn. Stayed here though, because—I'd hazard—it was easier to come and go than a room there or in somebody's house." Like a B&B.

"He had the reputation of being a . . . swordsman, if you know what I mean. Come down from town once a fortnight on an 'inspection tour,' like. To visit the three other fisheries police, get their reports, look things over.

"Widows, spinsters, married women. He preferred them, he once told me over a pint, since any little problem that arose would be cared for in her house, not his.

"This, though"—Riley raised his prominent chin, as though pointing to the bed—"is . . . *was* an outrage, with him the boss and her not even half his age and coming from one of the best families in the county. They'll be devastated. Destroyed." He shook his head. "They'll never get over it, to say nothing of her young husband."

"Name?"

"Ellen Gilday. Or at least it was Gilday up until last year when she married Quintan Finn, a fine local lad." Riley closed his eyes and let some breath pass between his lips, before glancing at McGarr. "I wonder if there's any way we could keep this part of it quiet? The way they are now?"

This second call for confidentiality rather surprised McGarr, coming from a man that Tallon had characterized as the town crier. He waited. Riley had more to say.

"This is a small town, a village. But a good place to live. And Tallon—gobshite that he is—runs a fine inn and pub here, even if it's on his wife's back.

"She had the money and . . . you know, the Continental touch. And it's her who makes it work while he plays at—what?—public relations, I think you'd call it.

"The 'Laird,' the locals call him, adding 'arse' behind a hand. Sure, it's part jealousy. Look what he's got. But it's how he carries himself that's off-putting, always playing the backslapping hail-fellow with the rousing laugh to a fault.

Goes fishing and shooting with the guests, stands the odd round of drinks, remembers names and sends greeting cards at Christmas with no more meaning to them than the cash in his till.

"That said, what Tallon and the wife have done with this building that was a near ruin when they bought it, has spilled out into the town. Any number of shops—fishing gear, gifts, the garage, the chemist—have bumped up their trade. And it's a steady increase with the same faces coming back year after year with new people in tow.

"Which makes this . . ."—Riley's hand flicked out at the bed—"even more of an enormity than it appears. For everybody."

They could hear footsteps approaching the door.

McGarr lowered his voice. "I want you to listen closely to everything that's said. Later, we'll talk."

The door opened, and Tallon appeared; there was a woman behind him, who looked as though she had been crying.

"What's this?" Indignant, with brow furrowed, Tallon pointed at Riley. "Why's he here? I thought we were going to keep this matter under wraps?"

Tired of Tallon's carry-on, McGarr pulled back the first of the two tall chairs that he had placed near the bed. "Close the door, and sit down."

"Well—I object. You and I were agreed. We had a definite understanding that you'd—"

"Look," McGarr cut in, "the only understanding that can be allowed in this room is that we have two dead people—officers of the law—who were murdered, and you either help us here or down at the barracks."

"Then it's plain you don't care about us, Peter." Tallon wagged his head, his face suddenly a tragic mask. "Nor this village. You're going to let this . . . thing"—he flourished a hand at the bed—"what we had nothing to do with, what was done by some outsiders, ruin our lives.

"Peter, I implore you. I beseech you. Don't let it happen!"

There was a histrionic element to Tallon's personality that was both curious and distressing and McGarr tried to remember if he'd always been that way. But the truth was—McGarr had had as little to do with Tallon as possible, and that little had been ugly.

"Peter, I appeal to you. Weren't we children together? Word of a thing like this"—again the hand gestured at the bed, as though trying to erase it—"why, we might lose the entire season.

"Declan," Tallon turned to the sergeant, "you tell him."

"I'll not tell him a thing," Riley said in a low voice. "I'll tell you, Tallon—sit your arse down and shut your bloody gob."

"What did I tell you, Peter? The man has it in for me."

McGarr was surprised by his own hand. As though in reflex, it shot out and seized Tallon by the arm, digging into the pressure point just above the elbow.

Tallon yelped, as McGarr walked him to the door.

"Christ—me arm!"

McGarr shoved him out the door.

"It's ruined altogether. I'm ringing up my solicitor this minute. I'm not without friends, you know. My father—"

McGarr shut the door, and the woman took a chair.

At the bed McGarr turned the second chair so that it was facing her.

"May I have your full name."

"Sylvie . . . Tallon, I call myself. Though"—her dark eyes, swollen from crying, flickered up at McGarr—"we were never married. Formally. My last name is Zeebruge." Late thirties maybe early forties, she was a pretty woman with wavy dark

hair, high cheekbones and a wide mouth. Large even teeth
made her lips look protrusive and pouty.

"How long have you been a couple?"

"Six years, ever since we bought this place."

"Why are you crying? Did you know these people?"

Her brimming eyes flashed up at him. "Why do you think?
Because I'm not an animal. Because they were two human
beings."

"You knew them?"

She nodded. "Him. Pascal."

"How did you know him?"

"He stayed here often."

"How often?"

Her face was now running with tears, and she had to pause
to blow her nose. "Once a month, since we opened. He was,
like you. A chief of police."

"What about the woman?"

She shrugged. "Of course, I knew her too. She's"—there
was a pause; she shook her head—"from town."

"Did they use this room, like we see them here, often?"

"Perhaps. I don't know. He always asked for this room.
We don't pry. What he did, he did."

"How long would he stay?"

There was another shrug and a sigh. She was a rangy
woman with square shoulders that a thin shiftlike garment
made all the more obvious. But it was equally apparent that,
although not portly, she had chosen the costume to conceal
her torso. Some tufts of hair had escaped from the dark bun
at the back of her head.

"At least three days. Sometimes a week, depending." There
was another shrug and a sigh.

"Depending on what?"

Her doleful eyes again met McGarr's. "Oh—many things.
He'd come for a holiday. For . . . women." She wrenched her

eyes away. "But usually it was the fish. The eels. Who was poaching them. Who was stealing from the licensed fishermen and the fishery, he would say. The IRA. Pascal would investigate those things."

McGarr remembered a police report that he had scanned maybe a year earlier. It said that former IRA toughs from the North, attracted by the huge prices that Shannon River eels could command, had tried to muscle in on the industry.

They had roughed up legitimate fishermen and stolen their catches, then demanded protection money from others. Even poaching, which required some actual work, was not beyond them, but only when the eels were running strong.

"You knew Mr. Burke well."

She only stared at McGarr in a way that he interpreted as an acknowledgment.

"How do you think this happened?"

Her eyes closed, and her nostrils flared, as though trying to fight back tears.

"Who did this?" McGarr encouraged.

"Are you going to do as Tim asked?"

"I'm no fan of the press, but you must understand—I have to ask questions."

Her eyes opened; she nodded. "The thugs, the IRA."

"Why do you say that?"

"They're bastards, gangsters. They'll do anything for easy money. You must know so yourself."

He knew that some former regular IRA—having abandoned their ideals and with no trade or occupation beyond the cudgel and the gun—had turned to crime. Gangsterism. Because they understood organization. "Anybody in mind?"

"Manus Frakes. And his brother, Donal."

McGarr turned his head to the sergeant, who nodded; he knew them.

"They stay here?"

"They have, but not now."

"How could somebody have entered this room and done this without you or your husband having known?"

"I was busy over in the inn with our fishing guests, I have my hands filled there. I never come here."

"What about your husband? Where does he work? What are his duties?"

She only shrugged. "You'll have to ask him."

McGarr remembered Tallon having to unlock the door into the archway from the inn and then unlock the second door into the B&B quarters. "Is there free passage up onto this floor?"

She shook her head. "The doorway to the stairs is in the bar. It's locked. A guest either has to use his passkey, or the barman can buzz it open."

McGarr pointed at the bed. "Was this woman registered with this man in this room?"

She shook her head. "No. I checked. You know, after—"

"Did you know she was up here?"

"No. But even if I did, I wouldn't have suspected that." With her chin she gestured toward the bed. "Ellen was newly married, and they were colleagues. Why shouldn't she come here? Perhaps they had something to discuss." A tear gathered on her high cheekbone before tracking down her face. "But . . . this. I never suspected."

"Was it usual for Mr. Burke to have guests in his room?"

"I don't know. I have the inn to mind and those guests. Tim"—she shrugged, saying the name—"is supposed to look after the bar and these quarters. And Benny."

"Who?"

"The head bartender. Benny Carson."

"He was on duty last night?"

She nodded. "He works the weekends. Always."

Again McGarr moved a hand toward the bed. "Who found them? Yourself?"

"No, the maid."

"And she came to you."

She had to pause and blow her nose. "Yes, of course."

"And not your husband."

Her head swirled, as though such a suggestion was absurd. "He was . . . out. Fishing, perhaps. Again, you'll have to ask him."

They could hear him now, roaring something that included the word "outrage"

McGarr stood. "So, I will."

# 5

# GRACE O'ROURKE

Out in the hall, McGarr pointed at Tallon, who had some other man standing with him. "You. Go with Sergeant Riley to the barracks. He'll take your statement."

"My *statement!* About what?" Tallon complained. "I can't be seen walking in the street with—"

The other man opened his mouth to say something, but McGarr cut him off. "And go out that way." He pointed to the door that opened in the archway that led into the inn. "This floor is now a police zone. And if I find either of you in it, you'll be charged with hindering an investigation."

But even after McGarr drew the maid into the room and closed the door, they could hear Tallon and his solicitor in the hall.

"May I have your name, please?"

"Grace O'Rourke."

She was a tall but slight woman in her early thirties, dressed in a light blue maid's uniform with dark blue piping, colors that matched the walls and trim in the hall.

"You discovered them?"

She nodded. "I'd finished doing the other rooms apart

from the one across the hall, of course—they're changing the carpet in there—and I knocked. When nobody answered, I tried the door." She took a key from her uniform pocket; it was yoked to a hotel-style tag.

"It was locked, so I used this to see if theirs was still in the door. It wasn't. So, I opened the door. And . . . there was Ellen. On top of him." She closed her eyes and turned her head away.

"You knew her."

Trembling now, she pulled in a bit of air to signify that she did.

"Well?"

"Didn't we go to school together? Her mother lives just up the lane from us."

McGarr waited, taking in her long plain face and lank hair. No rings on her fingers, no care taken with her appearance. The small towns of Ireland were home to many young women such as she, with no prospects or even hope of any. Unlike the woman on the bed, who had been a belle.

"Never would I have expected this of her," she continued, her hazel eyes swinging to McGarr. "Sure now, the boys were mad for Ellen at one time, and who could blame them. She was a catch, and Quintan Finn, her husband, was—is—the best." There was a pause, and she seemed to blush.

"But, you know, she wasn't said—ever—to be the easy sort that you'd expect this of, God rest her soul." She sighed. "But you just never know who people are, do you?"

"Work here long?"

"Since Madame Sylvie opened."

No Tallon in that. "How long ago?"

"Six years now."

"Did Mr. Burke have many women visitors?"

She closed her eyes and again drew in some air in affirmation. "Not that he made a show of it. Usually they'd be out

of the room before I began my work. But there'd be times
that a woman would tarry too long, and I'd see the back of
her fleeing down the stairs. And, of course, there was the evidence in the room."

"Of what sort?"

Grace O'Rourke blushed and turned her head away. "The
usual sort—the sheets, the bed. Condom wrappers. The . . .
odor."

"Names? Did you know any of these women?"

"I tried not to look. Sure"—she whipped her head back
at McGarr, suddenly exercised—"it wasn't any of my business,
was it? He paid the rate for the room, didn't he? He could
do whatever he wanted in here, once the door was closed."

"Let me ask you again—did you know any of the other
women or men who visited Mr. Burke in this room?"

She folded her arms across her chest. "No."

Plainly, she did. "You're sure."

"Yes, I'm sure."

McGarr let a few seconds pass. Through a window he
could see the Shannon; a sizable white boat—one of those that
could be rented and operated by tourists without a captain—
was struggling against the current as it motored north. Several
skiffs of fishermen had anchored by the bridge. "I want you
to look at those two people. At the wound in her temple."

"I can see them."

"No—look at them directly."

"I will not."

"Shouldn't whoever murdered them be caught and
punished?"

"Of course."

"Then—I want you to think about what I just asked and
ring me up at this number when you're ready to say more."
From his billfold McGarr removed a card and handed it to
her.

"Are you through with me?"

McGarr nodded. "I'll be expecting you to do the right thing."

Once the door closed, McGarr again took out his cell phone and rang up his wife, Noreen, telling her the general details of what happened and advising her that he wouldn't be home for at least a few days.

"Well, then—why don't we come down and join you? It *is* the weekend, after all, and we haven't had a decent getaway in the country for . . . for longer than I can remember."

McGarr glanced out the window that looked into the street, hoping he could get down to the bar and interview the personnel there before the tech squad and ambulance arrived. "Could I be mistaken, or didn't we just visit your parents?" Who owned what amounted to an estate and horse farm south of Dublin.

"Ah, but that's different. We know Dunlavin, yet I don't believe I've ever been to Leixleap. And surely Maddie hasn't." She was their ten-year-old daughter. "We'll need directions. Hold on, so—I'll get something to write on."

McGarr smiled and shook his head, knowing that a few days in another part of the country was not the cause of her eagerness but the fact that he was on a case important enough to take him away from home for some time.

Although they had been married now for over a dozen years, Noreen never tired of hearing and speculating about the details of his investigations. Such that he sometimes wondered if she had married him for himself as a person or because he was the country's top homicide cop.

"We'll be there in a jiff," she said, after he had given her directions. "Is it a cow town? Or would there be someplace nice to stay thereabouts?"

"I'll make the arrangements," McGarr said, resignedly.

"There's a good man. Ta."

After ringing off, McGarr surveyed the bodies one final time and conducted a cursory search of the room, careful to keep his contact with the objects to a minimum.

He noted, however, that while the contents of the woman's purse had been rifled and her service weapon was still in the holster under her uniform jacket, her service-issued beeper—which all field personnel carried—was nowhere to be found.

Whereas, Burke's beeper was firmly affixed to the belt of his trousers. His billfold was fat, stuffed with a sheaf of twenty new hundred-pound notes wrapped with a belly band and nearly another hundred quid in smaller denominations.

Otherwise, the contents were unremarkable—some dog-eared business cards from Shannon area fishing and tackle shops, marinas, boat-rental liveries, and a Dublin *24-Hour Adult Services* agency. He slipped them into his overcoat pocket, along with Burke's small leather telephone directory.

Pockets: a ring of keys, a packet of unopened cigarettes, some small change, and a nautical knife with a marlinspike to loosen uncooperative knots. Handy for somebody often in boats, McGarr supposed.

The woman's uniform also yielded little in the way of a lead: a tube of protective ointment for her lips, dental floss for her large even teeth, some tissues, and a biro.

Money was also visible in the woman's open purse on the carpet. A clump of notes of various denominations was protruding from a pouch within. McGarr squatted and, picking up the purse from the bottom, shook out the rest of the contents.

Among the clutter—compact, hairbrush, breath mints, a tin of acetaminophen, more tissues along with a packet of Thunderbolt condoms that pictured a golden lightning bolt piercing a suggestively shaped cloud mass. It was unopened.

There was a telephone directory and envelope that contained a number of photos that looked to have been taken from afar with a long lens at night. Both the light and the depth of field were minimal.

All pictured sometimes four—in other shots six—men working between a boat and a van that was parked on the riverbank. Only in two of the twenty-four was the face of the one man, who was in all of the photographs, fully visible.

He was dark and so hirsute that his cheeks, which he'd shaved, seemed almost blue.

McGarr put the photos in his pocket as well, along with her phone directory.

Back beside the bed, he studied the two victims again. They had been caught, like that, when they had to have been least aware of what was going on around them—she on top of him, her face against his chest, his head thrown back on the pillows.

How could the murderer have come through the door to the hall, which the couple—who had planned to have sex, as the neatly hung clothes implied—would surely have locked? How could he then have advanced on the bed without being seen or heard, and then held the gun so close to her temple that the skin around the entrance wound was thoroughly burnt from the muzzle blast?

And not have been heard? Or at least the report had not been so unusual that it had been brought to the attention of the Tallons.

Perhaps the murderer was already in the room before they arrived. Where would he have concealed himself in the sparsely furnished quarters?

Not in the closet where they'd hung their clothes. Under the bed? No, not there either, McGarr judged, when—back at the door, as though entering—he scanned the room. The bed, which was the only large piece of furniture, was so tall that he could see right under. And the light switch was right there by the door. He flicked it on. The bulbs in the globe on the ceiling were strong.

The toilet? The door was half-open, and McGarr left it like that, squeezing in to look around.

No tub, just a shower in a corner with three translucent glass panels, the commode, a medicine cabinet, and a bidet. Could the murderer have concealed himself in the shower such that the victims would not have seen him if, say, they had entered to use the facility?

McGarr couldn't tell without having another person get in, and he wouldn't touch anything until the tech squad went over the place. But, he supposed, it could be possible, if the party who came into the small room had been distracted and had not looked directly at the shower. And the lights had been low. The fixture on the ceiling was controlled by a dimmer, which had been turned down to a glow.

And what was he smelling? A toilet cleaner—pine-scented and rather strong. Yet the maid had said she only opened the door before rushing for the proprietress. How long would the smell of a disinfectant last in a small room such as this? A full day? McGarr didn't know, but it seemed unlikely.

The old octagon-pattern tiles on the floor near the toilet had a single prominent chip out of the surface that was somewhat whiter and looked fresh.

Stepping back into the room, McGarr realized that he had not seen a room key with a hotel-like tag, like the one that Grace O'Rourke had shown him. Another quick search failed to turn one up. Their commingled blood had soaked through the thick mattress so thoroughly that it was now dripping on the carpet beneath the bed.

Time. He glanced at his watch, wanting to get down to the bar and speak with Benny Carson, the head barman, before the others from Dublin arrived. Also, there was the register of other guests to go over. And he should make arrangements to stay in the inn.

Closing the door, he went over what he knew for sure so far: that Ellen Gilday Finn and Pascal Burke, two Garda fisheries officers with what was known as the "eel police," had been murdered. Somebody had either already been in the room before they arrived or had been able to approach them unawares while they had been locked together.

One shot to her temple had passed through her head, it appeared, and then penetrated his chest in the area of the heart. His handgun—which, McGarr supposed, was the same as her standard-issue Glock 9 mm—was missing. As was her beeper.

The murderer might have concealed himself in the stall of the *en suite* shower, where there was the odor of disinfectant, as though it had recently been cleaned. After the crime, the murderer had locked the door and taken the key with him, McGarr could only assume at this point.

Tim Tallon—McGarr's erstwhile nemesis and avowed (by Tallon) "boyhood chum" who owned with his common-law wife, Sylvie, the large and seemingly successful fishing resort, inn and pub—had tried to control McGarr's investigation from Tallon's initial phone call, reporting the double murder to McGarr's subsequent interview with the couple.

Tallon's main concern, he had told McGarr time and again, was to limit or even squelch any public report of what had occurred. Which was understandable from Tallon's perspective, but highly unrealistic.

Sylvie Zeebruge, on the other hand, seemed much more disturbed by the actual deaths of the couple in the bed. And her relations with Tallon appeared to be strained.

Without question the maid, Grace O'Rourke, knew more than she was saying about what other women Burke had bedded.

McGarr opened the door into the archway corridor that linked pub and inn, and—looking out the tall windows into the street in one direction and the courtyard in the other—he remembered having encountered the little curly-headed blond girl in the car park. She had been holding a beeper.

At the desk in the inn, McGarr asked the receptionist who the girl might be and where he could find her.

"Your guess is as good as mine," the older woman replied; she was using a scissors to clip coupons from a newspaper. "Her father and uncle drink in the bar—blow-ins from the North."

"Fishermen?" McGarr asked.

"And anything else with the promise of readies."

"Like the eels?"

She smirked. "It's said, but not by me." The woman stopped a passing waiter and ordered him to take the platter of petit fours he was delivering back to the kitchen. "Those are stale. Tell Kurt I said Madame Sylvie wants them fresh."

"Do they have a name?"

"Who?"

"The people from the North. The men in the bar, the girl in the courtyard."

"Frakes. What else can I do for you?"

McGarr arranged for accommodations for himself and his wife and child.

"You're the policeman?" the woman asked.

McGarr only nodded and signed the credit slip.

"Is it business or pleasure that brings you to Leixleap?"

"Fair day, in spite of the prediction," he said, turning toward the door to the courtyard.

"Not for long."

# 6

# Benny Carson

McGarr saw she was right, the moment he stepped outside.

Granted the day was now declining, but what he thought of as the hard shyness of Atlantic light had cast a kind of foreboding gloom over the riverscape. Usually the strange light—which he had seen only a half dozen times in his life and almost always while fishing—was caused by clouds racing in from the Gulf Stream.

Lighting a cigarette, McGarr glanced up. A leaden sky, frayed here and there with patches of brilliant luminescence, was sweeping to the east. And the pall it was casting had prompted one fisherman out on the river to weigh anchor and stroke toward shore; another was trying to start his outboard engine, as his skiff drifted south on dark, swift water. It would storm soon.

From the edge of the courtyard where the formal garden began, McGarr could see into the town—a housewife scurrying to fold her wash into a brimming basket; a shopkeeper stepping out of his door to carry a sandwich board inside, while his children—McGarr assumed—rushed out onto the footpath to pull in the goods that the shop had been offering passersby.

The little girl with the beeper, however, was nowhere in sight.

And yet for all its gloom and drama—what his wife, Noreen, called *momentous, immemorial light,* "the light of history and allegory"—the strange luminescence made the edges of things hard and sear.

Like the cobblestones under his feet, the foot-worn limestone steps that led up to the pub entrance, the old figured horse trough that now functioned as a litter bin in which McGarr stubbed out his cigarette, his "break" over.

Glancing up once again, McGarr hoped the dun light presaged nothing but a coming storm, history and allegory being two bogs difficult to traverse in a country that forgot little and forgave less.

He reached for the brass handle of the wide Georgian door that led into the pub. Like the door of the inn, it had an advisement in gilded scroll:

> *What harm in drinking can there be,*
> *Since punch and life so well agree?*

McGarr had no idea who said that. But surely for a publican it was an efficacious thought to put in the minds of patrons stepping into a bar. Which was proved beyond a doubt when McGarr pushed open the door.

A fug of hot air, smoke, talk, the mixed aromas of porter, hot whiskey, and mulled wine, and even music struck him. He stepped in.

Perhaps it was the impending storm. Or the fact that a warm pub of an early-winter Saturday afternoon in a small country town often drew a crowd. It was market day, and there would be little to do back on a farm. And didn't *punch and life so well agree?*

In the hearth a turf fire was glowing, and from some other room McGarr could hear a fiddle and tin whistle weaving a sprightly duet.

Nobody—the barmen in particular—seemed to take much notice of a middle-aged man in a twill cap and overcoat, stranger or no, and McGarr imagined that it was not unusual for guests from the inn next door to frequent the pub. Especially when a storm was threatening and fishing was over for the day.

In fact, he now heard French being spoken in one corner, and German at the end of the bar. But no word of murder in English as he listened, which would have been on every local tongue, had the news been spread.

At length he was asked, "What are you having?"

McGarr ordered a whiskey, and when it was delivered by a young barman, he asked, "Are you Benny Carson?"

Which brought a quick, sharp laugh from the young man. Like the other staff in the pub, he was wearing a light blue vest and white wing collar, as though Tallon drew no distinction between the level of service provided his local trade and the international guests on the tonier side of the building. "Another insult, like that, and—senior citizen or no—I'll chuck you out."

Those nearby laughed.

"He's here," McGarr insisted.

"Oh aye—he's the broth of a boy holding forth at the end of the bar." He pointed to a small thin older barman whom McGarr had noticed while waiting for his drink. Cigarette in one hand, glass in the other, Carson had been regaling the entire end of the large bar with jokes and banter, a peal of laughter going up now and again from the crowd gathered there.

Hawk-nosed with prominent cheekbones and sunken eyes, Carson's face was a sallow, liverish color that suggested too much drink or too many cigarettes or too little sleep and less good food. Or all of that. Yet his eyes were clear, and McGarr had known more than a few people—his own father one—who had lived to rare old age without a thought for their health.

Plainly, Carson was less the barman than host and raconteur; McGarr had seen him pour only one drink—his own—while the younger staff carefully milled around him, serving the throng.

And there was something familiar about Benny Carson. McGarr had seen his face or heard his name before, he was convinced, the closer he drew near. The man had a definite northern accent, with his voice running up in question at the end of a sentence. Down, he had pronounced, "dine"; around was "arind."

". . . sure, you heard of the young duffer who was out on the links, and didn't he hit a mighty shot so deep it sailed into the wood," Carson was saying. Like a seasoned performer, he paused to draw on his cigarette.

Yet proprietorially he was also scanning the rest of the bar and the pub, the staff, and the cash drawer. His eyes now fell upon McGarr, who was pushing through the crowd.

"And searching for the ball he found it had nailed"—Carson thumped his forehead with a finger—"the pate of a little creature. A pukka. Who, when he came to, said, 'So, you caught me fair and square, and what, pray tell, are your three wishes.' "

" 'Ah, go 'way,' says the young duffer, 'I'm nary a superstitious man nor one who could accept gifts from the little people. I'm only sorry to have troubled you, and I wish you and yours the very best of the day.' With that the duffer departed."

Now McGarr was standing directly in front of Carson, whose eyes shied from his gaze in a way that said he, at least, had placed McGarr. If not vice versa.

Sipping from his glass, Carson continued, "Said the pukka to himself, says he, 'A thoroughly decent chap, that young duffer, and, like it or not, I must do something for him. I'll give him what all young fellas need and want—a first-class golf game, money galore, and a vibrant sex life.' "

Some of the bar crowd now began chuckling.

But Carson glanced up at McGarr, "Help you?"

"I need a room."

"Ach—you'll have to come back. Can't you see I've got me hands filled?" He raised the cigarette and then the glass.

Which broke up the bar crowd, who were prepared to laugh. Some howled, others slapped the bar.

Said a woman standing next to McGarr, "Don't take it personally. Benny's a gas character altogether. He's just pokin' a bit of fun."

McGarr smiled as well, having no option, but he also presented Carson his Garda calling card.

Dousing his cigarette in the water of a sink, Carson shot the butt behind his back and it landed perfectly in a bin a yard or two distant, which was met with more approval from the crowd.

Accepting McGarr's card with his free hand, the older man glanced down at it and then up at McGarr, his smile suddenly brittle. And yet he continued with his story.

"So, a year goes by, and the young duffer is back out on the same course. And doesn't a long drive skip off a rock in the middle of the fairway and bounce into the very same wood.

"And there, when he goes to look for it"—Carson slipped the card into a slit pocket of his light blue vest, then reached below the bar and produced what looked like a leather-bound guest register—"who's there but the pukka?"

Carson placed the book on the bar and added a pen from his shirt pocket.

" 'Now, me young fella, tell me—how's t'ings,' said the Pukka. 'Grand actually,' replied the young man. 'Brilliant, if the truth be told.'

" 'And the golf game?' " Carson watched McGarr as he pushed into the bar and opened the register. " 'How's that?' "

" 'Couldn't be better. Every ball straight down the fairway, every hole below par, I'm presently the club champ.'

" 'You don't say,' said the Pukka. 'That's grand. And money—what about that?' "

The night before, the night of the murder—McGarr saw at a glance—seven of the eight rooms had been occupied, six by foreigners: two Dutch couples from the same city who were probably traveling together, two German, a Frenchman, and an American.

" 'It's magic,' said the duffer. 'Every time I put me hand in me pocket, I pull out a hundred-quid note. I've been able to help many a poor person with that, I'll tell you. It's done a great deal of good.'

" 'That's you. That's you, all right,' the pukka cheered. 'Don't I know you're a good man. The kindest and most generous.' "

McGarr thumbed back through the register, aware that Carson's eyes were now on him, in spite of the continuing joke.

" 'And what about the other bit. The sex. How's that going?'

" 'Glorious. Fantastic. Couldn't be better,' said the young fella. There was a bit of a pause, since the pukka, like all wee folk"—Carson raised his free hand to the top of his head to indicate that he considered himself diminutive as well—"are a manky lot, forever panting and always on the nob. I mean, job."

Yet more laughter greeted that.

McGarr found Pascal Burke's signature of the day before. And he noticed, turning back farther still, that a stay of a fortnight's duration had been usual for the dead eel policeman.

" 'Details, man,' the pukka insisted. 'Details!'

" 'Oh,' said your man, tallying up his scores in his head. 'At least once or twice a month.'

" 'What? You're jokin' me,' said the pukka, incredulous and hoping his powers weren't waning. 'Surely you must mean once or twice a *week?*'

" 'No, a month,' replied your man. 'Which isn't half-bad for' "—Carson paused to sip from the glass, his eyes twinkling as he surveyed the largely silent bar crowd—" 'a priest with a small parish.' "

The joke was an old chestnut that McGarr had heard countless times before. But the crowd was in a roaring mood, and Carson's delivery was practiced and skilled.

When they quieted, Carson turned to McGarr. "What about you, sir? Will you put up with this racket? Or do you prefer quieter accommodations? I can recommend the inn on the other side of this building where you can hear a pin drop and Tim Tallon will provide you with everything you want."

"And more," said one of the crowd.

"Like his company," said another.

"And a tab for two hundred quid," yet another added, which brought nods of the head and more laughter.

But most eyes were on McGarr. "I'll see a room first. Here."

Histrionically, Carson placed his glass on the bar and wrinkled his brow in puzzlement. "You'll . . . *what?*"

"A room, I'll see it," which by law a prospective guest

could view before agreeing to stay over. But McGarr understood he had become a part of Carson's continuing shtick.

"What's there to see, man? There's a door, some carpet,
a light, two windows, a toilet, and, of course, a bed. That's
it. End of story."

Which was humorous only in the way Carson said it and
yielded more laughs.

"Benny's on today," somebody said.

"You'd be better off to drink your drink and go over to
the other side, mister," another said to McGarr behind a hand.
"Before you're roasted and served on a plate."

But McGarr only waited until the others had quieted and
all eyes were on him, anticipating some angry response. He
then raised a hand, pointed his fingers at Carson, and snapped
them brusquely into his palm.

It was a universal cop gesture, and one which, like Carson's antics, had to be practiced; it said no more dallying,
come with me. Or else.

Carson glanced at the crowd, who were now watching
him, and shrugged. "Sure, he must be from Dublin. That's
how they say hello."

Which was an acceptable exit line and brought further
approval from the crowd.

Carson turned and reached for a key in one of eight pigeonholes that had been built into the back bar. "Liam—will
you buzz us through?" he asked one of the other barmen as
he moved toward the hinged flap of the bar. There was a door
just beyond.

As McGarr moved toward it, an obviously drunken older
man in a cloth cap and tattered jacket turned to him. "I hope
Benny and his mates breaks yehr fookin' legs fer yeh, yeh
city cunt."

When another man whispered something, trying to shut
him up, he roared, "I don't give a shite who he is—Nelligan

himself—he's a city fook, and Benny and Manus will chuck his arse in the river where it belongs. They're just the b'ys to do it."

After Independence in the early twenties one Brian Nelligan had headed up the notoriously brutal Special Branch of the Garda Siochana that had focused on rooting out the even-then-outlawed IRA.

But the statement jarred McGarr's memory, causing him to remember who Benny Carson was or, at least, had been: an IRA section chief who had spent a record number of years in solitary confinement in Northern Ireland's Maze Prison.

McGarr tried to recall Carson's story that had been much covered in the press. Something to the effect that he was the child of a mixed marriage, which had been highly controversial in the Ulster of Carson's youth, and he had sided with his Catholic mother's family after his Protestant father had abandoned them.

It was thought that, given his name, Carson believed he had to prove himself more completely than others in that organization, even after he had been arrested for . . . could it be? Murdering two Royal Ulster Constabulary policemen in the North. McGarr would have to check, but he thought so.

Later—after his release from prison on a legal technicality, McGarr now also remembered—Carson had gone on to become one of the IRA's chief tacticians. But that, too, was years ago. And here he was now decades later in charge of a busy bar in the Midlands of the Republic. Why? Or, rather, how? McGarr thought of Tallon, who had to have known of the man's past when he hired him. Or could their connection be more complicated still?

At the door, Carson signaled to one of the other barmen, who reached for a button near the pigeonholes on the back bar and buzzed them through.

"So, what brings you here, Chief Superintendent?" Carson asked as they climbed the wide stairs.

McGarr waited until they got to the top. "Put your hands on the wall and spread your legs."

"What?" Carson asked incredulously.

McGarr spun the older man around and shoved him toward the wall. "Hands. And feet." He did not know if the charges against Carson in the North had been justified—at the time, many people had been falsely convicted and imprisoned—but he would take no chances.

"Whatever you're about, you don't want to do this," said Carson, as McGarr patted him down.

Apart from a billfold and a sizable ring of keys, his pockets contained only a pen, a comb, and two objects that felt like clasp knives, one in either front trousers pockets.

"You should mind your manners. I'm not without friends. D'y'know who I am?"

"A cop killer, twice over. Or are you threatening me?"

"Call it what you will, it's fact. You should be wary."

"What's fact—that you killed two cops?"

Carson did not reply.

"Step over to that chair and empty the contents of your pockets."

"I will, but I won't forget this. Your day will come."

The object in Carson's left pocket was a shiny chromed waiter's tool with a corkscrew, a bottle-cap opener, and a small knife to cut off wine bottle top-wrap. The second was indeed a clasp knife with a rosewood grip; it had a marlinspike on one end, a stout four-inch blade on the other.

"That your shank?"

"Let me give you a bit of advice—it's none of your fookin' business what it is. Like the man said downstairs, you should get in your fookin' car and get the fook out of here, while you can."

Suddenly angry—perhaps because of what had happened down in the bar, or because he had been dealing with the

Carsons of the country for too long—McGarr said through his teeth, "You think so? I'll show you my business."

McGarr seized Carson under the arm and rushed him toward the door behind which the two corpses lay. Still powerfully built in spite of his fifty-plus years, McGarr threw open the door and shoved Carson in, grabbing a handful of the man's graying hair and pulling him across the carpet.

At the bed he yanked the head down hard, so it was nearly touching Ellen Finn's mortally wounded head that was lying on Pascal Burke's dead chest.

"There's me business, you gobshite. And the double murder of two cops has you written all over it." McGarr jerked up the head, then kicked Carson's legs from under him. The man came down hard on the carpet but in a sitting position.

Bending so his mouth was next to Carson's ear, McGarr whispered, "I could wrap this up right here and now. Not a judge in the country would think twice about putting you away for good this time. And one other thing. Never—ever—threaten me or anybody in my hearing again, or I'll put you down. Permanently."

Carson's blue and clear eyes darted up to McGarr's.

"My promise."

"And mine—you lay hands on me again, and I'll have you up on charges. I have a cast-iron alibi—three people—who'll tell you I only ever left the bar to piss, Friday noon to Friday midnight."

Flicking his hand, McGarr sent the man sprawling.

He reached for the cell phone in a jacket pocket; a function key dialed his office in Dublin. While waiting for it to ring, McGarr realized that the brewing storm outside had struck—wind was whining through the eaves of the large building, and a heavy rain raked the windows.

"Get me the sheet from the North on Benny Carson," he

said when a voice answered. And to Carson, "Is it Benny or Ben E.?"

But Carson, who had straightened himself up, was staring at the two bodies on the bed, and . . . could it be? Tears were streaming from his eyes.

"Don't have to," said the voice on the other end of the phone, "didn't I grow up with the yoke?" It was Bernie McKeon, McGarr's chief of staff, who was from County Monaghan, like McGarr's own father and his father before him.

"I thought he was from the North." Technically, Monaghan was part of Ulster, which was thought of as the north of Ireland by traditionalists and Republicans. But like Cavan and Donegal, Monaghan was firmly part of the twenty-six counties that now made up the Irish Republic.

"I think he always wanted to be," McKeon replied. "Relatives in Portadown. You know. Republican background. And he spoke that way—with the full Scots burr even as kids. Like he was really from there.

"And he carried it off, being a bit of a thespian. A great lad for skits and jokes. Tell you the truth, I liked him well enough, until he shot those two R.U.C. cops. But, sure, there were those who said he didn't, being too smart for something so . . . direct. There's that too—with his mates he was known as a backroom man, a planner.

"He with you?"

"Yah."

"And you're thinking he just shot two more?"

McGarr let silence carry the thought.

"I'll get the details. But there's this too: he's still a local hero up there—the whole IRA thing and his record in solitary. He was in on one of the hunger strikes, too. Takes a hard man to have lasted that."

McGarr glanced down at Carson, who looked anything but.

"When he got out, it was said by some he'd had enough. And he retired from active service. But me Uncle Mick, who's friendly with the family, said they're awash in cash from time to time. A new pricey car. They gussied up the old house. Mod cons, that class of thing. All from 'Benny B'y,' they call him over jars, though he's seldom seen.

"And then I think he's wanted again in the North."

"Check that."

"Something to do with strong-arm and protection schemes."

Perhaps here focusing on the lucrative eel trade. Or the busy inn. No—if the inn was the object of Carson and the Frakes's attention, why murder two police here? McGarr shook his head; he was getting ahead of himself. Now was the time to gather information, not draw conclusions.

He glanced back down at Carson, who was still starting at the bed, his face now streaming with tears. "Why don't you come down here too, Bernie?"

"You're kidding—along with Ward and Bresnahan? What would there be for me to do?"

"I think I need you." To poke around, to renew his acquaintance with Carson, to talk about old times or just talk. McKeon was a friendly sort, and there was never any telling what might come out over jars.

"But who'll handle the desk?" The question was pro forma; McGarr could hear the joy in his voice. McKeon was a desk man—the Squad's primary interviewer—and was seldom asked to leave the city.

"Swords. But tell him we want to keep a lid on this thing for as long as we can," McGarr said. "Have the other two left already?"

"An hour gone now. They should be there any minute."

McGarr switched off the telephone and slipped it back in his pocket.

"Know them?" he asked Carson, pointing to the bed.

Still sitting on the floor, Carson was using a handkerchief to blot his face. "Yes. I mean no. Not well enough, it's plain." He sighed. "People come in here, they talk to you come day go day, year in year out. You know the names of their mothers and fathers, their kids, the problems in their lives, their joys and sorrows, but it's all . . . mouth music. Nothing but form. A way of passing a few hours. All in all, it has no more meaning than birds in a tree.

"Take her—she and her husband, Quintan Finn, they had their wedding reception here at the inn, when . . . ? It can't be much over a year ago. A big splash with all the mucketymucks from three counties around to seal the deal. And look at her there on top of him." He shook his head. "Jaysus.

"And him." Carson paused to blow his nose; he then rose unsteadily to his feet. "Sure, he was a bachelor, moderate in his ways but one. You know, forever panting. Always up for a lark with a woman.

"And where was the harm? Maybe he brought a bit of joy into the lives of the odd widow or some others who were just playing out a bad hand for the sake of children and family. Divorce in Dublin may be common, but out here it's still a curse.

"This though." Carson cast his hand at the bed and shook his head. "This is hard to grasp."

McGarr waited, but Carson had said his piece.

"Quintan Finn—he come into the pub yesterday?"

"No." Carson closed his eyes and made a noise in the back of his throat, as though struggling with himself. "Of course, he came in. He comes in nearly every noontime and most nights. A couple of pints, some chat. He throws the odd dart, jokes with the lads. A happy openhanded sort with not an enemy in the world.

"*This,* though, will kill him. He'll never live it down."

"Could he have known about them?"

Carson hunched his thin shoulders. "If he didn't, he was the only one in town. They'd been at it since before she married Quintan, kind of like the father thing for her, I guess. But Burke could be persuasive."

"Could Finn have come up here?"

Carson sighed and shook his head. "I've said enough for the moment. You'll have to ask the others. I'm the dog and pony show. I chat people up. 'How's the missus? Has your prize pig ovulated?' That class of thing. Talk is, the only drinks I pour are me own."

"Are they?"

"Are they what?"

"Your own. Do you own a piece of this place?"

"I'd like to, I'll admit to that. But at present I'm a leaseholder. Sylvie owns the building and the license, since that's not on for me." His eyes swung to McGarr.

Because of his convictions, he meant. Felons were prohibited from owning a drinks license or even serving in a pub. But not from having a drink behind the bar, chatting people up, and knowing what there was to know in a small town. In many ways a popular barman was more knowledgeable than the local priest, since anything could be said to him. And was.

"What about Tallon? How does he fit in?"

"Here?"

McGarr waited.

"He's a bollox altogether. Without her he'd be just another Dublin blowhard. All mouth, no sense."

"Without his wife. Sylvie," McGarr clarified.

"*Wife?*" Carson objected. "Let's hope not, for her sake. When they opened up here, he had this side of the building, she the inn. Within a month there wasn't a person in town who'd come into the pub if he was there. It took me nearly a year to build up the trade again. I had to spread the rumor that I had banned him from his own pub."

Which was hard to believe, but maybe not about Tallon. "Manus and Donal Frakes come into the pub." It was a statement, not a question.

Carson nodded. "Aye."

"And what are they to you?"

"Mates."

"Colleagues."

"One time."

"And now?"

Carson paused before answering.

"Ach—they're younger than me, and regulars here. At different times we made the same mistakes, and we know some of the same people."

And perhaps the same techniques for getting on, thought McGarr. "Then, you're their mentor. They come to you for advice."

Carson's eyes were fixed on the corpses again. He shook his head slowly. "I never said that. Nor would they. Not a word."

"But I trust you know where they live."

Carson nodded.

"On your feet, then. Take me to them." With Carson in tow, no quick telephone call could be made. And McGarr himself would be safer with the jocular barman and convicted murderer as a shield.

Or so he thought.

# 7

# The Frakes

Like a brief impassioned kiss, the storm had been fierce and pointed. It left the countryside crushed and damp.

Water was sluicing in creamy streams down the narrow dirt road leading to the house that the Frakes were occupying, as McGarr—accompanied in his mini Cooper by a glum Benny Carson—skirted the puddles and tried not to get stuck in the buff-colored mud.

The road wove through a section of dense wood that was filled with a jumble of limestone outcroppings, too rocky and poor to farm in spite of its proximity to the water of the broad river. And yet the thick underbrush and tall trees had become a refuge for wildlife.

In the twilight, a cloud of crows lifted off a copse of beech trees, roused by the light from the headlamps of the small car that was jouncing over the rough path. A hare bolted in front of them. McGarr even thought he caught the fugitive glimmer of the eyes of a deer behind deep cover.

And there suddenly in front of them—about a long mile from any main road and hard by the eastern bank of the Shannon—stood a substantial older house with several outbuildings. Lights were blazing, but there were no cars in the drive.

McGarr turned the Cooper in a circle to scan the rest of the holding; nobody seemed to be about. Stopping the car, he switched off the lights and ignition, then reached for two objects that he kept under the seat.

"The Frakes own this place?" he asked, the darkness now lit only by the lights from the house and glow of Carson's cigarette.

"I wouldn't say so," Carson replied, "though I don't know. I think maybe they're 'sitting' it, like. For a friend."

Which was probably code for the friends that Carson and the Frakes had served with in the past. It had the look of a safe house, with a poor road in through cover and no near neighbors to gossip about who came and went. Also, there was the river for a quick escape. McGarr now saw the green beacon of a navigational light on the opposite shore.

Switching off the overhead light so the interior of the car would not be illuminated when he opened the door, McGarr turned to Carson. "Give me your wrist."

"Why?"

"Hold it out," McGarr did not wait. Grabbing Carson's arm, he clamped one ring of his handcuffs over the older man's thin wrist and then fixed the other ring to the steering column.

"Did you think I'd bolt?" Carson asked incredulously, as McGarr got out of the low Cooper. "Where would I bolt to? The river or the wood?"

"Pukkas in both places, it's said. And you're just the man to know them." Reaching beneath the driver's seat, McGarr removed the 9mm Walther that he kept there in a sling.

"Can't be too careful," Carson opined. "Once a soldier, always a soldier. You're a right man, McGarr. Always on watch."

"Aren't you mistaken?" McGarr asked in a low voice, turning his back to the house to check the action of the weapon and the clip, which was full. He slid the gun under his belt, then reached for the spare clip that was also under the seat. "Weren't you the soldier and a volunteer? Like them." McGarr canted his head toward the house.

Carson passed some air between his lips. "There's enough guilt to go round with all of us on the wrong side. It's just that we're a bit more advanced than you."

Intrigued, McGarr waited.

"We had to lose to win. As I said earlier, your day will come."

"Is it a threat I'm hearing?"

"Me threaten you? Not on your life. Or, rather, not on mine."

McGarr studied Carson before closing the door. "And so, if you won in the end, tell me—what exactly was the prize?"

"Our objectives were met. What about yours? Or don't you have any save your pay packet and whatever retirement the citizens of this country will be giving you? To make you go away."

McGarr closed the door and advanced on the lighted house through a mist that was thick there by the river, feeling . . . what was it? Vaguely meretricious, being—what?—a cop with a salary and a pension, as Carson had said. Not an idealist and romantic who could stick years of solitary and abuse. And whose idealistic goals had been realized, although the jury was still out on how completely.

It was—McGarr supposed, tugging the Walther from under his belt and thumbing off the safety—the old argument spun from the wool of a millennium of romantic defiance; that their tribe had a tyrannous enemy who was known. And any action, no matter how destructive of life—even one's own— was justified in ridding the country of the yoke.

The culture was steeped in the lore of insurgence. You couldn't switch on the telly or walk into a pub without some reference to rebellion in words, music, or the portrait of some famed martyr on the wall. No sacrifice being greater or more revered. And nobody who hadn't joined the struggle being considerable, it was implied.

But for those who had—like the Carsons and Frakes of the island—all else could be tolerated. Including perhaps the squalor that now appeared to McGarr as he pushed open the front door, which was ajar.

It was as though the center hall and two rooms that he could see had never been occupied apart from clutter and trash. Things like building materials, brick, tiles, slates were heaped in piles on what had only recently been gleaming beech-wood floors. In the second room, two sooty Aga cookers—one tumbled over on its back with its oven doors open and its guts pulled out—shared the space with fishing gear, an anchor, and what looked like a mound of trash stuffed into plastic bags. The warm air of the house, escaping through the open door, reeked of it. A cat had clawed its way into one and was picking at a chicken bone.

With the Walther cocked by his side, McGarr stepped in without announcing himself, knowing he was breaking the law. This one act alone could have him up on charges. He had to think of such things since he was a cop—a civil servant—with a pay packet and a pension to lose and no more romantic lore than the letter of written law to abide by.

Glancing back out at Carson, he wondered why he was smarting from the man's gibe. He had dealt with the IRA all his life, from family stories about the organization, family members who had been in it, the histories learned in school spoken of wherever people gathered. And then, later, he'd had to deal with the IRA professionally.

And to a man or woman—every last one—they had

seemed immature, as though they had never grown up in some major way. Maybe because they saw things in terms of black and white, when so much of what McGarr encountered was gray.

Water was running hard in the sink in the toilet off the hall and both lights there were on, as though whoever had been using the sink had simply bolted.

And so, too, in the kitchen, which was the source of the heat with yet another Aga torrid from having its flue opened wide. Wood was being burned and split right there in the kitchen. The tiles were chipped and cracked. A pile of beech saw logs was stacked nearly to the ceiling. An axe was nearby.

McGarr damped the flue, so the stove wouldn't be ruined or the house set afire. He turned to the table.

Tea had recently been poured and a plate placed before a child's highchair, which had been knocked over. The rashers, toast, and chips had not been touched, and the glass of milk nearby was half-filled.

A bib was on the floor, and the door leading to the back garden was also ajar. A large Grundig radio with a wooden cabinet of the sort that had been a feature of farmhouses in McGarr's youth was playing. Even the teakettle on a trivet still held heat.

They had been warned, but by whom? Somebody in the bar could have recognized McGarr, as had Carson. But why, then, would they have thought to phone the Frakes?

Or maybe they had installed a device at the top of the drive—an electric eye to warn them. McGarr knew of electronics shops in Dublin that sold such things.

But nowhere in the house—not in the child's room off the kitchen nor in any of the four rooms upstairs, one of which was locked, did he find a monitor or much of anything besides two mattresses and some men's clothes.

A plastic sign on the locked door said, "KNOCK FIRST"

in block capitals. McGarr removed from his pocket the brace of picks that he kept on a key ring and set about opening the door.

It was a skill that he had learned on his first police job with Criminal Justice in Paris. During the sixties, Marseilles had been a hotbed of drug activity, and senior officials decided that they needed several undercover cops—preferably young and non-French—to pose as buyers and target major drug traffickers.

As a young tough redheaded Irishman who spoke French execrably, McGarr fit the bill exactly, and he was then taught every sort of criminal skill, from picking locks through forgery and counterfeiting to the use of a gun, a knife, and his hands to kill. Drug testing and the art of negotiating drug deals convincingly came next. But over the years, of all the skills, picking locks—which was illegal in Ireland without a court order—had proved the most useful, if not the most critical.

It took McGarr perhaps five minutes to turn over the dead bolt and a moment or two longer to release the handle lock. And he had only just opened the door to view a surprisingly orderly bedroom with a four-poster bed and dresser to match, when he was stopped by the sound of a double blast outside.

The first report sounded like a collision of metal with metal, which was followed immediately by an explosion and howling, like a jet plane passing over the roof at Mach speed. Which could be only one thing.

A high-powered rifle. Louder here—McGarr realized when a second shot again concussed the windows—for having been fired over water from the opposite bank of the Shannon.

Down at the door McGarr discovered the target—his Cooper with Carson in it, handcuffed to the steering column. And nowhere in sight behind the shattered windscreen.

A third shot now slammed into the grill of the low car, rocking it back, and after the howling ceased McGarr heard

Carson moan or cry out, which meant that at least he was still alive. And such an easy target in the gleaming car lit by the lights from the house.

What to do? McGarr could try to find the fuse box, or he could rush out the other door and try to draw their fire with his Walther.

But the river was too wide for any shot from a handgun to carry effectively, and the shooters on the other bank might not even hear the report. Which was when he remembered the axe in the kitchen.

Three more high-powered rounds slammed into the Cooper before McGarr discovered the utility meter on the side of the house with its main power lead. Rearing back, he chopped it in two, and except for some sparking from the severed wires, darkness fell over the yard.

Rushing to the Cooper, McGarr found Carson huddled on the floor with only his shackled arm jutting up.

"You there?" McGarr asked.

"Where the Christ else would I be?" Carson replied. "Get me out of here. The fookers—they've got an infrared scope. And it's only a matter of time before they change to it."

McGarr had only unlocked the handcuffs and freed the clasp from the steering column when another shot screeched through the darkness and thwacked into the open door by McGarr's thighs with all the force of a sledgehammer. It knocked him down. Fortunately.

The next round blew through the window of the door.

Snatching up the now open end of the handcuffs, McGarr wrenched Carson from the Cooper and—on all fours himself—dragged the man into the lee of the house.

"You're hurt."

"Only the hand. And my pate, I think. Is that blood?"

McGarr pulled the penlight from his pocket; Carson's face

was streaming with blood. Tiny shards of glass spangled his balding head, which was showering blood.

McGarr trained the beam on Carson's hand, which had taken a sizable fragment of either bullet or glass—glass, McGarr guessed—to the fleshy part of the palm. The blood there was dark and slow-flowing, but the shard of a bullet would have gone through. "Anyplace else?"

"I don't think so. I don't know." Slowly Carson began trying to stand; McGarr helped him up, then steadied the man.

"Ah, fook," said Carson. "What a fookin' mess."

Indeed, thought McGarr, who glanced out at his car just as yet another round—a *coup de grace*—found the carburetor. And raw gas, spilling onto the hot engine, ignited.

With a blast, the Cooper went up in an oily ball of flame. The explosion staggered them, and Carson, bending his head, moved toward McGarr, as though seeking shelter.

And did he whimper? McGarr thought Carson did. After a while, as the conflagration raged, Carson straightened up and again tried to brush the blood from his eyes. "I'm too old for this shit. Let's get it over with. I did it."

McGarr slipped the Walther under his belt and glanced at his blazing car. "Hold out your arm." He tapped the one with the injury to the palm. "You did what?"

"Shot Burke and the woman up over the bar."

Using his handkerchief, McGarr fixed a tourniquet around Carson's upper arm. "Why?"

"Because Burke was a prick. A womanizer. D'you know that Quintan Finn is my nephew?"

McGarr had not.

"It's how I got here, you know—after prison. They took me in, gave me a place to stay."

McGarr waited.

"And I figured—the boy needed a clean go at life with no woman like her on the other end. So I gave him one."

"And you murdered them—how?" McGarr reached for the telephone in his coat pocket.

"Like you saw. One bullet, clean. Her being on top of him."

McGarr tied the binding tight, then reached for the phone in the pocket of his coat. "And you got into the room—how?"

"Door, of course. Don't I have all the keys at the bar?"

McGarr punched in a number. "They didn't hear you."

"Not being . . . engaged. You saw them yourself, her on top of him."

"Lights off."

"Aye."

"And in the hall, when you opened the door? Lights were off as well?"

Carson paused. "I must have switched them off. When I opened the door, it was dark. They didn't see me."

"And you have good eyesight. You knew they were . . . what was your word? Engaged. I like that. Is it a local term?"

"Ach—the two of them were like rabbits, her and him. Always at it. He'd only have to come to town, and she was on him like green on grass. A right bloody bitch."

"So you took a gun, the one you had—where?"

"Beneath the bar, of course. You can't be too careful these days." Carson was shaking now.

"And that gun is now—where?"

"Sure, I chucked it in the river."

McGarr nodded. "So, to recap—let's see if I have your confession straight. You decided to rid your young nephew of his adulterous wife and also—in passing—to do Manus and Donal Frakes the favor of getting Pascal Burke out of their lives. He was horning in on their illegal eel trade, right?"

"That's right."

"So, with sublime stealth you managed to open the door, approach them on the bed, and dispatch both problems with one shot. Then, you tossed the murder weapon into the largest and deepest river in the country where it probably will never be found. It's brilliant. When you get back to the drum, your mates there will call you a bloody genius."

"Me, Chief?" Swords answered on the other end of the phone. "Haven't I been telling you for years?"

McGarr ordered a car and rang off. Then, "May I make an observation?"

Carson was having trouble staying on his feet, and he leaned back against the house.

"The Frakes don't seem very grateful. Or do you think they were shooting at me?"

"Are you taking me up to Dublin then?" Carson asked in a hopeful manner.

"Not until your confession becomes more credible."

McGarr only led the injured man around the house to the kitchen entrance. He needed a cup of tea, and the Aga would still be hot.

In a very real way McGarr had loved that little car.

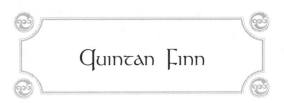

# 8

# Quintan Finn

The newlywed Finns—Ellen and Quintan—had shared a mews flat down an alley off the main road by the bridge.

Carson had a key to the door in a high wall that led into a flagged courtyard with a wrought-iron table; chairs and flowers traced the perimeter.

"How long did you live here?" McGarr asked.

"Three years with Quintan. I'm out the six months since they've been married."

"Where do you live now?"

"A flat at the front of the building. My brother-in-law owns most of the block."

Two rows of arched windows in the Georgian style had been placed one on each side of the doorway, and in all the makeover of what had formerly been stables or a commercial building was imaginative and inviting.

With his uninjured hand, Carson opened the door and stepped in. "They never lock it," he explained, before calling out, "Quintan—are ye about, lad? Quintan?"

Carson moved toward a flight of stairs and called again, but there was no reply. "Must be out. Would you care for another cup, Superintendent—I'm parched, and these things are giving me the business." He meant his scalp and hand.

Leading McGarr through a light and airy sitting room with stuffed chairs, covered in a floral pattern, and a smattering of tasteful antiques, they traced the length of a hall into what had evidently been a separate building. It now contained a large kitchen with sweeping views of the Shannon. Sliding glass doors opened onto a deck.

There was a note propped on a long kitchen table. Both men walked over to it.

*Ellen, you right bloody bitch. Before we were engaged you swore to me you were through with him. And now it's all over the county what a fool I am.*

*If you read this note before I find you, pack your gear and clear out. You should know this—you don't want me to find you.*

McGarr waited for Carson's reaction; from out on the river they now heard the droning of the horn of a boat.

Carson tried to reach for the note, but McGarr kept him from it. Straightening up, he glanced at McGarr.

"Yesterday, a little after noon, I'd make it, Quintan was in the bar when Manus came in to deliver a carpet for the room that's being refurbished."

"The room across the hall from where they were found?"

Carson nodded.

"Manus was all alone, so he asked if Quintan would lend him a hand. They carried it upstairs."

"Before Burke and Ellen went up?"

"Burke was already up there, I'd hazard, but I don't know. Ellen came in and had a couple of quick vodkas to steel herself, like. And then she must have gone up."

"Did you see her?"

Carson shook his head. "I get chatting with people. Burke must have had a key made for her, so she could—like—have a drink or two near the end of the bar. When others weren't looking, she'd slip upstairs.

"Then there were the 'planning sessions,' Burke called them, that were probably just . . . you know, *sessions*. He'd have a bunch of maps, sometimes even a third eel police, and they'd all go upstairs. The third party leaving before Ellen."

"What about this?" McGarr pointed to the, *Before we were engaged you told me you were through with him.*

Carson's eyes moved to McGarr's. He nodded. "I don't know what hold Burke had over women, even young women with . . . everything, including a future, like Ellen. But—"

Which seemed to contradict what the maid, Grace O'Rourke, had said about Ellen Gilday Finn. She had seemed genuinely shocked at having found her there, like that. And being the same age in such a small town, O'Rourke would have known practically everything there was to know about the murdered woman, especially a long-term affair with a much older man that had transpired above a large popular bar.

"You still haven't answered me why the Frakes tried to kill you."

Carson stepped toward the stove. "Because they knew I knew what I just told you, and there we were together and you out of the car."

"Meaning that you think Manus was in on it."

"How else could it have been done? The two of them burst into the room, catching them like that, and Manus—he's strong—held her down in place while Quintan shot her. Once being enough for the both of them." Carson bit his lower lip and looked away. "The carpet thing was just a ruse. They knew those two were up there."

"Why would Frakes do something like that for your nephew?"

"Because Quintan's one of them, I'm told. The eel trade, stolen cars, bootleg ciggies, building materials, anything not nailed down."

McGarr waited while Carson filled the kettle, since more of an explanation was in order—why a young man from a well-off family would link up with two known former IRA thugs.

"It's the romantic thing, I guess. Quintan's a . . . wee fella. And he's forever trying to prove himself. Spoiled like his mother was. Willful, you know. With the temper and all."

While Carson made tea, McGarr toured the rest of the dwelling. In the master bedroom he found a partly opened drawer that was filled with every manner of lingerie—teddies, garter belts, thong underwear—along with an assortment of vibrators and other items from sex shops.

Among them was a packet of Thunderbolt condoms with the lightning-bolt-and-cloud logo, the same as McGarr had discovered in Ellen Finn's purse. Like that packet, it was unopened.

Back down in the kitchen, McGarr refused Carson's offer of tea. "I'd like you to stay in town."

"I've nowhere else to go."

"Do you think you need protection?"

"Not now that I've been warned."

"I hope that doesn't mean carrying a weapon." Which for a convicted felon would mean immediate and lengthy jail time.

"I'm too smart for that."

By how much remained to be seen, thought McGarr.

"What about your head and hand? I could have you driven to hospital."

"Thank you, no. I'll ring up the local medic. He'll come and take care of me here. It's more my style.

"And Superintendent," Carson added as McGarr was nearly out the door. "Thanks for the bit at the car. It makes me grateful for my tea." Carson raised his cup.

# Part
# Two

9

# Winter Scene

Peter McGarr awoke the next morning to a wonderful surprise. Snow.

And not the snow that was usual to Ireland and often capped the tops of mountains during winter or coated fields with an inch or two of dampness that was gone in a morning. This was a deep abiding snow of the sort that McGarr could remember only a few times in his life.

Looking out the windows of the suite of rooms in the inn, he could see that, sometime during the night, the sleet of the night before had turned to fluffy snow. Perhaps a foot mounded the cars in the courtyard and the walls of the formal garden. And was still falling in swirling windblown clouds.

The white slope down to the jetty made the river look black and slick, and only the boats of two fishermen tending their eel nets near the piers of the bridge revealed that the surface was water and not dark polished stone. Gulls, looking like bright bits of kinetic snow, wheeled in their lee.

On the bridge itself, an articulated lorry was creeping along in what had to be its lowest gear with warning lights flashing. On the far side a car had gone off the road and was abandoned. And the sky above was the color of slate. It would rain soon. Or snow more.

And yet the sitting room of the suite that McGarr was sharing with his wife and daughter was snug and silent with the piped heat pinging in baseboard registers, the only sound at—he checked his watch—7:10.

Picking up the phone, McGarr ordered a pot of coffee, cocoa for Maddie, and a selection of buns. He then went back to the window to survey the unusual scene again. And muse.

After leaving Carson at Quintan Finn's flat the night before, McGarr had found the Leixleap police barracks where Declan Riley, the sergeant, was waiting for him. Together they walked the three blocks to the house of Ellen Gilday Finn's parents.

"I suspect you do this more than me," Riley said, as they were waiting for the door to open.

McGarr only drew in a deep breath, having known from his first days as a policeman that, while every job had some challenges, there was none in any occupation as troubling as this. Even doctors seldom informed parents that their child had been taken from them by a violent act.

"They only had the one," Riley whispered, as the door opened.

And like so many other parents in McGarr's experience, Ellen's were so shocked that they could be of no help, save to say that they had not been aware of any problems between their daughter and Finn. "They'd been together forever, you know. Since school. And getting married was like something they'd been waiting for all of their lives," the mother said.

"But did Ellen have anybody pursuing her?" McGarr asked.

"*Pursuing?*"

"Ringing her up, asking her out. That class of thing."

She had to think. "I can't say. Not after she was married.

But Ellen was a pretty girl, and all along there were boys wanting to take her to the ciney and all, even though she had her cap set for Quintan."

"What about Pascal Burke, her boss?"

Both parents only stared, before McGarr said what he knew for them would be the hardest part. "Your daughter was found with Burke in a room in the Leixleap Inn. Both were murdered. Shot with his gun."

Tears burst from her father's eyes. "The eels. The bloody eels and the bloody IRA. We never wanted her to take that job, but it was always the environment . . . the environment for Ellen. The kayak. The sneaking around in the dead of night. And look where it got her.

"Do you know who Manus Frakes is?" he nearly shouted through his tears. "Find that bastard, and you'll find Ellen's killer."

And her mother had broken down as well. After a while, McGarr and Riley withdrew, leaving them to their . . . what? Their sorrow? No, McGarr thought—having but one daughter himself—it was keener than that. More like desolation and the ruin of their lives.

Quintan Finn's parents lived on what could only be called an estate a few miles south of town. Built rather recently on a hilltop, the house was modern in design, with large bay windows on its four corners, rather like a glass castle, every pane of which was lit.

"Don't let the house fool you," Riley advised as the Garda car fishtailed up the slippery slope. "He's down-to-earth, Dermot is. If you ask him, he'll tell you he's got three degrees in what he calls plant nutrition. 'Bull shit, more shit, piled high and deep,' since it's the fertilizer trade that bought this place. Dermot's into it in a big way.

"But it's Honora, the wife, who wanted a spread like this.

And she's forever giving out to Finn for smelling like the money that bought it."

But neither knew the whereabouts of their son. And the father slumped into a seat in the posh living room that looked like something out of California when he learned why McGarr and Riley were searching for the young man.

"What about the Gildays?" was his first thought; he was a short man with a wide once-powerful body and a significant paunch. His face was windburned and his hair white. "They must be—"

"To hell with the Gildays," the wife cut in. "What about Quintan, our son? Where's he? Those Frakes—didn't I tell you they'd brought their trouble with them? Himself even gave them jobs." She pointed at her husband.

"Isn't that better than having them steal from me?"

"Ah—see how he thinks." She was a pretty woman in her early fifties with a trim body and a new perm. "He'd never think of calling you."

But Finn ignored her. "How can we help?"

"Find your son and have him contact us," said McGarr, handling Finn his card. "The sooner, the better." He then asked if they had any recent photographs of their son.

"Only the wedding pictures, and you can't have those," she snapped.

Finn got up and retrieved several. With tears in his eyes, he handed them to McGarr. "I'll find him for you, don't worry."

As they made their way back to their car, the wife called to them, "What about the Frakes? Aren't you going to arrest them? It's them, you know. It couldn't be anyone else. Quintan and Ellen were loved by everybody. Are! *Are loved!*"

Back at the barracks, McGarr scanned in the photographs and faxed the lot to Dublin, then told Riley to close up and go home. "I'll stay," replied the older man, pointing to the end of the room that led to cells that would have cots. "Finn is a man of his word, and he won't sleep. And then, we'll be having some information coming in from Dublin, I suspect."

McGarr nodded and bid him good night.

Back at the inn, he found Tallon waiting up for him. McGarr raised a hand to his questions and made for the stairs. "Please—I'm knackered. We'll talk in the morning."

"But, Janie—it's out, it's all over the country. We just had a phone call from an editor at the *Times*. He's got their names and who they were, and he even knows it was the Frakes that did it and how they tried to kill you only this evening. Blew up your car."

Which stopped McGarr, since it could only have been Carson who had phoned the Dublin paper. Why? To put so much heat on his erstwhile comrades that they would have to leave the area and go to ground someplace else? Carson, an old fox who had said he could take care of himself. And was doing so.

McGarr continued up the stairs.

"After the *Independent* called and RTE, we took the phone off the hook. Peter—I implored, begged, pleaded with you to keep a lid on this thing, and now—"

McGarr had closed the hall door and made his way to his rooms, where he found his wife in one of the two big beds and his daughter in the other. Rather than wake them, he took a long hot shower and slept on the couch in the sitting room.

Now looking out at the snowscape, McGarr moved into the bedroom, where he woke his daughter. Holding a finger to his lips so his wife could sleep, he motioned Maddie into the other room.

"Look at that," McGarr said, parting the curtains.

"Oh, *snow!*" Maddie enthused. "And it looks deep."

"Ever since I was a lad, we've only had a few days like this. See the slope down to the river? I bet the metal trays they've got downstairs in the dining room will go great in it this morning."

Which is how Tallon found them, puffing up the hill for another glide down the slope. "Is this what you're doing when I've got the place filled with press and everybody in town is after asking what gives?"

McGarr ignored him and tromped past, Maddie in his wake.

"They want to see you."

"Tell them I'm busy."

"I'll not tell them a thing."

"Good—then, you're covered."

"But what am I supposed to do with them about?"

"Here's something—I'll need a breakfast table set for six in one hour. Someplace private. No press, no staff." Nor you McGarr was tempted to add. "Ready?" he asked Maddie.

"One, two, go!" she shouted, jumping on her tray and skidding down the hill.

McGarr gave her a little lead before following, to make sure she'd win.

"You're a right bastard, McGarr—do you know that?" Tallon shouted after him. "You were then, you are now! A *bastard!*"

# 10

# Scenario

By ten that morning, preliminary reports from the tech squad had arrived.

A half hour later, McGarr gathered the three members of his staff—who would help him there in Leixleap—for a working breakfast in the dining room on the inn side of the hostelry owned by Tim Tallon and Sylvie Zeebruge. Noreen joined them.

Tallon himself served the group and kept hovering about, offering more coffee and tea, until McGarr asked if they could have some privacy "for official purposes." Even then they caught sight of Tallon from time to time, walking past the open doorway to the hall and stealing worried glances their way.

"What gives with that yoke?" Bernie McKeon asked. "Even without the feathers, he'd give Mother Hen a squawk for her tea."

"He found them," said Hugh Ward, distributing the photographs around the table like he was dealing playing cards; the pictures made the dead pair, who had been pitiful in death, seem grotesque in still life. There were also pictures of the suite, its closet, and toilet from several angles.

"Any bids?" Ward continued. "Two hearts is out until after the first rubber, because I've got news for you." Ward tapped a second envelope.

"And you wouldn't want any of us to go off half-cocked," McKeon added, fanning the photographs in front of him. A burly man in his early fifties with a thick shock of once-blond hair and dark eyes, he was the Squad's chief interrogator and—McGarr once declared—their "irrepressible wit." To which a junior staffer had added to the delight of all, "By half."

"I wonder," he now asked, "does blood flow to the lowest point after death, or did your man here just have a mickey that would make Uncle Mike proud?"

"You must be comparing it to your own, Bernie, since on the whole this one is only average in size," Ward quipped.

Detective Inspector Ruth Bresnahan traded glances with Noreen.

She had heard the Murder Squad staff gibes about other cases over the years and she well understood that the humor—albeit, black—provided them with some distance on the mayhem and carnage they encountered on a nearly daily basis. But the photographs of the naked and dead couple were nothing short of lurid.

"Poor woman," Bresnahan muttered, "out for a bit of a lark with a rotter who had pissed off the IRA, if the Chief can be believed. Pardon me, Chief—if a suggested avenue of investigation in the Chief's report proves accurate. It's a classic case of her being in the wrong place at the wrong time."

"Really? What about the two thousand pounds of crisp banknotes that said rotter had in his billfold?" Ward shot back. Bresnahan and he had only recently ended a longtime affair after a woman—who had borne Ward's child—came back into his life. And the relationship between the two staffers was still strained.

"As I seem to remember," Ward continued, "pissed-off former IRA gunmen are not known for their ideological stance in regard to quid. And these three"—he distributed three more photographs to the others—"have the reputation of nicking anything not nailed down."

The additional photographs were mug shots of two bearded and rough-looking men.

Replied Bresnahan, "Theft is one thing, murder another. What about their long-distance attempt on Carson's life in the Chief's car. If that wasn't attempted murder, I don't know what was. From near or far"—she shook the photographs— "these two are killers."

"Granted." McKeon was holding the photos in the light from a nearby window. "But why didn't they take her weapon as well? You know how the IRA trains its wankers—they can get kneecapped for leaving a gun behind." McKeon's youngest daughter had been killed in an IRA bomb blast, and he had little sympathy for their cause.

"They didn't take her weapon because they used his to murder them, and once it was fired they panicked and split."

"Ah, Rut'ie—you're all wet. When are you going to get the *hang* of this racket. If there's anything classic about this sordid . . . er, tale, it's a classic case of poor performance on the job. Just look at her position. Sure, it looks perfect for what they were doing, but as anybody with two eyes can see, there's no congruence."

"Can't you give your suspect macho illusions a rest, Bernie? Or could it be talk is all that's left?" A tall, statuesque redhead, Bresnahan forked a hand through her auburn tresses, and said to Noreen, "To think that I have to put up with this day in and day out."

But McKeon continued undeterred, "And when your

man—who was the boss after all—needed her to take a bullet for him, she botched that as well."

"Being soft in the head," Ward put in, reaching for a second manila envelope that contained the preliminary report from the tech squad and pathologist.

McKeon eased back in his chair. "Conclusion? Incompetence proved her undoing. Pity she had to take Officer Pork with her. And out of season."

"It's Burke. *Burke!*" Bresnahan groused.

But even McGarr, who had been musing over his coffee, glanced at McKeon.

"Doesn't Pascal mean Easter?" he asked. "Sure, Easter is whole months off." Where a large roast of pork was consumed in many parts of the country.

Eyes rolled, and McGarr tapped the table, signaling that it was time to get down to business.

Ward had arranged the tech-squad report before him and was now scanning it. Once an amateur boxing champ, he was a dark well-built man in his early forties, who had recently been promoted to detective superintendent and was widely regarded as McGarr's successor.

Always well turned out, he was dressed for the cold, wearing a heather brown tweed jacket over a tan cashmere polo neck jumper that had been a present from Bresnahan, all knew. His dark eyes glanced up. "Looks as though Bernie was right."

"Me *mahn!*" cheered McKeon.

"Shhh!" Noreen hissed, tired of McKeon's carry-on.

Ward shook his head. "I can't imagine how it could have happened, but the report from the pathologist says that they didn't die from the same bullet, and they didn't die together.

"In fact," plainly disbelieving what he was reading, Ward paused and raised a hand to his chin in a thoughtful manner, "it says here they died at least three hours apart. But the ballistics report claims they were both shot with the same weapon. A Glock 9mm.

"Him in the chest, her in the head. And both bullets were found to be lodged in him, the one that killed her having passed through her head and into his chest but in a slightly different place."

Said Bresnahan, "With his missing gun."

Ward snapped the pages taut. "We can't know that, can we?"

"Aw, c'mon—can't you at least be academically honest, Superintendent? How many Glocks can possibly be floating around this town?"

Ward ignored her. "And listen to this—there's evidence in and on the condom that they—or at least Burke—had sex sometime immediately before he was shot directly through the heart."

"What about her?" McKeon asked, struggling to suppress a laugh. "I mean, it's not difficult to consider the implication, if she died three hours later. When she saw he was dead, she doffed her duds and climbed up on your man for a wee bit of necro—"

"Bernie?" Noreen asked. "Would you please shut your bloody gob? We're all quick enough to understand the implication, your implication. But there are other implications as well. And your suspect humor is—"

"What about it, Hughie?" McGarr asked, cutting her off, since McKeon's question was apt, and often in the past the free flow of chatter had proved crucial to assembling the events of a difficult murder scenario. Also, Noreen—no matter how helpful she had been in other investigations—was not a staffer.

"Do you want me to leave?" she asked. "If I'm getting in the way, I'll leave right now. Just say the word."

McGarr reached for her hand, but she pulled it away. He'd hear from her later, he knew.

Which for some reason made him think of Tallon, who lived and worked with his common-law wife in the same building. He wondered how much time they spent together, and if they ever got the chance to get away from their work. And then, singly or together.

"Well, it was a line of inquiry that occurred to the pathologist, given how Ellen Finn was found, naked and on top of Burke. But the report says it's impossible to tell, since"—Ward canted his head, as though embarrassed—"since her vagina had been lubricated. But there was no trace of semen . . . you know, about her person."

McKeon held up one of the pictures. "It being as plain as the nose on your face why? A T'underbolt condom, which is where the lubricant would have come from."

But the others had fallen silent, trying to imagine the scenario that had led to the deaths of the two eel police.

Bresnahan was the first to speak. "Let me get this straight—he, Pascal Burke, Sergeant Pascal Burke—was shot through the heart after having had sex. Three hours later, Ellen Finn, his assistant, was shot through the head with the same gun while perched on top of him, as though they'd been having or just had sex."

"And as though somebody entered the room and shot them together. Once," Noreen put in rather breathlessly. "To make it seem like a crime of passion. There's the note from the husband about her affair with Burke, Burke's reputation as a Lothario, their clothes neatly hanging together in the closet. Whoever did this orchestrated the crime—a double murder— over the course of several hours."

Having noticed her animus, the others were now staring at Noreen.

"And, can I tell you something else?"

They waited. Like McGarr, she was a redhead, her hair a bright arrangement of copper-colored curls. Her eyes were green. Patches of red had appeared on either cheek. "I'm worried. Worried for Quintan Finn. Whoever did this is either strong, or there's more than one of them, and they're trying to pin it on him. Think of what it must have taken to get her into this position." Noreen jabbed at the most graphic photograph. "On top of a cadaver. She was young, she appears fit—"

"And she most probably resisted," Bresnahan put in.

"Without question. Unless they disabled or shot her someplace else, then arranged her like that and shot her again."

"Making three shots?" McKeon asked.

"Yes."

"And there's nothing about bruises on her body," Ward said. "The only other salient details about her are the butterfly tattoo and her being pregnant."

"*What?*" both women said together, Noreen adding, "Well—that changes everything, doesn't it?"

The three men only stared at her.

"Are they thick?" Bresnahan asked. "Or . . . ?"

"Thick. Veritable dunderheads!"

"Make that dunderbolts," McKeon quipped.

"Do you think she would have asked Burke to wear a condom if she was pregnant by him?"

"It's one of the few times in a young woman's life when something like that isn't necessary," Noreen put in, "when many women can allow themselves to be most passionate."

McGarr tried not to react, such having been the case between them when Noreen had been pregnant with Maddie.

"What about disease?" Ward asked. "Maybe she demanded he wear one because she knew he was . . . messing about with who knows who?"

"And she was out for a bit of a lark, like you said earlier, Rut'ie." McKeon shook his head and tsked.

Cocking her head, Bresnahan raised a hand as though trying to grasp something. "Let me tell you two boobs something"—

"Now there's a start," McKeon muttered.

"And get this straight." Head cocked, Bresnahan leaned over the table, her sizable breasts—which today were swathed in sea-green cashmere—splaying to either side, her smoke-colored eyes darting from Ward to McKeon. "I'll bet my last farthing that Ellen Finn, this victim, was not that kind of woman. I'm from a small country town myself, and if she was pregnant, she was pregnant by her husband and nobody else. And if she got murdered like this"—her hand slammed down on one of the forensic photographs—"it's because it was fooking arranged."

Having succeeded in nettling her, both men were smiling slightly. "Maybe they both just liked the feel of the thing," McKeon said to Ward. "Thunderbolt Condoms—the name's a stroke of genius, if nothing else."

"Bernie," Bresnahan said, two bright patches having risen to her cheeks, "sometimes you're a flamin'—"

"Anything about the toilet?" McGarr asked, cutting her off.

They waited while Ward found the entry; a party of fishermen passed by the open door and looked in. Several were speaking Dutch.

"No. Only that it had been cleaned 'most thoroughly,' " Ward said.

"No tile chips, no blood."

Ward shook his head. "The chemical analysis of some wetness discovered behind the commode says the cleanser was Ever Fresh. An empty bottle of it was found in the waste bin and is being examined for fingerprints."

"I never heard of that," said Noreen.

"A note here says it's a commercial product, sold in bulk by restaurant and hotel suppliers."

"Anything further in the report about her wound, Hughie?" McGarr asked.

Ward scanned the sheet, and the next, and the next. "Yah—here's something—the pathologist says that she would like to explore the possibility that the amount of bruising around the wound seems excessive, and there are tears in the flesh of her temple not usual to bullet wounds."

Ward read some more. "The second bullet—entering Burke's body was just slightly offcenter from the first. But this is only a preliminary report. We could put a rush on the final and get the full thing pronto."

"By tomorrow morning, if we make it high priority," said McKeon, who handled such things.

McGarr nodded his approval.

"Finally, a single strand of blond hair was discovered on the pillow beside the two corpses. Dyed blond and not belonging to Ellen Finn, whose blond hair color was natural. As with the condom, the lab will perform a DNA analysis."

Another moment of silence passed, as the five considered what they knew of the crime.

"Oh the other hand," McKeon finally said. "We have two thousand large in Burke's uniform jacket and the snapshots of the Frakes rustling eels down by the river, the pix that were found in her bag."

"Which could have been planted," Noreen shot back. "If you were the Frakes and you did this, would you have left that stuff lying about?"

"Murderers are seldom neat," said Ward. "They almost always leave something lying about."

"And there's this." McKeon held up a Garda fact sheet and passed it to Ward. "I did some checking before I came down yesterday afternoon. It seems Ellen Finn was a kayaker and could get around the river without making much noise.

"Last month in the middle of the night she came upon the Frakes poaching eels. They jumped in their van, and when they wouldn't stop for her, she shot out two of their tires. They kept going, but they'd left their woman behind—"

"Gertrude McGurk, her name is," said Bresnahan, who was scanning the tech-squad report.

"And she resisted arrest. Maybe you remember the picture of her appearing in court the next day." McKeon had a photocopy of that as well. "Our woman there—Ellen—thumped her bloody, and Gertrude McGurk swore out a complaint charging her with police brutality."

More silence ensued, as each of the five tried to put the case together. Or, at least, tried to understand which avenue of investigation should be pursued first.

"Also there's the matter of the other guests—who they are, what they might have heard," said Ward. "We've got an all-points out on them."

"And the personnel in the inn and pub," McKeon said, almost wistfully, adding. "Didn't you mention in your report, Chief, that you didn't think the maid was telling you everything she knows about who Burke had been bedding?"

Lost in thought, McGarr only nodded. He was trying to marshal the facts, even though he knew it was too early to draw any conclusion but one: that the ballistics report and autopsy made the dynamic of the double murder apparent. Ellen Finn's murder had been staged to mislead them about who had slain Pascal Burke three hours earlier.

Why? To implicate the Frakes, who subsequently tried to murder their erstwhile comrade, Benny Carson?

Plainly, they didn't know enough. But in McGarr's experience, murders of such premeditation and . . . craft seldom occurred without some animus. Having been known eel poachers as well as regulars at the bar—to say nothing of having carried a carpet upstairs at or around the time of the murders—at least Manus Frakes would have been a suspect in Burke's death without the money in Burke's jacket and without the photographs of the Frakes poaching eels.

Why, then, murder Ellen Finn?

The husband, Quintan Finn, had been with Frakes at the time. Finn of the note on the table, Finn who was missing.

McGarr also remembered the little girl he first met in the courtyard, the one with the beeper of the same brand as issued to Garda personnel. Manus Frakes's daughter, as it turned out. But not by the woman, Gertrude McGurk, whom Carson described as "something close to a professional woman."

"Also there's this—where are Ellen Finn's undergarments?" said Bresnahan, holding up the page of the tech-squad report listing all items found in the room. "No bra, panties, stockings."

"Maybe she was just dressed for action," McKeon suggested.

The two women glared at him.

"Don't look at me—you know yourselves, it happens."

Tallon had appeared in the doorway. "Sorry—but there's a gentleman from the Shannon Regional Fisheries Board to see you."

Thanking him, McGarr waited until Tallon had left the room before he passed out assignments, sending Bresnahan and Ward to the house where the Frakes had been living to see if they could find some lead as to where the three might have fled. McKeon was dispatched to the bar to renew his acquaintance with boyhood chum, Benny Carson.

"Ah, no—Chief, please—anyplace but the bar on a Garda Siochana expense account." McKeon grasped his throat. "Send Hughie, send Ruth—anybody but poor parched Bernie McKeon."

Signaling that the meeting was over, McGarr stood but

not without pain. His right leg was now a mottled whorl of bruises where the door of his erstwhile Cooper had slammed into his thigh after having been struck by the high-powered bullet. It reminded him of his loss. And the Frakes.

Out in the hall McGarr shook hands with Chief Officer Eamon Gannon of the Fisheries Board and expressed his condolences on Gannon's having lost two of his staff.

A bearish man in early forties with a full beard and mustache that had just begun to gray, Gannon looked off. "I still can't take it all in. It's so hard to believe. Do you know who . . . ?"

McGarr shook his head. "But you can help us."

"Anything. Anything at all."

McGarr then introduced Noreen. "Would you mind if my daughter comes along? She's very interested in fish and the environment."

"What about me?" Noreen demanded. "Do you think I'm not?"

McGarr knew for a fact that her only concern for fish was limited to the one that might appear on her dinner plate. Also, any environment lacking horses was for Noreen not considerable at all, she being profoundly a land person. "I thought perhaps you'd like to poke around town here, like Bernie. Who knows what somebody might have seen."

He watched admiringly while his impulsive, intelligent, and beautiful wife sorted through the probability of enjoying an outing with her husband and daughter or the possibility of discovering something critical to the investigation on her own.

Twelve full years younger than he, Noreen was a trained art historian and restorer who managed her family's fine arts gallery in upmarket Dawson Street in Dublin. But her hobby—where she had the most fun—seemed to be his career, which, however, she would be the last to admit.

No item of information regarding a current investigation

was too small to be of interest, and any request for "word on the street"—meaning Dublin gossip—was pursued with a diligence that few on his staff could equal.

Now wrestling with the pleasant trade-off which either way promised an enjoyable day, tiny crow's-feet—new now in her forty-second year—appeared at the corners of her green eyes.

Noreen was a diminutive, well-formed woman with fine features. Today she was wearing jeans, flats, a cable-knit green cardigan that matched her eyes over a white turtleneck jumper—what McGarr had dubbed her "off-duty" uniform.

Gritting her teeth—her eyes sparkling nonetheless—she asked, "Do you think Maddie would mind?"

McGarr pretended to demur. "It's an agonizing decision, I know. But somebody has to make it. And there's the possibility that you need your own time." To *investigate,* he knew she knew he meant, marriages being largely about the first language—the unspoken language—that was forged in intimacy over many years. The McGarrs had been married for an even dozen.

"Yah," she agreed. And to the Fisheries Board Chief, "Excuse me. I'll fetch our daughter. She's up in our rooms doing her schoolwork."

"Dress her warm. It's cold and wet by the river."

# 11

Eels

While waiting for Maddie to join them, McGarr took Gannon into the room that functioned as the library, saying, "You're not going to like what I'm about to show you. But it's necessary. I have some questions."

The sky had cleared, and a ray of strong sunlight was falling across a table near a window. Into it McGarr placed the least graphic of the forensic photographs taken at the murder scene, one that showed the victims plainly but from afar.

Gannon gasped, and his body flinched.

"What do you know about their relationship?" McGarr asked.

Gannon had to put a hand out to steady himself before sitting in a nearby chair. And it took a while before he could speak.

McGarr pulled up another chair and listened to the contrapuntal ticking of two competing grandfather clocks in the overfurnished room.

Finally, Gannon glanced up at McGarr. "I feel rather nauseous. It's almost worse than their having been . . . murdered. I don't mean that, but . . ."

McGarr considered easing the man's pain by telling him about the three-hour interval between their deaths and the supposition that the tryst had been staged. But what he was seeking was a confirmation of that theory. "Burke was a Lothario, I take it."

"Oh, aye—desperate. But I would never think, I *could* never think that Ellen and he were . . ."

"Did you ever see her with Burke after working hours?"

Gannon hunched burly shoulders that were wrapped in a waxed-cotton waterproof jacket of the sort that had been in the boot of his Cooper—McGarr only now realized—and would now have to be replaced. "Our 'working' hours are mainly at night at this time of year. It can be dangerous, so I often pair the staff. But not with Burke. I didn't pair her with him. Ever."

"Why not?"

Gannon's eyes met McGarr's for a moment before shying toward the door. "I know it's wrong to speak ill of the dead, but Pascal Burke was an unsavory character altogether and possibly a bad man."

McGarr nearly smiled at the innocence of the assessment. "Forever on the make, if you know what I mean.

"At first I dismissed it as a midlife crisis, but it went on for"—Gannon opened his palms— "years. Also, there was the suspicion—which I was never able to prove—that he was taking backhanders."

"From poachers?"

Gannon nodded.

"What about this? It appears that Ellen's husband thinks her affair with Gannon had been going on before and during their marriage."

Gannon shook his head. "I can only say that, of all the women I know, including my own loyal wife, I would have expected that of Ellen Gilday Finn least."

Asking for Gannon's confidence, McGarr then told him about the time lapse and the fact that Burke had been shot twice—once through the heart three hours earlier than the young woman, who had obviously been arranged on top of Burke before being shot herself. "That bullet entered Burke, too, but not as perfectly as the murderer or murderers planned. Was Ellen working Friday night?"

Gannon nodded. "I had her paired with another officer patrolling the riverbanks about ten miles south of here."

"Can I speak to the . . . man, woman?"

"Man. I 'll take you to him."

Outside, McGarr had to dodge a clutch of reporters, photographers, and cameramen who had gathered in front of the hotel.

"You know as much as I know," he told them. "The investigation has only just begun. When I know more and can tell you, I'll call you together."

Which was greeted by a chorus of, "Yeah, *right!*"

Cold air from the fallen snow—meeting warm vapors off the water of the river—had created a funnel of cottony fog over the Shannon, and the ruts of an informal road along its eastern bank were brimming with meltwater, slush, and a thick slippery mud.

Through it Gannon drove his battered Land Rover at a snail's pace, the four-wheel-drive gear clattering in its box.

McGarr sat beside Gannon, and Maddie had hopped in back with Gannon's dog, a friendly black Lab that reeked of river muck and reeds.

As though sensing that Maddie was a dog lover, O'Leary— as he was called—immediately moved toward her and leaned his considerable weight into her shoulder.

Like her parents, Maddie would not grow tall, but she was a pretty girl with regular features and hair such a deep shade of red it was nearly brown. And where her dark brown eyes came from, nobody knew, since the only dark-eyed ancestor on either side was McGarr's grandmother. Today, her hair was braided in a long pigtail.

"I'm glad I wore my slicker," she observed. "No offense, O'Leary, but I've got one word for you—SOAP. And your breath! Tell me true—how many eels have you et today?" And yet the diminutive girl, who was ten, had an arm around the friendly beast that was panting in the warm truck.

"I'll put the lad outside, if he's bothering you," Gannon said.

"Ah, no—O'Leary's fine right here," Maddie replied, patting the dog's wide glossy chest. As though to thank her, the dog turned its head and tried to lick her ear.

"Oooof! You're a basilisk, you are, O'Leary. And you like it that way, I can tell."

Basilisk was obviously a term Maddie had picked up from her mother, who had an intellectual bent, and McGarr tried to recall just exactly what a basilisk was besides, obviously, having bad breath. But without yet another cup of strong coffee he was locked in the kind of half-cognizant stupor that one of his older friends called, "Senior stasis—don't expect it to get any better. It won't."

Thus, McGarr was paying only half a mind to Gannon's narrative of how difficult it was to police the Shannon eel fishery.

"The eels, you see, migrate during the fall, and they move mainly on windy, moonless fall nights when the current is favorable. That's when the fishing is best and most poaching takes place. In the dark off roads, like this. Which makes the poachers very difficult to catch."

"Using fyke nets?" McGarr asked, if only to prove to himself that he was conscious.

"Sometimes, if they're well-organized poachers. And many

of them are. They wear masks and have lookouts with walkie-talkies. No numbers on their boats and no license plates or tax stamps on their cars. And operating down here along hundreds of miles of riverbank in the dead of night . . ." Gannon shook his head. "They're harder and slippery-er than the very eels to catch. That's why Ellen's nabbing the Frakes, like she did in her kayak, was brilliant, God rest her soul."

"Weren't they jailed?" McGarr asked.

"Sure—for a night. Irony is, in morning their woman, the blond—"

"Gertrude McGurk."

"Came down with a fistful of readies—doubtless got from poaching—and bailed them out. It was their third time in court for poaching, so the judge threw the book at them—a two-thousand-pound fine apiece, and the promise of doubling that if they were ever hauled in again."

"And they paid it?"

"Without a word, like they were buying a round at a bar. Eel wholesalers buying for Japanese and Chinese brokers are currently paying two hundred pounds a kilo for eel elvers. In one pass, a fine-mesh fyke net with a motorized winch can pull in nine to fifteen hundred kilos. Deployed several times a night with a lorry nearby to carry them out." Again Gannon shook his head. "You don't need many nights like that for a packet of money, tax-free."

"What are fyke nets?" With a sleeve Maddie wiped the condensation off a window so O'Leary could look out, but it was as though the Land Rover were passing slowly through a dense but brilliant cloud. Overhead the sun had to be shining.

"Nets that form big bags and can stretch across the entire river," Gannon explained. "Because fyke nets catch all the elvers migrating inland, pretty soon there would be no eels left to procreate. That's why fyke nets are illegal."

"So anybody using them has to be a poacher," McGarr put in.

Gannon nodded. "We only issue about three dozen licenses a year by lottery. And applications require the kind of personal and business information that thugs don't like giving. Instead, they horn in on the fishing sites of legitimate eel fishers, who've paid hundreds of pounds for the exclusive right to fish there.

"Beatings, cars and boats shot up. One had his fishing shack bombed."

"By the Frakes, you think?"

"Ach, who knows—the Frakes are not alone, and, really, I've always thought of them as small fry, not nearly as organized as some. You heard about the report of high-powered weapons fire at a shooting range near Mullingar?" It was a Midlands city about forty miles distant.

McGarr nodded, having read the report that later appeared in newspapers. When the local police arrived, they found whoever it was gone but the ground littered with a mass of shells fired from a Kalashnikov rifle. Could it have been a Kalashnikov that had been used to destroy his Cooper the day before, he wondered.

"What's an elver?" Maddie asked from the back.

Gannon turned his head to her. "A baby eel. Do you know about eels, Maddie?"

She made a face. "I don't think I want to. They're slimy, aren't they?"

"Well—the slime is actually a very important slime. It's a mucous membrane that protects their tender skin and allows them to wriggle and squiggle after food and find shelter in rocks."

"Do people actually eat them?"

"Any way they can—fresh, smoked, barbecued, and even

jellied. In many countries, smoked eel commands a much hirer price than premium-grade smoked wild salmon."

"Now salmon I like," said Maddie.

"O'Leary even likes to roll on them, but only when they're dead."

"Ooof." Maddie tried to push the dog away, but it wouldn't budge.

Gannon and McGarr both chuckled.

"Now, don't knock what you haven't tried." A pleasant man, Gannon winked so only McGarr could see. "I bet you didn't think you'd like salmon, when you first tried it. And consider this—the elvers that arrive here to Ireland are some of the bravest and hardiest creatures on earth. Haven't they swum all the way from the Sargasso Sea without eating once?"

"Where's that?"

"Way down by Bermuda, off the coast of America. On their way, dozens of species of predaceous fish take their toll, and then—here in the river they've got to get over fish ladders at dams and past legal fishermen and poachers, like I was just telling your dad.

"But they don't begin to eat—not so much as a single zooplankton—until they've spent twenty-four hours in fresh water. And then they'll only eat what they've first tasted, which makes a Shannon River eel taste different from, say, a Lee River eel."

"You mean, eels from each river have their own distinctive taste?" McGarr asked, not having known that.

"That's right. And something else that's unique to eels— opposite of salmon, shad, sea trout, and sea bass, they're the only fish that breeds in salt water but lives in fresh. It's called being catadromous."

There was a pause as the three thought about what had been said.

Finally, Maddie asked, "How far is the Sargasso Sea?"

"It's a big still spot in the middle of the Atlantic Ocean about three or four thousand miles from here."

"And they come all the way from there on no food?"

"And no parents to guide them, either. Their digestive systems are devised for freshwater eating only, so they can't feed until they find the river that their parents lived in. Which is why they're called glass or silver eels. If you catch one when it first enters the river and hold it up against the light, you can see right through its body and the tube of its digestive system, which is empty."

"What happened to their parents?"

"Ah, now—there's the sad part of the tale. After spending up to fourteen years in a freshwater river or lake, adult eels reverse-commute, so to speak, to the Sargasso Sea again on no food. There they spawn and die, the cycle of their lives being over."

"But how do the elvers know which way to swim to get here?"

Gannon hunched his broad shoulders. "Nobody knows for sure. It's one of the great mysteries of nature. They're only five or six inches long with a brain the size of a grain of sand, and yet they get here, year after year. Or, at least, we hope they'll continue to arrive, year after year.

"Do you know about the new pressure we have on this fishery?" Gannon asked McGarr.

He then explained that in the past the Fisheries Board had to worry only about poaching in the river. But recently because of just what his staff was trying to end in Ireland— overfishing that had stripped stocks in Asian waters to near extinction—commercial fishing fleets from China and Japan had begun netting glass eels off the coasts of the UK, France, Spain, Portugal, and Ireland.

"They use electronic sensors to spot the eels and enormous

nets, some of them stretching up to twenty-eight miles. In one pass they can take an entire school of fish."

"Like our salmon," McGarr put in, since schools of salmon returning to Irish rivers to spawn had been faced with the same threat for over a decade now.

"The new technique is to ship them live back to the Orient where in aquaculture plants they're 'educated' to eat a secret diet that makes them taste the way Chinese and Japanese eels tasted."

"When they had them," Maddie said with an angry edge to her voice.

"Exactly. They're also stuffed and treated with hormones so they reach maturity in about two years instead of the usual fourteen. Fattened up, like that, they go for around a thousand American dollars apiece. In Japan, the eels are barbecued for a special dish called *kabayaki* that's considered a rare culinary treat, rather like Beluga caviar is to European palates. Or truffles."

"But can't we stop them from stealing our eels?" Maddie asked, her eyebrows knitted with concern.

"Not really, if they're fishing in international waters, which begins at twelve miles off the coast."

"Or our Taosieach. Can't he go to their Taosieach and tell them to stop?"

"It's been tried, but . . ." Gannon pulled the Land Rover off the road onto a laneway, and a building that resembled a fishing shack suddenly appeared through the cottony fog. A small boat with an outboard motor was tied to a dock. "Which is all the more reason that we have to stop the poaching here—so the elvers that get through can live long enough to make the trip back to the Sargasso Sea."

Yet two of those who had been trying to accomplish that had just been murdered, thought McGarr, getting out of the car and helping Maddie from the back. And were there tears in her eyes? When he bent to look more closely, she turned her head away quickly, the braided pigtail whipping over her shoulder.

McGarr tried not to smile, realizing how difficult it must be to arrive at an age when suddenly you could understand complexities but were still very much a child emotionally. Wrapping a hand around her shoulder, he pulled her into him so Gannon wouldn't see the tears that were now streaming down her cheeks."

O'Leary, the Lab, bounded ahead of them and scratched at the door of the shack.

"I've asked Paddy Keating, Ellen's partner, to be here to speak with you," Gannon explained. "He was with her Friday afternoon when her beeper went off. But he'll tell you himself."

The interior of the shack was toasty from the ruby glow of an electric fire in one corner. But apart from a silvery light streaming through the only window, the room was dark.

At a table sat a man in his thirties who was dressed for the weather much like Gannon. There was a mug and Thermos before him with a pencil, a pad, and a two-way radio nearby. After introductions, McGarr and Gannon took the two other seats, and Maddie wandered over to the window.

"Can you tell me about Friday?" McGarr asked.

Keating hunched his shoulders. "What's to tell? We'd just got here and were planning how we'd handle the night." He glanced up so the light fell across his face, and McGarr caught sight of a long fresh scar on his forehead.

"We'd got a report from a farmer saying he'd found tire tracks and footprints all up and down the riverbank, and the field was filled with dead coarse fish."

"There's no concern for other species," Gannon explained, glancing over at Maddie and lowering his voice. "When they pull in the fyke net, they just trash the other fish and make no attempt to put them back in the water. Unless it's a salmon, of course."

To be sold over the bar at some pub, McGarr well knew.

"And we thought we saw a pattern in how they were working the river," Keating continued. "Using the same sites on the various rivers but jumping from the Brosna to the Shannon and then the Blackwater." The other two rivers were tributaries of the Shannon. "That's when her beeper went off.

"Ellen didn't recognize the number, and the one cell phone we had is a dud." Keating pointed to an equipment rack on one wall. "It hasn't worked in a dog's age."

"Budget," Gannon explained, shaking his head.

"So, after being paged twice more, she decided it had to be important, and she drove into town. It was the last I saw of her."

"Did she write down the number?" McGarr asked.

Keating shook his head. "The first time she asked if I recognized it, and she said the number to me. And don't think I haven't been trying to remember what it was." He turned the pad and showed McGarr what appeared to be several telephone numbers. "Not one of them rings."

"What about recent investigations? Were you concentrating on anybody in particular?"

Keating glanced at Gannon, and nearly together they said, "The Frakes," Gannon adding, "They're scofflaws of the worst sort. It's the whole bandit thing from the North—laws were made by other people to keep you poor and oppressed."

"And should be broken on principle," Keating put in. "You should see them in the pub—they get jarred and start singing all the old rebel songs. And if you should so much as look at them sideways, they're on you. The both of them."

"What happened to your forehead?"

"I got thumped in Leixleap three months ago in the courtyard in back of the inn. Broke my leg, bruised my liver. This"—Keating pointed to his forehead—"was the least of it."

McGarr waited, the man obviously having more to say.

"Two men in balaclavas and eye masks. Northern accents.

Told me they'd kill me unless I quit this job." Keating paused before adding, "I guess they made good on Ellen."

"You reported it to the police?"

"Declan Riley, the sergeant at the barracks?"

McGarr nodded.

"He pulled in the Frakes, Manus and Donal. He's the younger wild one. It's said he's killed five men with his hands alone. But nothing came of it. They swore they were in the pub when it happened."

"And got Carson to confirm it," said Gannon.

"Benny Carson, the barman?" McGarr asked.

Both men nodded. "He's one of them," Keating added. "More than that—he's the brains of what they do and how they can keep doing it without landing in the drum."

Not anymore, McGarr thought. "Could it have been somebody other than the Frakes who beat you? Who else from the North is active here?"

Gannon closed his eyes. "Who isn't? The chance for quick cash profits, either poaching or ripping off some poor defenseless fisherman in the dead of night having brought them."

"Or both," added Keating.

"Most come down for a day or two of 'sport,' so to speak, then blow back across the border with a few thousand quid in their pockets. But around here, only the Frakes stayed, that I know of."

McGarr wrote the main number of the inn on a business card and handed it to Keating. "If you think of the number of the call—or anything else—phone me.

"May I take this sheet?" McGarr pointed to the pad with the numbers.

Keating handed him the piece of paper.

# 12

Nightware

Ruth Bresnahan and Hugh Ward had not conducted an investigation together for nearly a year, ever since Ward had moved in with Lee Sigal, the woman who had given birth to his son fourteen years earlier but who had kept the birth secret from Ward until recently.

Granted Ward had been recovering from gunshot wounds at the time, and the moving in had been more de facto than de jure—Lee having the leisure, money, and inclination to nurse Ward back to health. Bresnahan, of course, had to work.

How it happened was Ward, during the course of an investigation, discovered that a woman—who had seemed familiar to him but had given her name as Lee Stone—was actually Leah Sigal, who had been his history instructor during the one semester fourteen years earlier that he had attended university. They had a torrid affair, but Ward had not seen her since.

But when she had introduced him to her fourteen-year-old son whose name was also Hugh and looked so much like Ward that it was like looking into a time-warped mirror, she had to tell him. And Ward was glad she had, all children needing to know—and to have the benefit of knowing—their fathers.

Gravely injured in a gunfight shortly after the revelation, Ward had arranged for a licensed nurse to tend him in his bachelor digs as he was being released from hospital. And in retrospect probably should have, since Bresnahan and he were still very much involved. But Ward had come close to dying, and his perspective on life had changed dramatically.

And so, when Lee had revealed how much she loved him—never dating other men and maintaining an album of press clippings from his days as an amateur boxer and his career with the Garda—and asked that he give her another baby "with no string attached. Not one," Ward had complied. Knowing in his heart of hearts that it was no mere string that would bind him to her, his son, and the as-yet-unborn baby. But rather an unbreakable chain of affection.

Also, at the time Ward's affair with Bresnahan had grown flat, with both maintaining their own digs and neither owning up to the reality that they should be married. In other words, what Ward believed to be the *moment* that occurs in all affectionate relationships, when something greater could have happened, had passed.

Yet for some reason that Ward only vaguely understood, he still felt deep guilt about how and why they had broken up, perhaps because he had made the decision when he was still recovering from his wounds and his judgment had been clouded. But he could not go back on it either, which made the deep affection he still felt for Bresnahan all the more maddening.

At times he told himself that it had just been . . . you know, *events*—what had happened while he had been on the mend and beginning to feel better while living in the house of his former lover. Which was the rekindling—no, the immolation—of a torrid passion that dated back to his youth.

The heat had simply been too much to deny and had over-whelmed him.

At rare other times, when Ward could view things dispassionately, he acknowledged the truth, which was not pretty: that he was probably a semiferal male who could love two women simultaneously and equally—Lee, who was dark, diminutive, considered in her ways, and the mother of his child and soon children.

And Ruth, a tall angular redhead, who was feisty and visceral, and whom Ward could not bear the thought of other men . . . dating. At night his dreams—erotic and otherwise—were still filled with her.

Bresnahan's own feelings were not dissimilar. Hurt and angry after Ward had chosen the other woman for what she knew was the best of reasons—since she could not bear the finality of the thought of marriage and was surely not the motherly type—she had gone out with a spate of other men. But it had not been the same. The certain something that was Hughie Ward in the particular was always missing.

Probably it was his utter maleness. How sure he was about who he was and what he was doing, from his long tenure as one of Europe's best amateur boxers, which the recent injuries had probably ended. To how he pursued his chosen career; someday he would run the Garda, she was certain.

And then, of course, he was darkly handsome in a way that was Bresnahan's cup of tea exactly.

Thrown together now in a car on the wet and slippery cart track leading to the safe house that the brothers Frakes and Gertrude McGurk had occupied, the tension between the two was nearly palpable.

Bresnahan was at the wheel. A powerful, four-door car with a sun roof and spoiler, the Opel *Vectra* had been selected because it did not look like an unmarked Garda patrol vehicle. And Bresnahan drove the automobile as its designers intended.

Born and raised in the mountains of Kerry, she had learned to drive a tractor when she was only ten and with her father's permission had plied the narrow and often perilous roads of that mountainous county even before she was old enough to apply for a learner's permit. Thus, a slushy Midlands farm track posed her little problem.

Ward, on the other hand, was a confirmed Dubliner who never drove when taxis or public transportation were available. In fact, he did not own a car and only took the wheel of a Garda vehicle when absolutely necessary.

Working the gearshift and the accelerator with Eurotour skill, Bresnahan slammed and bucked the Opel through the mire that became, like the fog, all the deeper as they approached the river. Until the house with the cinder of McGarr's Cooper nearby suddenly appeared out of the gloom, and Bresnahan swung the passenger side of the car in a juddering skid as close to the front door as possible.

"*Olé!*" Ward cheered, if only to break the silence.

"Hop out, Super'. I've still got to bring meself in for a landing." It was the *breezy* manner that Bresnahan had decided to adopt when alone with Ward, as though the past didn't matter, that what they had was just water-over-the-weir, so to speak. Such an approach would allow them to continue as an investigative team, and also perhaps just drive him mad, which was a happy thought.

"Why don't you just hop over that and get out on this side?" He pointed to the drivetrain and leather-swathed gearshift.

"Surely, you jest. What you have here—*had*, shame on me—is a sizable woman and a small car. In spite of our mutual experience, you are deceived if you think I'm a contortionist."

With that she pulled shut the door, and Ward knew enough to move away, as she hit the gas and twisted the wheel, sending a rooster tail of creamy mud into the yard.

Ward didn't know what to think. Was she making fun of him and what had been for him the only other important love relationship of his life? Feeling suitably compromised—at once understanding that they couldn't have the same relationship as before but mourning the fact—Ward snugged his oilskin cap over his brow and drew his Glock from under his all-weather jacket.

It was unlikely that the Frakes had returned to the house, but they would take no chances. Keeping down so as not to be seen passing by any of the first floor windows, Ward worked his way around back.

"Hah-loo," Bresnahan called out, twisting open the handle and pushing the door open while concealing herself on the other side of the wall. She was nothing if not professional. "Is anybody about? Hah-loo! It's Ruth from the village, wondering if you'd like to contribute to our football effort."

Meanwhile, Ward had found the back door open, which would not have been the case, he assumed, had the Frakes been present. Yet he kept his weapon drawn as he moved into the kitchen. The pantry. And obviously a children's room off the kitchen.

Glancing down the hall, he saw Rut'ie—as he referred to her himself—entering the residence, gun first. He waited until she saw him, then he moved toward her. Now inside, they would check the rest of the house together, backing each other up.

But Ward had little hope that either of the Frakes or their—what was she?—companion Gertrude McGurk had returned. Situated on a shelf of raised ground on the riverbank, the house had soaked up the moisture of the Shannon and the cold of the wintry day like a stone sponge, and he imagined that a hot stove was a necessity there year-round.

And all that was contained in McGarr's report of his visit the day before appeared to be untouched—a collection of nets and what seemed to be building material in the sitting room that contained no furniture.

Like all other rooms save the well-fitted-out kitchen with its large Aga cooker, the crib in the child's room, and a rather ornate bed and mirrored armoire in the room that obviously the McGurk woman inhabited. The Frakes slept on mattresses on the floors of separate bedrooms, with their personal belongings strewn about them.

Ward dug a coin from the pocket of his trousers. "Heads or tails?"

Bresnahan slid her Glock back into a kidney holster. "You know me—I'm easy." Smiling, she glanced at him in a way that suggested she was having him on.

"Which?" Ward demanded, looking away.

She shrugged.

He slid the coin back in his pocket. "You lose." He pointed toward the stairs.

"Whatever you say, Super'. You de mahn."

"What's that supposed to mean?"

"Just what I said—you de mahn."

As she moved away from him he perused the curve of her hip and the line of her legs. Today the entire smooth package was contained in skintight sweats of the same forest green color as the cashmere sweater she was wearing, and which—it now occurred to Ward—she had chosen to wear just to taunt him with her body, what he could probably never ever again have. Which also accounted for her provocative allusions.

Well, he decided—wrenching his eyes from her back—he wouldn't bite, so to speak. He'd treat her as he treated the rest of the staff—with what he thought of as distant familiarity.

And yet, could the tights be Gore-Tex, Ward wondered as he turned toward the heaps of dirty laundry in the first bedroom. If so, where had she gotten them?

Skiing in Norway, he decided. It was a favorite venue of hers, and she had just returned from a fortnight holiday about which she'd been uncharacteristically mum in the office. Could she have spent it with another man? Ward wondered, feeling the sharp sting of jealousy.

How could he be jealous? he asked himself. He had no right to be jealous. Still, if he could just get a feel of that material he'd know if it was Gore-Tex. But when he looked back, she was gone.

And so they passed an hour going through everything they could find in the house. What struck Ward was how poor and comfortless was nearly everything that the two brothers had owned, from the absence of furniture to their clothes that were the tawdrily stylish gear seen on the covers of rock-group CDs—tight jeans, tighter (he imagined) jerseys, square-heeled boots, even what looked like an imitation leather bolero jacket.

It was stuff that could be had—and he could see from the labels had been purchased—at cut-price shops in Derry and Dublin. Even the collection of thin gold rings in differing sizes for different pierced parts of the body, Ward imagined, were only gold-filled, as if they considered themselves unworthy of anything of quality or substance, no matter how much tax-free swag they pulled in.

Mattresses with dirty—no, filthy—sheets on the floor. Beer cans. A brimming bowl of stubbed-out cigarette butts with a crack pipe in the ashes, lids of aluminum foil from same, and a roach clip complete with roach.

In the second bedroom, which had been used by Donal Frakes—Ward assumed from a court summons that had been thrown away—he found snapshots pasted on the wall of women striking provocative poses mainly in the buff.

In others, Donal Frakes had been captured having sex with two women who were also having sex with each other. And a final large and grainy blown-up shot pictured Donal Frakes having sex with Gertrude McGurk—Ward believed she was—against the door of the room. Life-size, it had been hung, of course, on the door of the room where the event had occurred.

Art shot, Ward thought, moving out into the hall and toward her room, the door of which was open but contained the advisement, "KNOCK FIRST" in block capitals. The door had also recently been equipped with a new lock and dead bolt, the one that McGarr had just finished opening when the shots rang out that nearly killed Benny Carson and destroyed McGarr's car.

But the room was an island of order and comfort, with fresh paint on the wall, a recently hoovered imitation oriental rug on the floor, and a high posted bed. There was not a sexual reference in sight, not even in the small desk by the bed, where Ward found some bills that were unpaid and letters from McGurk's mother, who lived in Newry, urging her to come home.

> *"Niall McGrath just got divorced from that woman who left him and has been asking after you. As he has no children and a good job with the Council. You could do worse. Drop that gypsy life you're leading and come home, Trudy."*

Ward slipped the envelope with its return address in his pocket. As well as the 32-caliber Beretta with a full clip and the safety thumbed off. Gertrude McGurk had been afraid of someone or something, and had concealed it between the mattress and box spring on the side of the bed farther from the door.

An answering machine was attached to the telephone in the room, and the light was blinking. Ward tapped the playback button. A man's voice said, "It's me, and I'm baaaaack!

And just devastated that you seem to be busy now on Thursday evening about"—there was a pause—"half eleven. What about a wee visit tomorrow morning. You name the hour. I've just got to see you. You know where I am."

Ward took the tape as well, before turning to the armoire that functioned as a dresser. And it was while he was going through the top drawer that was filled with what he thought of as "nightware"—chemises, bustiers, boas, thong-type underwear, the silk stockings and garter belt that she had worn when being serviced against the door—that Bresnahan entered the room.

"Hard at it, I see."

Ward was holding a handful of the tawdry items in one hand while rifling through the drawer with the other.

Bresnahan snatched a strapless brassiere out of his hand and wrapped the cups around her own breasts. "Great form, this woman—wouldn't you say? Good breasts, thin hips, nice legs as displayed on the back side of the door in the next room.

"Can't imagine what she sees in those two erstwhile military yokes, unless I'm missing something. Privates Dirty and Dirtier."

Just that, Ward was moved to say. How often had they seen it in their work before—the slide down into degradation and death. Some fast, others slow. Gertrude McGurk would wake up one morning a toothless addicted or diseased old hag in some slum or doorway.

But he was staring down at the white brassiere spread across Bresnahan's green cashmere jumper. And a longing that was beyond dreams swept over him—for Bresnahan and what they had been together, the good *young* and innocent times they had spent discovering each other and what their lives could have been together. And could never again be.

Before he was shot and nearly killed. And before whatever

genetic mechanism it was kicked in and made him decide that it was procreation that mattered. The next generation. Life, after all, being short and made up of a concatenation of quick hard choices.

Sensing his mood, Bresnahan tossed the brassiere into the drawer. "Look at these." From her jacket pocket she removed a number of photographs and spread them across the nightwear. Captioned obviously by a child, they pictured, "MA AND ME IN HOSPITAL," which was an overexposed Polaroid of a wan young woman in a hospital smock holding a newborn baby lovingly in her arms.

The second shot showed the woman, who looked increasingly thin and suddenly gray with a toddler, the next with a young child, and the final photograph pictured the pair back in hospital with roles reversed—the child clasping the mother's shoulders and bandaged head, which she was kissing. The woman's eyes were not open. The caption read, "MA AND ME BEFOR MA WENT TO HEAVEN." Each caption was signed, "Cara Frakes."

"Ma being Manus Frakes's wife," Bresnahan said, placing two wedding rings on the final photograph. She turned the underside of the larger one into the light from the window nearby. "Names, wedding date. His wife's last name was Carson. Nelly Carson."

"Benny Carson's . . . daughter?" Ward asked, picking up the rings and the photographs and closing the top drawer of the armoire. He reached for the handles of the second.

"Could be. Or it could be a coincidence. But if Nelly Carson was Benny Carson's daughter, it would make Carson this little girl's grandfather."

"Whom Manus Frakes—if it was Manus Frakes—tried to kill when he destroyed the Chief's car."

"So it would seem."

"Why? A . . . falling-out?"

"Obviously."

"Over what—the eel trade, whatever else they were in-volved in? The murder?"

"It occurred to me as well."

Lost in thought, Ward opened the second drawer.

And Bresnahan gasped. "Oh, my—what have we here?"

Ward looked down on a variety of whips, chains, a pair of handcuffs with "NYPD" engraved on the stainless-steel surface of each clasp. And probes of various sorts, some with complicated tenebrae of straps.

"Tools of the trade," said Ward, reaching toward the packets of condoms that filled the other half of the drawer. There seemed to be every brand and type—ribbed, colored, flavored, tasseled, extended—but of all the brands Thunderbolt was not among them.

"Something there you fancy?" Bresnahan asked. "I wouldn't think such items interested you any longer, daddy-o."

Ward ignored the oblique reference to his family situation. "Ever come across Thunderbolt condoms?"

There was a pause during which Bresnahan seemed to have to gather herself. "I assume you're asking that question in a professional . . ." she almost said vein, "way, not—you know . . ."

"Know what?" Ward kept pawing through the inventory. "I'm not following you."

"Can I say something?"

"Anything you want."

"Sometimes you're an incredible . . . incredibly obtuse."

"As opposed to acute? Well." Ward glanced up and rubbed an eyebrow, as though considering the justice of the remark.

Combined with a widow's peak, his eyebrows, which met in a dark line, were the feature that made his face so differently handsome. And so irresistible for Bresnahan. She would—she now realized with a pang—never love anybody again as totally as she had Hughie Ward. He had been and, she feared, still was her first and only true love.

"I'll take that. Sometimes, I suspect, I can be a little thick. But then again, we all can."

"Do you mean me?"

He turned to her and noted the glowering brow, the quivering upper lip that was just slightly protrusive and which he had traced with his own lips he couldn't count the times. "Do you think you're exempt?"

Maybe an inch or so taller than Ward, she stepped in on him, making sure their eyes locked. "Can I tell you something?"

"Shoot."

"I don't know one condom from another, and the only person that I've known in my life who did is you. You . . . slut."

Ward reached for her hip to pull her into him, to comfort her—he told himself—and she chopped his hand away. "Don't even think about touching me. Ever."

Ward raised his palms. "Sorry. I understand."

"*No!* You don't understand. You'll never understand. You only ever think of yourself, and what I don't understand is how you could have done what you did to . . . us." Turning, she moved toward the window.

Ward had known it would be difficult having to work with Bresnahan again, and he had even approached McGarr about somehow avoiding the situation. But McGarr had been intractable—"If you want to be reassigned, it's your call. But Ruth has told me she wants to stay, and I won't reassign her because of your personal life. *Lives,*" he had added pejoratively.

Not finding Thunderbolt condoms among the collection, Ward closed the drawer and opened the last, which contained a number of jumpers, skirts, slacks on one side and a photo album and a packet of tampons on the other. None of the photos had actually been inserted into the plastic sleeves; the brace of, say, three or four dozen had simply been stuffed into the volume.

All pictured Gertrude McGurk standing alongside a different man, who was usually older and shorter and looked a bit embarrassed to have been caught on film with the younger woman. For her part, McGurk—wearing some tawdry outfit, in several, a leatherette miniskirt with high black boots to match—appeared triumphant. One of the only two men taller than she had been Pascal Burke.

In that she was seen with his Shannon Fisheries uniform cap on her head, and she had inserted one hand between the buttons of his shirt, as though rubbing his chest. Without question a pretty woman, she had dropped open her wide mouth and closed her eyes, as though to say, Can you imagine if any one in Dublin saw this? She had raised one long thin leg, so that the brilliant red high-heel shoe was dangling casually from her toes, and the knee was firmly inserted between Burke's thighs. He looked drunk.

The packet of tampons had been opened, and the lid looked a bit worn. Opening it, Ward found the "works" needed to prepare and inject heroin—stainless-steel spoon, strap, lighter, and five disposable needles.

Ten minutes later they discovered the "stash" of drugs— on a ledge above the door inside the armoire: five glassine packets that contained heroin as well as a half dozen lids of crystalline cocaine. Four prescription-size vials also held a variety of nonpharmaceutical-grade tablets and pills. A hatbox nearby on the topmost shelf contained a large Ziploc bag of marijuana.

"At least she keeps the goodies out of the reach of children," Bresnahan observed.

Ward nodded. "All three of them."

"And notice who controls the goodies."

"The sign on the door. It's the only neat and clean room in the house. And that." Bresnahan pointed to the bed. "Her . . . throne, so to speak. Where, doubtless, she controls her subjects."

"They'll come back for the drugs," Ward said, "now that their mug shots are circulating. They'll be afraid to buy in a city."

"But not with our car parked outside."

"Know who I worry about?" Bresnahan asked.

Ward nodded. "Cara, the child."

"Among this"—Bresnahan waved at the collection of drugs— "trinity of unholy shaggers."

"At best. We better phone this in and find someplace to conceal the car."

"With ourselves in it."

When Ward glanced at her, Bresnahan added, "Don't take that wrong, pops. It's just that I don't fancy a stakeout *en plein* air. Not in these conditions."

Out in the side yard, water was still sluicing toward the Shannon.

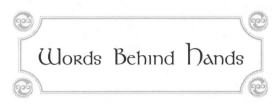

# Words Behind Hands

Water was rushing through the cobblestone gutters of Leixleap as well, especially in the low area by the riverfront and its shops.

Under a strong sun—made all the brighter by the cover of snow, which was melting—the streams gushed down side streets and merged with other torrents headed toward the river.

It was warm. And the sour odor of melting snow and damp earth was everywhere, Noreen McGarr noted as she tried to step off a curb and across from the chemist shop, where she had bought some needed toothpaste, to the green-grocer where she would purchase an apple. "O'Rourke," the intaglio sign declared in Celtic script over the door.

Fortunately, Noreen kept a spare pair of Wellies in the boot of her car, since her widest step brought her only to the middle of the torrent; blithely she pushed on, the water crystal-line and clear against the black rubber of her galoshes.

And it struck her—not for the first time that morning—that life in a small country town, like this, could be very good indeed, what with everybody knowing everybody else. There was a level of familiarity in the chat, which she had overheard this morning while prowling the shops, that was unattainable in Dublin.

Granted, in the city she knew nearly all of the other business owners in the immediate vicinity of her own shop. And with the Dail Eireann (the Irish parliament), Trinity College, and corporate and professional offices close by, many of her daily acquaintances were the movers and shakers of the country.

But Dublin was so . . . raucous and gruff, she decided, reaching for the brass handle of the greengrocer's door. The gentility that the town had obtained even as recently as her own undergraduate days at Trinity two decades earlier had fled the city. With the recent prosperity, Dublin seemed to have assumed the mantle of other large commercial centers, like London, Paris, and New York.

Well, maybe not New York, she decided, closing the door. New York was another category of urban animal altogether. In recent years, Noreen and her well-off mother had shopped in New York, where everything could be had in greater variety and more cheaply than anywhere in Europe. But she would never consider living there, the most basic urges—for money and power—being all too evident, even on the streets.

"Good morning, missus," the shopkeeper called out, as Noreen turned to survey the shop that was heaped with fresh produce grown, she assumed, in the hothouses that now dotted agricultural Ireland and had been paid for through grants from the EU.

"Morning to you," Noreen replied, cheerily.

"And a fine morning it is, in spite of the snow." An early middle-aged countrywoman with broad shoulders, the greengrocer was wearing a bib apron over a cardigan sweater and she had a bandana around her head to protect a recent perm, Noreen suspected. With arms folded across her sturdy chest, she continued to speak to another older woman in hushed tones.

It was cool in the shop and damp, the concrete floor having just been hosed out; the aroma of fresh vegetables was like a bracing perfume.

But when a snatch of conversation came over a heaped bin of cabbages—". . . bloody hussy coming in here saying, bold as brass, 'Pascal prefers this,' and 'Pascal can't stomach that,' to me, mind, knowing how close . . . and in that accent of hers, as though she was actually going to cook for him, well. . . ." Noreen decided to move closer, ostensibly to reach for a basket.

"Can I help you with anything?" the greengrocer asked.

"No, thank you. I'm here for a little of this and that, whatever catches my eye this morning."

"Well, then, work away. I'm here if you need me."

Not moving far, Noreen continued to hear a snippet or two of the gossip. The customer saying, "I know you don't like hearing this, Moira, but to think that Ellen Finn with her new husband was throwing a leg over him, too, to say nothing of . . ."

And, "Certainly, Quintan had cause. And how could you fault him, if he did. I mean, I know it's wrong but . . ." Also, ". . . missing now, the uncle is telling people over at the inn. He's beside himself, like the parents."

With the greengrocer saying, ". . . who else could be capable of such a thing, and her with the background and all. Didn't the bloody bitch take my Tony's last pound with trips to Madeira and wherever."

"And even suing after his death," the customer put in. "Tony Moran being yours and everybody knowing it."

"She threatened me, she did," the greengrocer went on. "Rang me up and said her 'friends' would take care of me if I contested her action in court."

"Do you think that *she* . . . ? How?"

"Key, of course. She's in the inn more hours than Grace herself, overnighting so to speak."

"Everybody knows . . ."

"And how is Grace taking it?"

"Ach—not well at all, the shock . . . tells me she's not sure she can go back."

"Who can blame her? But what will she do for money?"

The greengrocer shrugged. "There's always the Compensation Board, and I'll not be tending this place forever."

She meant the government panel that awarded cash grants to people who had lost their livelihoods through no fault of their own.

"Has she filed a claim already?"

"No, of course not. She's too upset . . ."

The other woman turned toward the door and had to speak louder. "And deserved, too. Imagine—opening the door and coming upon that with no warning. It would be enough to put me in my grave."

"And nearly did Grace, I tell you."

"I'm off, Moira."

"Cheerio, Breege."

When the door of the shop closed, the greengrocer turned to Noreen. "How are you coming along?"

"Dandy—I think I've got what I need."

"Can I interest you in some fresh organic claytonia? Have you ever tried it? It's—"

Noreen begged off and paid the woman, saying, "I couldn't help overhearing what you were saying, when I first entered the shop. Could I ask who was the woman who was cooking for Pascal Burke?"

Without responding, the greengrocer handed Noreen her change and stepped back. "Are you the police?"

"I don't work for the police."

"Then, who? The press?"

"I'm a shopkeeper, like yourself."

"In Dublin, from your accent."

Noreen nodded.

"Then—may I ask your interest?"

"I'm staying in the inn, and, of course, I heard."

"You have, have you?" The woman turned to straighten up the baskets near the register. "Well—you'll not be hearing from me beyond my saying, she could have been one of any number of women in this town.

"Pascal Burke may have been a bit of a rogue. But he was a thoroughly charming rogue, who never harmed a soul. And he had the best intentions, I'm sure. He brought joy into the lives of some who would never have known otherwise. He'll be missed." When she glanced at Noreen, there were tears in her eyes.

By you or by Grace O'Rourke, Noreen was tempted to ask. Perhaps forty, she was a pretty woman in a big way, with an expanse of bosom and a broad back. "You're Grace's mother?"

"Aunt."

"Would it be possible to speak with Grace for a moment?"

"I thought you said you weren't with the police or press."

"I'm not."

"Then—good day to you, my good woman. And I thank you for your custom."

Out in the street, Noreen looked for the person named Breege who'd been speaking to Moira O'Rourke. But she was nowhere in sight.

Not far away in the Leixleap Inn, Detective Superintendent Bernie McKeon was ensconced at the end of the pub bar. Benny Carson was standing across from him, reminiscing about old times in Monaghan Town, where they had grown up together.

They had already been over who of the many they knew had done what in the past and was doing what now. Who had passed away. And who had simply "dropped off the scope," as Carson had put it, so many of the "kids" they'd grown up with in the fifties and early sixties having emigrated, leaving little knowledge of their progress in the world once their parents died.

The two had also already discussed their own lives and the curious paths that had brought them to be sharing a drink in the small river town on the Shannon, Carson mentioning his sister, Honora, who was Quintan Finn's mother and exactly McKeon's age.

"The prettiest girl by far in all Monaghan Town," McKeon enthused. "And it pains me to know what she passed me up for."

"Fertilizer," Carson put in. And they both laughed.

In the nonce, McKeon had quaffed more pints of porter than he cared to remember, and Carson had kept pace with what appeared to be whiskey and water. And the afternoon had worn on, such that—when McKeon turned to glance at the street door that kept opening now, as farmers began to appear for a wet before their tea—he saw that the day was declining.

It was time to get down to business. "So," he asked. "What went on here?"

"You're the pro, you tell me."

McKeon sipped from his pint. "You first. You know the turf and the players. Then I'll tell you what we know so far. I wouldn't want to influence your opinion, which I value."

"Fair play." Carson reached for the bottle of Powers he was drinking from. Always wiry, he had kept himself trim, McKeon had noticed, and appeared to be in good health in spite of the constant glass and the cigarette. "Like I told your chief, McGraw"—

"McGarr."

"That's him." Carson splashed a tot of the amber-colored liquid into his glass and replaced the cork. The spectacles he had donned at lunch, when ringing out tabs, made Carson appear owlish and wise, given his beaked nose and deeply set eyes, which were ringed with dark skin.

"All I know is what I saw from here. The bar. And I have three witnesses to prove that the only time I left this room was to water the trough, which makes it a—" He glanced at McKeon.

"A cast-iron alibi."

"Ah, there now—that's communication for you. Spot on."

"So?"

"So, I think it was a classic love triangle gone wrong."

Carson raised the glass to his lips and drank. "Quintan, the new hubby"—he had to wait for his voice to return— "was browned off that the marriage hadn't put an end to the affair that his wife had been carrying on with Burke since . . . well, now, that I think of it, since pretty close to day one of her joining the eel police. Burke, you see, having the knack with women." Carson dipped his head to McKeon and winked over the top of his glasses.

"And I can remember him chatting her up right there where you sit, Bernie, and then the two of them—a bit lit, don't you know—slipping upstairs. Him with the Cheshire cat look and her with the big bright eyes and slight smile, knowing that a skin-adventure was in the making. If you're in this business long enough, you can always tell."

"How did Finn, the hubby, get upstairs then?"

"The day it was done?"

McKeon nodded.

"With Manus Frakes and the delivery of the rug, of course. They had it all set up, the two of them."

"Why would Frakes go along with something like that? Money? You think he was paid?"

Carson canted his head, as though considering. "Could be, Manus forever on the trot for quid. But it could also be a recruitment thing."

"For what? The army?" McKeon asked, meaning the IRA.

"Not the real thing. Manus got drummed out of that long ago."

Again McKeon waited; he'd let the other man talk unprompted the night long, if necessary. His decades of interrogating people, like Carson, told him that something was coming. The barman and former terrorist had something new to say.

"For being a whack-job, I think the saying is these days. Undisciplined, undependable. A loose cannon. Do any damn thing he pleased. And he's the sane one. The brother, Donal, is from outer space. He was called 'the Quark.'

"And I think Quintan admires that, coming from the steady background that he does. Father being the fertilizer mogul in these parts with the big house and all. And I suppose Manus is a . . . you know, romantic figure. Maybe Quintan wanted to emulate him, prove that he'd take no bullshit, like a philandering wife."

Carson paused to sip from the glass and draw on the cigarette.

And then, "I hate to conjecture this about me own nephew, mind. But the facts are the facts—he was on the scene upstairs, he had Manus with him, and then there's the note that McGarr, your chief, and I discovered when I took him to Finn's flat. What more do you want? To a mere mortal, such as I, it looks open-and-shut. Case closed."

"One shot through her head and his heart."

"That's what I saw."

"What if I were to tell you that there were two shots three hours apart?"

Carson's eyes appeared over the rim of his glasses. "Go 'way, now."

"The first through his heart at close range, probably fired by whatever woman he'd had sex with, since there's evidence that he did have sex. The second through her head."

McKeon raised a hand and formed the likeness of a gun with forefinger and the thumb, then "shot" himself through the temple. "After she came to the room and been incapacitated in some way, then stripped and arranged on top of your man. And finally shot.

"The other unlikely possibility is that she was shot someplace else, then put on top of him and shot again—to make it appear that it was one shot. As you say. As you said." McKeon reached for his own glass, regarding Carson all the while.

Who drew on his cigarette. "Given that, want my guess who did Burke?"

McKeon nodded.

"The bloody bitch, the Frakes's bitch—Gertie McGurk."

"Was she on the premises, too?"

"Didn't she hold the door for Manus and Quintan, when they were carrying up the carpet? And I know for fact Burke was mad for her, wanted her to quit the business and move in with him, she told me."

"Business?" McKeon asked.

"Well, let me amend that—I shouldn't slag the woman—*profession*, if you catch me drift. She's young and quite the looker, and I think that mattered to Burke."

"Did you see her go up with them?"

"No. It was quiet then, and from time to time, I actually do a bit of work around here—go over the tabs, check the stock, make sure the inevitable larceny is kept to a minimum. I work in the cubby office over there behind the far end of the bar. She could have gone up while I was in there."

"But how could she have got into Burke's room. We assume he locked it, while he was engaged in . . ."

"The sex thing," Carson completed, nodding? "Well, Gertie plies her trade mainly on the other side, and, pounds to pies, she's got her own set of keys to the place. She's a canny thief, that one, who'll lift anything not nailed down. Didn't I catch her right here, reaching across the bar for one of these bottles.

"When I asked her what the feck she thought she was doing, she said, 'Service is terrible around here. I was only after a drink.' Aye, I replied, one big one for the road. And didn't I have to pull the bloody thing out of the bloody big purse she carries with all her goodies in it, her complaining all the while that she'd bought it in the off-license up the road."

Chuckling, McKeon finished his pint and shoved it forward; Carson signaled, and one of the other barmen began readying another.

"The Tallons let her carry on there?" McKeon asked, folding his arms and leaning back on the stool.

"Nothing they can do, really. She comes on to some German or Dutchman who's drinking in here. He's dropped a few thousand quid for a fortnight's stay over in the inn. And it's late, there's nobody about, and he's got his key. They're two consenting adults, and if some money changes hands, who's to know? The room is paid for, and Hans or Henrik goes back to the Fatherland with a happy memory of a Celtic tigress. I hear she can get rough."

Carson stood back, so the brimming pint could be placed before McKeon.

Who asked, "So, where is she now, this wild woman? And

the Frakes? At this point, a word with them would be helpful."

Carson sighed and rested his back against the bar. "I knew it would come to this . . . that you'd ask, Bernie. And it's not in me to grass on me mates or nephew. But that poor little girl had a right to her life, no matter what she was doing with Burke—and no outraged macho ego should have taken it from her.

"And so," Carson's eyes swung to McKeon, "I'll tell this to you and nobody else. They can be only one of two places."

"The house."

Carson nodded.

"Where they'll return, sooner or later, the three of them having the nastiest of habits, if you catch my drift."

"And the second?" McKeon prompted.

"There's a certain old mill upriver on the other side. Manus has a *private* lease on the place, and they keep their boats in a raceway there, out of sight."

"Could you show me how to get there?"

Carson smiled. "Why not, I'll get a pen and paper. It's a bit of a drive from here, since there's no near bridge." Turning, Carson began working his way down the bar toward his office, saying hello and bantering with this one and that.

The moment he was out of sight, McKeon reached for the glass Carson had been drinking from and took a sip. Tea, as he had suspected.

Returning, Carson drew a rather detailed map that included mileage and how to get there without being seen. Handing it to McKeon, he asked, "You'll keep my secret."

"Which one is that?"

Carson pointed to his glass.

"You must have eyes in the back of your head."

"I knew you'd taste it. Once a cop, always a cop. But don't get me wrong, I drink my share. It's just that I'm about to consummate a deal to buy this half of the business from Tallon, and I've got to keep my wits about me."

"Go 'way! Really? Tallon would sell this place." McKeon glanced around the bar that was filling up, now as the day declined. "Why?"

"Sure, he doesn't need the headache. And he's doing a roaring trade on the other side where, he says, 'The gouging is better.' His quote."

"Be Jaysus, Benny, you're doing grand," said McKeon, pushing the full pint away. "How can you manage?" Being only recently out of jail, was implied.

"I wasn't entirely stupid in my former life and put a few pounds by. Tallon will hold the mortgage, and, sure, I'll be in debt to the grave. Are you off, lad?"

McKeon stood up. "That I am, and I thank you for the conversation, the drinks and the tip. You should go easy on that stuff." McKeon snapped a finger at Carson's glass with its ersatz whiskey. "I hear it's hard on the kidneys."

"Nonsense. It's a diuretic, the very best, and keeps me in shape, jogging to the jakes."

Out in the car park, McKeon reached for his cell phone and rang up Dublin, asking them to put him through to McGarr, who might possibly be closer to the mill, having left on a tour of the river earlier in the day.

14

RIVER DANCE

After receiving McKeon's message, McGarr slipped his phone back into his jacket pocket and glanced out the window of the Shannon Fisheries Land Rover at the broad river.

A fiery twilight had cast the Shannon in the color of blood. The snowy banks were the walls of its artery, while a cataract—gushing pink from the top of a bluff—looked to McGarr like nothing more than some consequential terrestrial hemorrhage.

Overhead scores of seagulls were working the current for bits of edible flotsam that might have washed off the land into the floor. And from afar—as the Fisheries Land Rover skidded and slid through the muddy ruts of a riverside cart track—the pattern of the graceful white birds assumed the darting intricacy of wind-driven snow.

"At one time, the Frakes were using the copse up ahead as a base of operations," explained Eamon Gannon, the Chief Fisheries Officer who was at the wheel. "They had everything in there, including a bucket loader for the nights when their fyke nets pulled in every migrating eel from the river."

As the Rover moved closer, they could see a car midst the tree trunks.

"Could that be them?" Maddie asked hopefully, pointing past the nose of O'Leary, Gannon's black Lab. Following her hand, the dog saw the car as well and let out a low growl.

"If it is, they've already seen our lights. But it's too late. For them."

"Why? Can't they start the motor and take off? That's a big car."

"A Volvo," said Gannon. "A turbo and powerful. But it's only got two power wheels, and I can't understand how it could have gotten in here under these conditions, unless—"

"Unless it was driven in here before the storm," Maddie concluded breathlessly.

McGarr, who was sitting in the passenger seat beside Gannon, reached back and patted her knee. What were the chances, he wondered, that because of outings like this she would go into police work when she grew up? He hoped not.

McGarr pictured his daughter in some pleasant profession—or, at least, pleasant as perceived by him—medicine, the law, teaching in some university with the summers off and sabbaticals. That would be best.

When McGarr himself was a lad, he had an uncle who had been with the Ulster Constabulary. But his family seldom saw the man. Could it be, he mused, that there was something genetic at play in career selection?

"There doesn't appear to be anybody in it," Gannon said, as he directed the vehicle down an even narrower road into the small wood.

"No tracks," Maddie enthused. "It's been here a while."

O'Leary's growling grew louder.

"Uh-uh," Gannon admonished. "You growl when I say, O', and only then."

And the dog stopped, lowering its ears and turning its eyes to its master.

"That's brilliant," Maddie enthused. "He stopped. Daddy—did you hear that? Does O'Leary understand you?"

"Every blessed word, I swear. If he could pass the written test, I'd have had him in a uniform long ago."

McGarr tapped Gannon on an arm. "Stop, and you two stay here." On one of the knolls that they jounced over, he had caught sight of what he appeared to be a head between the front seats.

"But it's a bog out there. You'll destroy your shoes."

"What did you see, Peter?" In the last few months, his daughter had begun addressing McGarr as her mother did.

O'Leary had begun to growl again.

"I'll be all right, but after I get out—could you back up?"

"How far?"

"Back to the road."

"'But we won't be able to see anything."

Or get shredded by shrapnel, McGarr thought. They were dealing with surds here. Or, rather, surds that not even the IRA could tolerate. True, the car had been in this place at least since the night before when the snow had fallen. But booby traps were an IRA specialty.

"Can you at least tell us why?" Maddie sounded so much like her mother that McGarr hesitated before opening the door.

"I will, after I have a look. In the meantime, please back up."

Gannon nodded, obviously sensing the gravity of the situation.

"But—what about you? Will you be all right?"

McGarr was tempted to say, Well, I have been for fifty-plus years, based on what I feel, why I want you to back up, what this situation could be. But he only reached back and patted her hand. "Don't worry. I'll be fine."

And to Gannon, "Could you manage to get out of here without your headlamps?" The last thing McGarr wanted was to be silhouetted against brilliant lights in a dark copse on the banks of the Shannon. The trap—if a trap—could be much simpler than a possible bomb.

The shoes that McGarr had worn were actually the boots he wore when fishing, which were kept in the back of Noreen's car along with fully waterproof stockings.

Yes, his feet might get cold, and surely his trousers would get wet, but . . . he thought of his Cooper, as he approached the Volvo. How it had been destroyed, how it probably couldn't be replaced, at least not in the condition that he had maintained his own. Which had been with much care.

But he was thinking too much of himself and something as evanescent as an automobile, when, in fact, life itself was ever so much more precious and fragile. Witness what he now saw in the car—a body with a wound to the temple. It had slumped away from the wheel, the bullet having exited the head and shattered a side rear window, which was covered by blood and brain. The gun—a Glock—was resting in the young man's right hand, which was stretched across the passenger seat. A note was on the dashboard.

Even though the lock latches were raised, McGarr stepped around the back of the car and reached for the door handle of the rear passenger-side door, which was less likely to have been touched. There would be no bomb, he decided—not with a note.

Sliding in, he carefully reached over the body and picked the note off the dashboard, holding it by a corner. That was when he heard footsteps behind him, and his hand jumped for the Walther automatic under his jacket.

But it was only O'Leary, the dog, followed by Maddie,

who snatched up the leash, explaining, "He had to get out of the van, and I asked if I could hold him. But he's strong, he is, and quick."

They heard a sharp whistle in the distance, and the dog bolted off into the darkness.

McGarr thought to ask why she had disobeyed him; the car could still be wired, for all he knew. But he thought better of it when he saw her looking beyond him at the corpse. This—her first experience with violent human death—would be chastisement enough, he imagined.

"Is he dead?" she asked.

McGarr nodded, holding the note in the dome light.

"Did he kill himself?"

The note said, simply, "This evens the slate." The handwriting looked similar to that on the other note that had been propped on the table in the Finns' flat.

"How old would you say he was?" Maddie asked, matter-of-factly.

"Twenty-six," said McGarr.

She pulled in some breath. "Young, to take his own life. Or was he . . . murdered?"

McGarr didn't know. He'd have to get an expert to compare the handwriting, the tech squad to go over the gun and Finn's right hand to learn if he had been holding the weapon when it discharged. The blowback would have covered it with spent gunpowder.

"Was it his wife that was found with the man in the room?"

McGarr glanced at her and noticed that she seemed rather pale and was staring down at the man's shattered head as she spoke. The bullet had been either hollow-tipped or had shattered on bone. The exit wound was a red wet hole, as though something sizable had taken a deep bite from the skull. "You've been reading the papers."

She nodded. "You never say anything to me about what you do."

McGarr reached the slip of notepaper over the corpse and dropped it back on the dash. "Now you know why, I hope." Getting out, he closed the door and wrapped an arm around his daughter's thin shoulder.

"Do you think it hurt?" she asked, as they made their way slowly back toward the lights of the Rover. At ten, Maddie was just old and young enough to ask questions that older people thought they'd answered for themselves.

"Only for the shortest time, I should imagine."

"Why would somebody do something, like that, to himself?" They took a few more steps. "Or commit murder?"

It was, of course, the question that McGarr had spent nearly all of his adult life trying to answer. "Because they can no longer believe in themselves."

"You mean, those who commit suicide. What about those who commit murder?"

"Because they can no longer believe in themselves. And they become angry that others not only believe in themselves but they believe in life so thoroughly that they attract love or money or power."

"But aren't some people just . . . damaged? And they don't know any better?"

McGarr nodded. "But the real damage is that they can't believe in themselves. For whatever reason."

Maddie thought about that for a few steps. Then, "Do you believe in heaven?"

McGarr glanced up at the night sky that had cleared and was visible through the leafless bowers of the tall trees. And with no other lights but the headlamps of the Rover, the stars were layers deep.

McGarr thought of something that he had read about the formation of the universe and how planets and life, as we know it, could not have developed without the violent collapse of early stars, in the furnaces of which all the heavy elements—carbon, iron, silicon—were created. And in such a way, the writer had continued, human beings are essentially star dust. "I will when I get there."

"Oh, you will. You'll get there," she said with perfect confidence.

Back in the Land Rover, McGarr asked Gannon if he knew of an old mill farther up the river.

"I do, of course."

"Perhaps you can drop me there and take Maddie back to the inn. It's getting late."

"I will, surely. But you'll not find anybody there. It's been abandoned for years."

In another car—the Opel *Vectra* with the sun roof and spoiler that had been selected *not* to look like an unmarked Garda patrol car—Ruth Bresnahan and Hugh Ward had been staking out the Frakes's safe house for all of ten hours from a laneway not far from the drive that led there.

A few hours earlier the pair had agreed to nap in shifts, tossing a coin to decide who would sleep first. Ward had lost, and Bresnahan and he had traded places, Ward getting behind the wheel, and the tall redhead climbing into the passenger seat.

"Wouldn't you be more comfortable in the back?" Ward had asked.

"Not with these legs," she had said, smacking her thighs.

Ward had looked down upon her legs, which he could not see because of the sweatpants she was wearing, but he knew . . . intimately, he could not keep himself from thinking.

"And the seats don't go down."

Precisely, Ward had thought.

Dropping back the seat, Bresnahan had arranged herself

and nodded off almost instantly in a way that had always bemused Ward during the time that they had been together.

It was as if her early formative years—living on a farm perched on a mountainous bluff above Kenmare Bay and consorting with the beasts of farm and field—had imparted to her a spontaneity that not even a dozen years in Dublin could change. Ruth was always in . . . *touch* (was probably the operative word) with her own needs. And how to achieve them.

Ward was in a self-pitying mood. Because no sooner had she fallen asleep than her body turned to him, one of her long legs insinuated itself over his ankle, and her hand reached out and took hold of his left arm, as she had slept with him—he tried to compute the total number of events but couldn't— literally hundreds of times over the four years that they had been together.

Then. And hugely provocatively. In the midst of her sleep, Bresnahan had suddenly raised her body off the reclined seat, turned her back to Ward, pulled up her cashmere jumper and said, "Can you unsnap this? It's pinching me, and I can't get any rest." By which she meant her brassiere.

All while still asleep, Ward had few doubts. But they were nagging. What if she wasn't really asleep? What if her turning back to him and taking his arm again and folding a leg over his but more completely this time, what if it was a conscious act? Or at least an unconsciously conscious act of the sort you do when you know something is wrong but you conveniently tell yourself you forget why and do it anyway.

No, Ward told himself. She was asleep. In the near-total darkness with nobody about but some cows that were continuing to graze in a nearby field under a brilliant half-moon, he could feel her slow, even breathing on his neck. And the familiar warmth of her hand and breast against his arm convinced him that she was.

Until her head moved across the small space between the two seats, and her mouth rose to his ear. "Kiss me," she whispered. "Life is short, and we should not allow this foolishness to go on any longer. I know you love me."

Taking his right hand, she raised the waistband of her jumper and placed it on her bare breast.

"But I also love Leah," Ward blurted out.

"That's your problem. I don't care who you love, as long as you love me." Her lips jumped for his, and their kiss was a long passionate kiss that was as much a kiss of recognition and reaffirmation as one laden with the possibility of gratifying sex.

But when Ward opened his eyes again, he saw a figure silhouetted against the half-moon, standing in front of the bonnet of the car. He was holding something like a bat across one shoulder.

As were the two other figures on either side of the car.

"Ruth," Ward said, trying to push Bresnahan away and reach for the Beretta in the holster under his jacket.

But the man in front of the bonnet yelled something like, "Right, lads—now!" And he and the other two swung what looked to be heavy sledgehammers at the car—the bumper and the sides—and there was an instantaneous explosion, as the front and side airbags inflated and Ward and Bresnahan were crushed together.

Ward couldn't move, and what was he hearing? It sounded like the whine of a diesel engine in a small tractor or van. Or two diesel engines.

"God—what happened?" Bresnahan managed to say, her voice muffled by the pillowy bags.

"Airbags," Ward explained. "See if you can push back so I can free my hands."

"I don't think I can breathe."

Which was when something big struck the roof of the car,

and with the sound of shrieking metal, the sunroof was pried off the car by what appeared to be, as Ward looked up, the heavy metal teeth of a backhoe.

And before either of them could struggle free, Ward heard the same man's voice say, "Now—they want eels. Give 'em a taste of eels, boys."

With that there was further engine noise, and Ward watched as the scoop of a bucket-loader appeared over the ripped-open roof of the car. It tilted, seemed to hesitate for a moment, then swung down, dumping its contents into the car on top of Ward and Bresnahan—a mass of slithering eels.

As Ward fought to push himself up through the writhing creatures toward the night sky, he heard gales of laughter, along with the voice saying, "Ah, Jaysus—it was perfect. Perfect! I could die right now, happy!"

Then Ward heard the engines again, moving away.

"Hughie! Hughie!" Bresnahan fairly screamed. "Get me out of here. The bastards are everywhere, and they're biting me."

No more than an hour later, Peter McGarr heard the clatter and whine of a tractor or tractors approaching the former riverside mill that—Benny Carson had told Bernie McKeon—Manus Frakes had purchased and used as the base of his eel-poaching operation.

Earlier, McGarr had picked a stout lock on a narrow door to enter the only part of the large complex that was still roofed.

There on the second floor he found all the impedimenta of poachers: rolls of netting material, several outboard engines, some small boats, anchors, and—concealed under a tarpaulin—two packing crates of Kalashnikov assault rifles. All had been brought in through what looked like a large elevated hay door on a barn; it was locked from the inside.

Only one Kalashnikov, however, had been unwrapped and cleansed of Cosmoline, the paraffin-based preservative in which, since W.W.II, guns and munitions worldwide were often packed for long-term storage.

Contained in a bulky gun case, the one assault rifle was also equipped with a high-tech night-seeing scope and was probably the weapon that had been used in the attempt on Benny Carson's life that had destroyed McGarr's Mini Cooper.

Back downstairs, McGarr leaned the weapon against the wall where the door, when opened, would obscure it. Next he found the electrical utility box and disabled all the lights.

Returning to the second floor by the dim light of his tiny pocket torch, which was failing, McGarr had to struggle to open the interior lock on the hay door. But once it was open, he used the thick rope of the winch—which the Frakes had employed to hoist the bulkier items into the building—to let himself down.

There on the ground floor, he slipped the lock through its hasp and clamped it shut. When they returned, they would think the building secure.

But letting himself down was one thing; climbing back up the thick rope another. Thoroughly middle-aged now at fifty-four, McGarr had acquired a paunch in recent years, and his workouts in the gym—where Noreen insisted he go thrice weekly because of high blood pressure—consisted of a couple ambles around the track to loosen up, fifteen minutes on the speed bag, and a half hour of weights.

There was nothing aerobic about his workouts, McGarr discovered as he labored to pull himself back up. Sure, he still had enough strength in his arms, but by the time he reached the lip of the open hay door, he thought his lungs would burst.

With one final heave, he rolled his body onto the well-worn planking in front of the door and just lay there, gasping for breath.

Which was when he heard the diesels in the distance and saw lights jouncing down the cart track that led to the mill.

"Shite!" he roared, clawing himself to his feet. And he only managed to pull the rope back inside and close the door before first one engine and then another were switched off. And he heard voices and laughter, two men, a woman, and—could it be?—a child.

McGarr scuttled downstairs mainly by feel now that the batteries in his penlight had nearly failed, and he threw anything he could find in the path between the door and the fuse box. Reaching for the Walther PPK that he kept in a shoulder holster, McGarr took three steps away and squatted down, handgun at the ready.

At length, he heard voices again, closer now. They seemed in a festive mood, apart from the child who kept asking, "But I haven't et yet. Is there any food?"

"Is that all you ever think of?" the woman's voice asked.

"But I'm hungry."

"Hush now," the woman said. "There's no chance of food for a good long while, so put it out of your mind."

McGarr then heard whimpering.

"Look—stop that, and stop it now. You'll just make yourself miserable."

"Don't you tell her that," a man's voice replied. "She would've had some fookin' thing to eat, if you hadn't been tending your fookin' traps."

Now the child was crying.

"Which is my business, isn't it? And she's not my child, is she? Do I look like a nanny?"

"You look like what you are—a whore," said a second man's voice.

"Well, I'm not *your* whore, am I? And you remember that."

"Not to worry. The memory is bad enough."

McGarr could not hear what the first man said to the child, because it was low. But the crying quieted, and the next sound was that of a key being fitted into the lock.

McGarr braced himself, as a cone of dim light expanded into the room. The child complicated things, but there was no help for that.

The first figure to step into the room was that of a rather tall, well-built man. He tried the light switch beside the door. "Bloody fookin' hell, when I get hold of the yoke who wired this place, I'll throttle the bastard, so I will. Or, did you not pay the bill again, Manus?"

"I paid the bill," his brother—McGarr assumed—said.

He could now make out a second man, who was holding the child.

"Where's the torch?"

As though weary, Manus, the smaller man, said, "It's in the boat, Donal. You know that. And you know where the circuit breakers are as well. Maybe there was a power surge, and they switched off. Could you check the box, please?"

"Why me?"

"Because I'm holding Cara."

"Ah, fook—why's it always me?"

"Because you're the *mahn*," the woman put in. McGarr imagined she was the fabled Gertie McGurk.

"Shut your bloody gob, woman, or I'll—" Having stepped into the deeper darkness of the room, Donal tripped over a box that McGarr had set in the path from the door to the circuit breakers. *"Fook!"* he roared.

"Ah, there it is," the woman remarked. "The colorful cry of the truly feral male."

Which caused Donal to roar again. Standing, he began

feeling for objects before him and throwing and kicking them out of the way.

Until he arrived within a yard or two of McGarr, who rose from his crouch, kicked the tall man's legs out from under him, and then brought down the heel of his palm—weighted with the Walther—on the back of his neck. And again for good measure.

Donal Frakes groaned or moaned, and McGarr, who had crouched back down, felt the body go limp.

"Donal? *Donal?*"

The woman began to laugh.

"Sh! Donal?"

But she continued chuckling. "What a night! This is better than the eels. Don't I wish Benny was here."

"Well, I don't. The bastard is trying to hang a double-murder charge on me and you, too, just you watch. Unless you did it."

The woman did not answer.

"Benny here?" the little girl asked.

But her father only handed her to the McGurk woman and turned to enter the darkened room, his eyes—McGarr imagined—by now having accustomed themselves to the darkness. "You two stay there," he said in a low voice. "If anything happens, leave in the car. I put the key in the switch, just in case."

"In case of what?" McGurk asked. "What could possibly happen, you fool? The fookin' door was fookin' locked," she said with such an edge to her voice that the child again began crying. "You're thicker than your fookin' brother."

"We'll see." Pulling what McGarr assumed was a handgun from under his belt, Manus Frakes stepped into the darkened room. And McGarr, who was still in a squat, holstered his own weapons and moved toward the advancing figure.

Once past the boots of the unconscious brother, McGarr

turned around, so his back was to the oncoming figure, and then eased himself onto hands and knees.

"Donal?" Manus Frakes asked. "Donal?"

"Can y' hear that, Cara? Your daddy is afraid of the dark." Which caused the child to wail.

"Donal?" he asked yet again, louder this time.

"Here," McGarr said in a hoarse voice, as though injured. He did not want Frakes to move beyond him.

"What's wrong, Donal? Where are yeh, lad?"

"Here," McGarr repeated. "I'm hurt."

"How many times have I told you that your fookin' temper will be the fookin' death of ye?" Frakes said in a broad Ulster burr.

And when McGarr felt Frakes's hands touch his back and then move under his arms, as though to help him to his feet, he let his body go limp, so that the other man had to struggle to raise him up.

Which is when McGarr struck, seizing the wrist that held the gun and twisting it so sharply up and away that he felt bones break as the weapon clattered to the floor.

Frakes screamed only once before McGarr spun him around and chopped both hands simultaneously into the base of his neck. Pushing him away as he slumped by his brother, McGarr debated rushing the door. But he no longer knew where all the obstacles were, and there was the child to consider. Time was of the essence. He could not tell when one or either of the Frakes would come around.

Instead, he reached for the electrical supply box and the circuit breakers.

"Manus?" the McGurk woman asked, concern now in her voice. "You there?"

McGarr's hands fumbled in the darkness. "Yeah," he answered.

"What happened?"

While the fingers of one hand searched for the main switch, McGarr drew out his Walther with another, only hoping that the last person to touch the light switch in the room had left it up. On.

No luck.

"What happened, Manus?" With the child in her arms, the woman took a step away from the door.

McGarr moved toward her. "Shock," he muttered. "The fookin' thing burnt me."

She stepped back again. "Manus?"

McGarr tried to move quickly, but he banged into one thing, and then another, and the woman was no longer visible in the doorway.

Stepping outside, he saw her rushing toward a car that was parked near two tractors that were maybe a hundred yards distant. "Halt! Police!" he roared, reaching for the Kalashnikov with the night-seeing scope.

Switching on the device, he had to wait a moment or two while his right eye accustomed itself to the greenish glow, but gradually he saw that the McGurk woman was now walking backward toward the car with the bawling child held out before her. As a shield.

She then shifted the upset child to a hip and opened the car door. But instead of placing the child in the car before sliding in herself, the woman pushed the little girl away from her, got in, and slammed the door. Without lights, the car bolted away.

What to do? He could try to stop the car with the rifle, but he'd have to act fast before the vehicle moved into a nearby wood. Then there was the child to consider, who had fallen but was now picking herself up. He could hear her crying, and he watched as she toddled off into the darkness toward the river. And behind him, he heard some stirring.

Setting down the Kalashnikov, McGarr did not switch on

the lights for fear of making himself a target. Instead he used
his penlight to find his way back to the Frakes in time to catch
Manus reaching for the handgun on the floor.

Kicking it out of the way, McGarr plunged both hands
into the man's leather jacket and hauled him to his feet. "You
broke my wrist," Frakes said in an even tone. "I won't forget."

"When I break your head, you will."

McGarr clipped one end of his handcuffs to Frakes's unin-
jured wrist and the other to a stout pipe. He had to hurry.
Moving back to the brother, McGarr stood well away.
"Donal. Donal!" he shouted.

The man didn't move.

"Nudge him in the ribs. He'll come round," his brother
suggested.

Which McGarr interpreted as an invitation to move closer.
Instead, he stomped the large man's outstretched hand, and
Frakes rolled over quickly and began to stand.

But McGarr's foot, lashing out, caught him on the side of
the head, sending the man skidding into the wall beside his
brother. A second kick slammed the head against the stone
surface, and Frakes's eyes drifted up into his head as he
slumped to the floor.

"Your daughter is in the field, walking toward the river,"
McGarr said, removing the handcuff that was attached to the
pipe and clamping it to the wrist of the brother. If only he
had a second pair, he could clamp both of them to the pipe.

"Get her, man! Go, now!"

"I'll try." McGarr reared back and slammed his fist into
Frakes's face, knocking him over his brother's outstretched
legs.

Snatching up the handgun and the Kalashnikov in case
either of the men came around, McGarr rushed outside.
"Cara!" he shouted. "Cara!"

God, if he found her in the river, he didn't know what

he'd do, having failed to protect the one person on the scene worth the effort. Once in the field he shouted again and again, but there was no answer. Nor could he see her.

But the Kalashnikov—it was still in his hands. Like the handgun, which he now dropped.

With the night-seeing scope to his eye, McGarr scanned the field, then the riverbank. Then the river. No child. Despairing, he was about to turn back and rush around the mill to peer downriver, when he remembered from his early reconnaissance of the place that the old structure had a walled millrace where the Frakes kept several of their boats hidden.

There he found her, standing on the lip of the crumbling wall with the boiling millrace below, still sobbing, both hands to her eyes. "Cara," he called to her gently, so as not to startle her; she was only a half step from the edge.

"Cara—it's me, the man," from the inn, he rejected; she might think he was Tim Tallon, "the man who spoke to you about your beeper." He was closing the gap as quickly as he could without rushing her. Hating himself, he added, "The one who thinks he can put you in touch with your mother."

The girl's hands came away from her eyes. "Me mammy?"

"Yes. Remember me? The man with the toy car. At the inn."

"I still have the beeper. Can you ring up me mammy?"

In the light of the half-moon, McGarr watched her pull the small black device from the belt of her dress. But in stepping toward him, her foot strayed into the pocket of a missing stone, and she dropped the beeper. Reaching for it, she pitched sideways and tumbled from the parapet into the boil below.

McGarr did not hesitate. With the Kalashnikov to his eye, he caught sight of her head drifting toward the millrace grate that had snagged a wide apron of flotsam. If he could just get to her before she sank beneath that, maybe he could save her.

Dropping the gun, he jumped into the abyss and rose to

the surface in time to see her head sinking under the ragged edge of the floating debris. Forcing himself down, he pumped his arms and kicked and kicked, the swirling current pulling his larger body away from her.

He thought he felt some material, some textile like her skirt, and he pulled it toward him.

No. It was a seed sack.

One foot had come up against the grate, and he pushed off, ducking his head under the flotsam and sweeping his arms. Trying to find her and pull her in.

But the current was so string it kept slamming him against the grate. And would her, too, he reasoned; her body had to be stuck, as his was, against the grate. Which is where he found her. And he had to tug with all his strength to rip her body off the thick teeth and hold her up into the air.

But now what? Could there be a ladder? Was she still breathing? Holding on to the grate with one hand, McGarr brought her face to his ear. He couldn't tell; the sound of the water rushing through the grate was too loud.

McGarr looked around. There was no ladder. But there were boats tied farther up the wall, if only he could fight the current and get her to them.

Which was when he was startled by a voice above him. "Tie her to the rope." Looking up, he saw two figures standing on the wall, silhouetted against the moon, their arms yoked together at the wrist. The brothers Frakes.

"Tie her to the rope," the larger yelled again, and his free arm whipped out, sending a skein of rope sailing over the millrace.

Dropping into the water a few yards above McGarr, it nearly shot past him. He had to release his hold on the grate to snag the rope, and the child and he went under again.

While securing the line around her waist and tying a sturdy knot, McGarr found he had to submerge, just to keep her head out of the flood. If she fell in again, he did not think he could save her.

"Right, now!" he hollered, and the larger brother—holding his arm and one of his bother's well over the lip of the millrace so the child's body would not scrape the wall—quickly had her to the top. And they were gone.

McGarr was relieved, but he wondered how long it would take the Frakes to return. All they had to do was discover the Kalashnikov, which was lying about somewhere in the field where McGarr had dropped it; using the night-seeing scope, they would shoot him like a rat in a barrel.

McGarr looked around. It was time to think of himself. The boats. Perhaps without the child he could fight the current and the slippery millrace wall and make it that far.

But they were open wooden boats, and even if he concealed himself behind the bow of one, the 7.72mm rounds from the assault rifle would punch right through the planking.

The flotsam. Maybe he could conceal himself under that when they returned, holding on to one of the logs and ducking under. Only his fingers would be visible, which among the clutter might not be conspicuous to them.

McGarr did not know how long he waited there midst the river wrack, concentrating on the funnel of light at the top of the millrace. But it was long enough to realize that his body was growing numb, his breathing labored, and he would have to get himself to the boats after all, if only to keep from succumbing to hypothermia.

Even the moon had nearly passed out of sight, when finally another figure appeared at the top of the wall—rotund and compact with something that looked like the Kalashnikov in his hands.

He raised it to his eye, but McGarr paused before submerging. "Bernie," he managed to call out, slapping the water with one unfeeling hand.

After quickly tying one end of the rope to a nearby bollard, McKeon had to throw it twice before McGarr managed to grab the line up. Securing a knot around his waist proved more difficult, and he went under several times more.

Then there was the wall. After his climb earlier in the night, it took McGarr some time to reach the top, even with McKeon's help. He had to pause again and again to rest his weary arms, and by the time he hoisted himself over the lip, he was exhausted, and every muscle in his body seemed to be aching.

Resting there while McKeon rushed for the blankets that were contained in the Garda emergency kit, McGarr suddenly found himself shaking uncontrollably. He had to get himself someplace warm. Fast.

Reaching out to push himself up, his hand fell upon something square and hard. It was the beeper.

McGarr was neither suspicious, nor did he believe in imminent justice. But finding the device was like a reward for all he'd been through.

"What about the Frakes?" he asked, when McKeon returned.

"Gone. I only passed one car on the road, getting here. Must have been them. But I'm glad I didn't try to stop it.

"At least we got the Kalashnikov."

"And this." McGarr handed him the beeper, his fingers being too weak to hold it any longer.

15

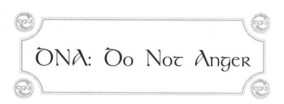

ONA: Do Not Anger

When McGarr opened his eyes the next morning, he could see
that it was late. A dun sky freighted with lowering clouds was
sweeping past the windows. Yet the room was well lit.

It had to be at least nine, the hour that he had scheduled
a staff meeting in the dining room of the inn. He should make
himself presentable and get downstairs. Pronto.

But attempting to throw back the covers, McGarr was
visited with the reality of the night before which had ended
about three, after fending off the press, who had still been on
the job at such an hour, God bless them. And more crabby
than usual.

Scribbling a brief report and a hot bath had come next,
so—McGarr tried to compute the hour that he had finally
closed his eyes—it must have been closer to four. Five hours
was not enough recuperation after what he'd been through.

No wonder he felt like the case was about to claim a
fourth victim. Himself. Already it had destroyed his antique
car, a Vacheron-Constantine timepiece that had been a wedding present from Noreen and would need restoring, maybe
his Walther PPK, and his Garda cell phone, which he would

replace temporarily with Noreen's. Added to those losses were a hat, a pair of shoes, and probably a sports jacket and trousers because of all the scraping on the walls.

Also, never had his arms felt so sore or weak, and a weal of pain shot through his torso as he sat up. Finally and ominously, there was a squeezing sensation in his chest that made him think heart attack. Or was he merely having the usual problem with his lungs that he felt before the first cigarette of the day? Enhanced by all the high jinks of the night before.

Behind him, McGarr heard a door open. Then, "Mammy says you're to make yourself presentable and come down to the dining room as soon as possible."

His thought exactly. "Everybody there?"

"No, just Mammy and Bernie."

"Where's Hughie and Ruth?"

"Mammy is trying to rouse them. She sent me to you."

Kind of her, thought McGarr. And more charitable still, when what he needed was now placed on his lap by Maddie— a small tray with a brimming bowl of muddily black French coffee, from its smell, and a smallish snifter that contained another aromatic fluid.

Ah, McGarr thought, the advantage of having an understanding younger wife, one who had witnessed the decrepit return of her aged hero. How he had removed his sodden ruined clothing and then subjected his equally ruined body to the balm of hot water, only to . . . whimper, ño it wasn't quite a whimper, climbing in bed.

And sleep? It had hit him like an articulated lorry.

Now, all he needed was: "A smoke—you don't happen to see my smokes about?" he asked Maddie, who was still in the room somewhere behind him. McGarr didn't dare turn his neck more than a few degrees to either side.

"Even if I did," she informed him, "I would not be your enabler."

School, he thought. He sent her to perhaps the finest private school in Dublin—one of her mother's alma maters, as it happened—that cost much of his annual salary. And what had she learned there? Verbal parent abuse.

"Well, I suspect I'll just have to get them myself." McGarr had to rock back and forth, just to test his legs and his arms—holding the tiny tray out before him—to rise off the bed.

Which was when a packet struck the tray with a suddenness that rather frightened him. Ditto, the matches.

"There—have your death," said Maddie, her tone as histrionic as the voice on a television advisory condemning smoking. The last line of which was, "The Irish smoke more than any other English-speaking nation."

Maybe it was the fault of the language and not simply an oral fixation, as McGarr had long thought. You know: English not being theirs, having to speak the oppressor's language made the Irish resort to smoke.

"And don't expect me to witness your attenuated suicide. Smoking is so incredibly banal. And alcohol at this hour? Well . . ." With that, the door closed.

McGarr breathed out the smoke and reached for the snifter, deciding that, after all, he was getting value for the enormity he was paying for her wonderful education.

"Attenuated" and "banal"? Maddie was only ten.

"Where's Hughie and Ruth?" McGarr asked, taking a seat at the round table that had been set in a corner of the spacious dining room. He signaled to a waiter and pointed to his coffee cup.

No other guests were nearby.

"I knocked on Rut'ie's door to deliver the daily activity sheets from yesterday, but there was no answer," Noreen said. More suspiciously still, when she tried to slide the sheaf of memoranda under the door, she discovered it was slightly ajar.

Pushing it open, she found the bed still made up. But there was no Bresnahan in the suite, nor any sign that she had stayed there.

Then, knocking at Ward's door, she asked him if he had seen Ruth. There was a definite hesitation before he replied.

"Hughie said he'd be right down," she now told McKeon and her husband. "And that he'd just seen Rut'ie out his window, walking in the street." Glancing at McGarr, Noreen raised an eyebrow in a way that told all.

Perhaps five minutes went by before Bresnahan and Ward arrived under the archway of the dining room, their appearance so extraordinary that a passing waitress slowed to stare at them.

On Ward, whose skin was olive in tone, the bites and nicks from the eels were not conspicuous. But Bresnahan looked like she had chicken pox or measles.

"Is it contagious?" McKeon asked. "Or have you two been at each other again?" But when nobody responded, he added, "Oh-kay—do I continue, Chief? Or commit hara-kiri right here on the spot?"

"What a brilliant idea," Noreen said, affecting a smile. "May we watch?"

"Thank you, Shogun Noreen. Your encouragement is acknowledged." McKeon shook out the lab and other reports that had been sent by courier from Dublin. Fitting on half-glasses, he looked down and read for a while.

In the silence, Ruth jotted a note on her pad and showed it to Noreen. "*I want you to know: the only reason I slept with the rotter again is, after the eels, I needed somebody to hold.*"

And was it a healing experience? Noreen was tempted to ask in a big-sisterly way. But she only nodded, as though understanding; they would, of course, talk later.

"Not to keep yous in suspense, b'ys and gir-rills," McKeon

said, exaggerating his brogue. "But it says here the Frakes have rap sheets that would make career criminals proud. Including charges—but not convictions—of murder.

"Likewise their boon companion, Gertrude McGurk, whose own past encounters with the criminal law include arrests for loitering, pandering, and prostitution. Also, there was the punishing run-in with our victim, Ellen Gilday Finn.

"In civil actions, Ms. McGurk has twice sued to receive bequests from wills that had been denied her by the solicitors of the deceased. Both men. The earlier action failed, but she was successful to the tune of twenty-seven thousand pounds against the estate of a certain Antony Moran, late of Leixleap.

"Then, we have two opinions about the note that Peter discovered on the kitchen table in the Finns' flat, the one that casts suspicion on the husband.

"The first analysis says that the note is genuine, but that Quintan Finn wrote it while distraught or in some way impaired or both. Although smudged, his fingerprints are also on the sheet.

"The second says no, it's a forgery, albeit, a high-quality forgery. The lab has sent the note out to an independent expert for a third opinion."

"Don't we have it somewhere that Carson was a forger for the IRA?" Ward asked.

McKeon nodded. "Their best. He specialized in financial instruments—negotiable bonds, stocks, letters of credit—that class of thing. And was never caught. It was manslaughter that put him in the poky."

"But isn't Carson a slight older man?" Noreen asked.

"Ten stone tops."

"How could he have disabled Ellen Finn and then accomplished her murder on top of Burke, like that?"

"Speaking of which, the lab says Ellen Finn had a preexisting contusion and gash on her temple before she was shot there, evidently in an attempt to cover up how she was disabled."

"And cover up when Burke was shot," Ward put in. "As always, murderers try too hard."

"Or murderer," said Bresnahan, who was doodling over the note that she had shown Noreen earlier.

Ward turned to her. "Aw, c'mon—it's got be the Frakes in collusion with Finn. Who else would have been strong enough? And they both were on the scene."

"As placed there by Carson," said Noreen.

"And by one of the guests." McKeon leafed to the back of the report. "All have been interviewed, all shown photographs of Manus and Donal Frakes and Quintan Finn.

"A certain Georgette Freuling was in her room down the hall from the murder scene. She says that while her husband fishes, she 'grouses,' her quote, meaning she takes walks and reads outside.

"But because the weather was closing in, she returned to the room and was disturbed by the sounds of the carpet being delivered and later all the banging as it was being fitted to the room.

"Opening the door, she looked out, which was when she definitely saw Manus Frakes and maybe—she's not entirely sure, since he only passed by the open door—Quintan Finn. But she heard Frakes call the other man Quin!

"But—get this—after the banging stopped, she then heard a short sharp report that she thought was the backfire of a car in the street. Unfortunately, she then dozed off for a while, and she doesn't know for how long. But she was awakened by the sound of a man and woman—or it could have been two men and two women—in the hall and the rather loud closing of a door.

"Nodding off again, she was awakened yet again by another backfire, and she saw it was around six and time to get ready for dinner, since her husband would be returning soon.

"He took over the interview here, saying he bumped into Tim Tallon, the proprietor, in the hall, and Tallon showed him the new carpet, in addition to discussing the day's fishing.

"He added that, since the wife and he were leaving and heading north, Tallon told him to fish Lake Gowna in Cavan, which was where he was found and was proving a great stay."

"What was Tallon doing there? Didn't Carson tell Peter at some point that he ran that side of the operation?" Noreen asked.

"More than that." McKeon paused to remove his half-glasses. "Carson told me yesterday afternoon that he's been negotiating with Tallon to buy the pub half of the business.

" 'Tallon doesn't want it and doesn't need the headache,' he told me. 'He's doing a roaring trade over there on the other side, where the gouging is better.' "

Observed Noreen, "Not bad for an older man only a short while out of prison—a good business and a premier property."

"Also, there's the pretty riverbank house he's now in solo," said Bresnahan.

Noreen nodded. "And he might even get his cute little granddaughter to keep him company, if the Frakes go to jail."

Bresnahan turned her notepad; she was drawing a picture of a glass eel, the face of which looked very much like Ward's. "But Carson's not the woman who had sex with Pascal Burke. Find her, and we'll find our murderer."

"No," Ward objected. "We'll find our murderers, who are the Frakes and their trollop. The body of evidence points to them."

"Really now?" McKeon secured the bows of the glasses over his ears. "Says here that the Kalashnikov I found in the field near the millrace—the one with the night-seeing scope—has not been fired recently."

Ward hunched his shoulders. "Maybe they have another. Didn't Peter's report say they have a case of them?"

"Of assault rifles that are still wrapped in Cosmoline," said Bresnahan, still working on her drawing. "Nightscopes are quite another item, altogether. As I said, when we find the woman who had sex with Burke, we'll find our murderer."

"Speaking of which—woman, that is—we have this bit of disappointing information," McKeon continued. "There's now proof positive via DNA that Ellen Finn did not have sex with Pascal Burke, nor was the fetus his.

"And while we're on DNA, the DNA on the outside of the condom was not hers either, nor was it the DNA of the woman who left the bleached blond hair with hair follicle still attached on the pillow beside the two bodies."

"Which means—there're *three* women involved?" Noreen asked. "Ellen Finn"—she counted on her fingers—"whoever had sex with him prior to his death, and now whoever left the hair in the bed."

"If the maid changed the covers," Ward noted.

"Mr. Tryster," McKeon said. "Remember—he'd only just arrived that morning after being a fortnight away. And there was Leixleap's special Welcome Wagon, beating down the door to greet him."

"In triplicate," Ward put in.

"Pity he had to die and take his secret with him."

"His comeuppance, entirely," said Bresnahan.

"Twice over. First literally and then figuratively." McKeon glanced back down at the report.

"Also, the lubricant that was found on her person is not the same as what's applied before packaging to Thunderbolt condoms—love that name—at the factory in Morristown, New Jersey, where genius obviously resides.

"Here again, as in the earlier report, it's said that the condom on Burke was another brand made by Sheik."

"Is it too early to know if the baby was her husband's?" Noreen asked.

McKeon nodded. "All we know about Quintan Finn's death so far is that it occurred in his car, where Peter found him, and that in all likelihood he pulled the trigger. There's a bruise on his left index finger."

Which was an indicator of suicide, McGarr well knew, the shock of bullet tensing all muscles in the body. Briefly.

"What's the possibility of somebody inserting his finger through the trigger guard and pulling the trigger for him?" Noreen asked. "You know, after they drugged him or got him drunk."

"And we all know it's happened before," Bresnahan put in.

"What about his blood?" Ward asked.

McKeon scanned the next page. "Don't you just hate it when amateurs are right? I mean, beautiful gifted talented amateurs with a friend in a high place. Finn had a blood alcohol level of two point oh three."

"Locked," said Bresnahan. "He probably couldn't have told you where his temple was, much less put a gun to it."

Pleased with herself, Noreen enthused, "And since it's not on for me as a civilian to write reports, I have me own bit of information to add to the pot."

She then related what she had overheard in the greengrocer's shop about a certain woman who used to cook for Pascal Burke.

"I couldn't make out everything that was said, so I'm not sure it's the same woman, but later the O'Rourke woman— Moira, I believe her name is—said, 'Didn't she take Tony Moran's last pound with trips to Madeira and wherever.' She also speculated that the woman, whoever she is, must have had a key, too."

"To what?" McKeon asked.

Noreen shook her head. "By what she said to me later she might have intimated that her niece, Grace, had some involvement with Burke. Or she had herself at one time. In any case, she spoke highly of Burke and seemed to be upset in a contained way. I mean, the store was open for business."

Bresnahan shook her head. "Maybe. But Gertrude McGurk surely has a well-furnished kitchen. Apart from her locked . . . fortress on the second floor, it's the only complete room in the house. Also, Ellen Finn busted her."

"Literally." McKeon began reassembling the reports. "Only a few months ago. She could have been the one who put Burke's biscuit in the oven and baked him to a turn."

"Really, Bernie, must you?" Noreen complained.

"McGurk is a big strong woman, twice Ellen Finn in every way." Bresnahan was now doodling a substantial black brassiere that had attracted Ward's attention.

"Yet it was Ellen who thumped her, wasn't it?"

"Probably because she had a gun at the time."

"And McGurk could have had Burke's before and after shooting him," observed Ward. "You know the bit—it's over for the moment, and he's closed his eyes and is snoozing.

" 'I'll be right back, luv,' she tells him. 'I've got to get something from me purse.' Instead, she fetches his Glock, tiptoes back to the bed, and plugs him through the heart."

"Which only works with those who have hearts," Bresnahan whispered to Noreen.

"Hughie, son—I commend you," McKeon nearly chortled. "It takes a brave man to utter a thought like that to a mixed and possibly a mixed-up gathering."

The two women only eyed him.

Unperplexed, McKeon slid the reports into a folder, looked up at them, and smiled. "Lads and lassies, if that's all there is, let's keep on dancin'. Namely, it's time for me to get back to the bar."

Their eyes were now on his throat.

McGarr straightened up and reached a closed hand to the center of the table, where he placed the beeper, the one that the child had dropped at the top of the millrace wall.

"Is it Ellen Finn's?" Bresnahan asked.

McGarr nodded. "And the last three calls were made from the same phone number. Here. From the inn side of the premises. Not the public number, but one that is available to staff and registered guests."

He stood. "Everybody have a lead?" he asked, since it had come to the time in the investigation when McGarr allowed his staff, given their experience, to follow their own hunches.

"But who will take Maddie today?" Noreen asked, when the others had departed.

"I will, if you like."

"But you took her yesterday."

McGarr let the silence convey his reply.

"And I suppose it's unfair—you were up half the night and being in charge and all. No," she decided, 'I'll take her, I will. So, you can do your job of work."

Reaching out, she took his hand, her turquoise-colored eyes fixing his. "It's just that I get so caught up, and guess what?"

McGarr canted his head, suspecting what was coming.

"I know who murdered them, and I know the scenario— how it happened and why."

McGarr wrinkled his brow inquiringly.

"I just have to prove it."

McGarr waited to learn more.

"No, no." She released his hand and made for the stairs. "I don't want anybody, like Bernie, carping about amateurs. When I have all my ducks in line, I'll present them."

"I'll try to phone," McGarr said to her back. "Maybe I can spell you later."

At the reception desk, McGarr asked the attendant who had treated him so officiously the day before, "Is Grace O'Rourke on duty today?"

"Upstairs in the pub. She's making up the rooms left from the day of the tragedy."

"And where is Mr. Tallon?"

"Below in his office in the basement."

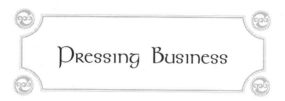

# 16

# Pressing Business

Since he did not possess a passkey to the two doors at either end of the archway that linked the halves of building, McGarr had to step outside, cross the cobblestones of the courtyard/car park, and enter the pub through the rear.

And curiously, not one member of the Fourth Estate was in sight at such an early hour, not even in the bar, which was shocking. Must all be sleeping after their taxing vigil waiting for him to return with some more bad news the night before, McGarr mused sourly.

A young barman, who was cleaning up, asked him if he needed something, but McGarr only waved him off, wanting to discover for himself how difficult it would be for somebody to admit himself to the staircase that led to the rooms upstairs.

But at the end of the bar, he could not quite reach the button that buzzed open the lock. A taller person with longer arms might, he speculated, and one whose body was less ancient and sore. He tried again, lunging this time.

"Yo! Get out of that!" the barman yelled, moving toward him. "What do you think you're doing there?"

The tip of McGarr's finger, however, had grazed the button, and the bolt clicked back. McGarr eased his battered form off the bar and reached for the door handle.

"You can't go up there."

But the look that McGarr now fixed the barman with stopped him.

"You're the police."

McGarr stepped into the stairwell and glanced up at the long flight to the top. Arriving there slowly, he found Grace O'Rourke standing by a service cart at the end of the hall. But upon seeing him, she stepped into the room she had been cleaning and closed the door, throwing the lock.

McGarr rapped on a coffered panel. "Grace—I'd like a word with you, if I may."

"Why?"

"You know why."

"Do I, now?"

"Because it's the only right thing to do. There's something you should have told me when we last spoke, and it's critical that you tell me now."

"Right for who?"

"Just right. Can I tell you about wrong?" She did not reply, so McGarr continued.

"Wrong was last night. Two of my staff could have been killed, and a little girl—Cara Frakes, perhaps you know her—nearly drowned in a millrace because I don't know enough about what went on in the room across the hall before Pascal Burke and Ellen Finn were murdered.

"You do. And right most definitely is your telling me. Now. How much blood do you want on your hands?"

There was a pause, then the lock slid back.

McGarr stepped into the room and closed the door. Turning around, he beheld a Grace O'Rourke far different from the dowdy maid he had spoken to on the day before. Gone were the uniform smock, the lank hair, the serviceable shoes.

Instead, her hair was permed, her face made up, and this Prussian blue uniform had been tailored to her figure, with the hem raised well above the knees. Her stockings were black and patterned, and the matching shoes were pointed with enough heel to set off her narrow ankles.

In all, the outfit made it plain that Grace O'Rourke, while not a pretty woman, was youthful and shapely. And surely somebody whom—what had been Benny Carson's term for Pascal Burke?—a *swordsman* would have found fetching, being so close at hand.

"Pascal preferred me like this," she said self-consciously, her hands touching her thighs. "And it's the least I can do to honor his memory."

McGarr shook his head. "No. The least you can do is answer my questions. Who else slept with Pascal Burke on a regular basis?"

Her head was quivering, and McGarr could see tears welling up in her eyes. "Apart from you."

As though having been slapped, she spun around. "What if I did? You didn't know Pascal—his kindness, his caring. He was not at all like the men down in the bar with their carry-on about themselves. Always themselves and what they need and nothing of you.

"He remembered little things—my birthday, my aunt's, what looked good on me. Brought me presents, nothing grand but . . . And he could and did love me . . ." Her shoulders lurched, as she broke into sobs. ". . . in his own way. I'm certain of it.

"And what we had was special. I don't give a damn who else he shagged or was shagging."

McGarr waited for the sobbing to cease. "Like Gertrude McGurk."

"That whore! That slut! There's not a man in town she hasn't shagged."

Wheeling back on McGarr, Grace O'Rourke spread her hands across her stomach, pulling the material of the uniform dress taut. "See this, you bastard. See it?" Her face was running with tears, her features were contorted.

"This is Pascal's child, what he left me. It makes me not like the others, and I intend to love and care for his baby. But what am I to do? You tell me. Work down in the shop with my aunt, as she wants, where every bloody woman in town would know my shame? At least here in the inn I'm in the company of strangers, and I can come and go without notice."

"Except for Madame Sylvie, of course. Sylvie Zeebruge, your employer, whom you're protecting. Tim Tallon's wife. How many nights did she spend with Burke?"

Again Grace O'Rourke pivoted, turning her back to him, her shoulders heaving, her head down.

"Talk about access, Madame Sylvie lived here, while you had to go home. She had passkeys to the archway, even a key to his door. And with Tallon always out with his guests, fishing, having a jar, Burke and she lived like husband and wife.

"I wonder—could she be pregnant by Burke as well? She's still young enough, I gather. And a handsome woman. Junoesque."

"So help me, if you don't leave this room this minute, I'll swear you tried to rape me," she managed through her sobs.

"Your pleasure—there's nobody about to hear you." With her back still turned to him, McGarr stepped forward and, reaching up, plucked a small amount of hair from the back of her head.

Which was when she spun around with her arm outstretched and something in her hand. A knife.

McGarr lurched back, and it clipped by his face.

"Rape!" she screamed, cutting the knife this way and that, as McGarr backed toward the door. "He's trying to rape me! Rape! Rape!"

When McGarr reached the hall, she kicked shut the door, and the blade of the knife punched through the coffered panel of the door, splintering the veneer.

Into one of three envelopes that he had removed from the writing desk in his room, McGarr deposited the several strands of hair that he had taken from her head, noting that some were complete with follicles, which were essential in revealing DNA. It was extremely difficult to determine DNA from a strand of hair alone.

While listening to Grace O'Rourke's muffled sobs, he wrote her name across the front, then made for the stairs.

Down in the pub, McGarr yet again had to dodge several members of the press, who were drinking at the bar.

"Early for that, isn't it, lads?" he asked, while moving toward Benny Carson, whom he could see at the other end of the long room.

"If you'd give us something to write about, there'd be no need for drink," said one, sliding off his stool and following McGarr with pad and pen in hand.

"I'm sure you'd find a need," McGarr shot back over a shoulder.

"Did Quintan Finn murder his wife and Pascal Burke and then commit suicide?" one asked.

"We're waiting for the reports from the postmortem exams."

"If it wasn't Finn, do you have any suspects?"

"What about Donal and Manus Frakes, are they still suspects now that Finn has been found?"

"Have you made an arrest?"

"When I do, I'll clear it with Phoenix Park, then gather you together as usual." It was the location of Garda Siochana Headquarters in Dublin.

"Don't tell us you've been down here—what?—three days now, and you've no leads?"

"Why not? I have no leads. I am categorically stumped, and that's for attribution." Arriving at Carson's side, McGarr took his arm, and said, "Show me your office."

"Ach—don't give us that shite again, McGarr. We won't fall for it a second time."

Some years back during a case in which the press had been particularly intrusive, McGarr had told the most obnoxious reporter—"This is strictly off the record, is that understood?"—that he hadn't a clue who had murdered a nun visiting her mother's grave in Glasnevin Cemetery. "All my leads have turned out to be dead ends."

The day after banner headlines proclaimed, "CHIEF COP STUMPED," McGarr arrested a former priest for her murder. And the press reviled him for being duplicitous.

"Is Mr. Carson a suspect?"

"No."

"Have the Frakes been arrested?"

"No."

"Do you know of their whereabouts?"

"No, but if you do, please tell me."

"Does that mean the Frakes are still suspects?"

"At this time, there are no suspects, and whoever reported that was doing you no favor. Like I said, I'm stumped."

McGarr was now behind the bar with Carson, who used his unbandaged hand to open a low door; the two men stepped into a small room that contained only a desk, chair, and a rack of pigeonholes. There was also a door that appeared to lead farther into the building.

"C'mon, McGarr—we're only trying to make a living here."

"There are other occupations," he observed, closing the door.

Carson eased himself against the desk and pointed to the chair. "Chief?"

"Why'd you ring them up with the story about Ellen Finn and Burke? And the Frakes."

Carson touched his chest histrionically. "Me? Janie—I'd never do such a thing, considering how shabbily they've dealt with me in the past."

"Why?"

Carson pulled a cigarette from a packet, then held it out to McGarr, who had remained standing. "Don't tell me they're not still suspects."

"Why?"

Carson lit the cigarette, then batted the smoke from his eyes. "To speed their arrest and conviction on its way, I suppose."

"Even though Manus Frakes is your son-in-law."

Carson's light blue eyes flashed at McGarr. "Manus Frakes is a murdering, thieving lout of a liar, and the sooner I can get my granddaughter out of his hands the better. That much I'll admit to and no more.

"Manus and Finn murdered Finn's wife and Burke, and then Finn did the decent thing and killed himself, just like I told your sidekick and my old friend, Bernie McKeon. I don't care how many hours' lapse it was between their deaths or how many bullets were or were not used.

"And as for the possibility that some other woman had been in bed with Burke shortly before Burke was shot, then that could be nobody other than Gertie McGurk, who'd fook a snake if you held its head."

McGarr regarded the small older man, who was again wearing a hand-tied bow tie and Prussian blue tuxedo jacket. If nothing else, his police instincts told him Carson had been involved in one or all of the murders. "You told me you were the manager of this place, a leaseholder of the space. You told Bernie that you're now thinking of buying it."

"Sure—I only just decided myself, after Tallon came to me and said he was sick of the problems it's given him over the years, the murders upstairs being the two final straws."

"Where'd you get the money?"

"Now, what money would I have, Chief Superintendent? Me just having left the brig."

"You tell me."

"Not a lot, to tell you the truth. But Tallon likes my style and—apart from the recent tragedy—I run a quiet place. Tallon will hold the paper, and I'll pay him from the profits of the place."

Profits that Tallon would have been receiving anyway? Somehow, that did not scan.

Reading the doubt in McGarr's face, Carson added, "What I mean to say is—the portion of the profits that had been going to me as salary for managing the place will now pay off the principal. And Tallon will continue to participate in the profits on a sliding scale, according to the percentage of the business that he owns."

"The building included?"

"Half of the building from the middle of the archway down."

"And the principal is?"

As though swearing to truth, Carson raised his bandaged hand, his eyes fixing McGarr's. "I'd like to tell you that and more, really I would. But I've already said too much, Tallon having sworn me to silence on that score, since he's rather a secretive chappie who doesn't want the locals knowing his finances. If the figure gets out, it's a deal-breaker, says he. And I believe him."

"Why would he do something like that for you?"

"Money, plain and simple. The principal? What I can say

is I probably won't pay it off in my lifetime. But this place will be here and ticking on all cylinders, I'll make sure, for my granddaughter in her time."

"When are you taking over?"

"Soon. Sometime next week. Tallon wants out of here and fast. 'The whole thing disgusts me,' says he to me. His solicitor is working out the details as we speak."

"And how will you live on no salary?"

"Sure, on air. It's the big lesson you learn in the drum—not to want much. And to be honest, I don't require much. No car, I only live around the corner for little or nothing, since I take care of that place, too. And I've got the only girlfriends worth having—they go home to their parents and husbands at closing time."

"Why did you tell me that Tallon's wife Sylvie actually owned the business, and not Tallon?"

"Because that's what he told me. Ask any local, and they'll say the same."

"What about your nephew?" McGarr suddenly felt like one of the reporters that he could hear grousing about his own ". . . stonewalling," one now said through the door.

Carson cocked his head and took a final drag before stubbing out the butt; the small room was now filled with smoke, which only made McGarr crave one for himself all the more. "Do you want the, 'Of course, we're all broken up over poor Quintan' or the truth?"

"Which is?"

"That he was a miserable little guttersnipe from birth, a truly bad seed, and Honora and Dermot are well shed of him. Too bad he had to take Ellen and Burke along with him."

"How's your sister taking it?"

Carson only hunched his thin shoulders. "Poorly, I hear. But right from the start Honora was a child of glass, forever complaining, always thinking of herself alone. And you know how women make too much of things."

McGarr waited.

Carson's pale blue eyes flashed up at him. "Because they can give birth, they think life is the answer, while men know that death is the only truth."

They held each other's gaze for a moment or two, before McGarr asked, "How can I get to Tallon's office in the inn? Through there?" McGarr pointed to the small door behind the desk.

Carson shook his head. "Unfortunately for you—one way and one way only: through the pub, across the courtyard, and in through the inn. It's down in the cellar."

"What's behind the door?"

"Storage."

Stepping back into the bar, McGarr found at least a dozen faces glaring at him.

Master stonemasons must have built the premises, McGarr decided, as he descended the long flight of wide stairs into the basement of the inn.

It was cool there, but dry, the grain of the blocks of gray stone having been selected in such a way that moisture was carried out of the building, he assumed.

The ceilings of each of the small rooms that he was passing were vaulted and made of brick, like the magazines in a fort, and it occurred to McGarr that the first use of the structure might have been military, given its position of command above the river.

Finding Tim Tallon in one of the larger rooms, he paused in the doorway and looked around: a computer, faxes, and several telephones on one long table; rows of filing cabinets; and one cushioned reading chair with a light behind it.

On the phone, Tallon was sitting at a large oak desk;

behind him was a sizable and ornate safe with gilded scroll-work on the door, which was open. Seeing McGarr, Tallon raised a finger, meaning he would be only a moment, then pointed to a chair near the desk, before the hand descended. It closed the safe door and spun the combination lock.

"Ah, good, Hans . . . great . . . wonderful . . . grand. We'll see you, Britta, and the family on the tenth then. I'll have the car waiting at the airport. No problem, none at all. My pleasure. G'luck to you, too."

Hanging up, Tallon glanced at McGarr and smiled. "Peter, lad, how goes the sleuthing?" He picked up some papers on his desk and shuffled them. "What can I do you for? The Frakes, now, have you nabbed their sorry arses yet?"

McGarr wondered why even those few remarks set his teeth on edge. Was it their past history? Or was Tallon so lacking in social skills that he struck everybody that way?

"Something in there you don't want me to see?" McGarr asked.

"What? No, of course not. Your walking in only reminded me that it was open. And let me assure you—*friend*—had the bloody Pope himself walked in, I would have closed it—as a matter of habit. But you didn't search me out to discuss my finances."

"But I did. Benny Carson tells me that you're going to sell him the pub half of the inn, building and all."

Tallon's brow was now a field of furrows.

"Is that true?"

Tallon nodded.

"Why?"

"Why what?"

"Why are you selling it to him?"

"Because it makes good sense, business-wise."

"Aren't you making money there?"

Tallon stood and moved away from the desk. "I am, yah—but not enough. Can I tell you the history of the pub?"

McGarr nodded, noting the MacDonald-plaid twill shirt that wrapped Tallon's paunch, the tight blue jeans, the tooled-leather cowboy boots that rather accentuated his curious shamble. His belt buckle was made of silver with a large turquoise stone in the shape of the head of a longhorn steer.

"We're open now six year come Christmas, and, as I think I've told you, it's taken that long to get the inn half of the operation off the ground.

"Oh, I know, I know." Both fidgety and demonstrative, Tallon flapped a hand, "people will tell you, I tried to make a go of the pub, too. But, the plain truth is"—he stopped his strange perambulation, turned and faced McGarr—"I'm not much of a publican. People don't like me very much."

He paused, his dark eyes searching McGarr's face, as though for a denial. "You don't yourself."

Another pause.

"You didn't when we were kids, you don't now."

Tallon waited further, before dipping his head and shoulders and continuing to pace. "And the pub was a bust.

"Then along comes Benny Carson—ex-convict and murderer—asking me . . . no, *begging* me to give him a chance to pump up business.

"Says I to him, not a chance. Don't even think about it, until Dermot Finn—his brother-in-law and a man of his word—comes by and says he'll cover any losses. 'Just give Benny a chance to get on his feet. You won't be sorry.' "

"Nor was I. Because—who do the Culchie pricks in these parts think is so brilliant beyond words that they're willing to splash out their last pound come-day-go-day as long as he's there behind the bar, like . . . like some fallen priest in a public confessional? Benny effing Carson, is who. I tell you it's hard to fathom."

"Aren't you making money?" McGarr asked again.

Tallon nodded. "Like I said, I am, yah—but not enough. First, there's his salary, which we've negotiated and renegotiated thrice now, always up. And then he's stealing, I'm sure he is, even with the new computer. But I don't know how.

"And I dare not fire him. There isn't a bar in these parts that wouldn't hire him in a blink, and I'd be back where I was. Behind the bloody bar, and I don't want that.

"So, here's the deal," he continued. "We own it together on a sliding scale, as he pays me the sum that we've agreed upon. If he misses a payment—a single payment—we go back to square one. I keep what he's paid me, and he begins all over again.

"But if all goes according to form, I'm rid of the place with a handsome purchase price in me back pocket. And the pub is still there, perking along for my guests here in the inn. Some of them like consorting with the locals—the music, the *crac*. You know, the *wild* Irish thing."

"How much?"

"Excuse me?"

"How much is Carson paying?"

Tallon laughed silently. "Now, answer me this—how smart would that be? Tell you, tell all. Only two days ago I asked you to keep a secret for me. And look what happened— we have press all over town."

He paused, his eyes narrowing sagely. "But, I suppose, Peter, we all have our flaws, and I'm a big enough man not to blame you for yours."

What was it about Tallon that was so off-putting, McGarr asked himself again. His need to make the other person feel guilty in regard to him? Or, at least, indebted?

In Ireland, of course, guilt ruled all, but the entire *shtik*, if it was that, was an attempt at control. From schoolyard bully to emotional bully wasn't a great leap, McGarr well knew, and he wondered at Tallon's relations with those closer to him, like his wife and employees.

"Gertie McGurk—is she one of the wild Irish things your guests consort with?"

Tallon stepped back to his desk, where he sat. "It has been known to happen."

"In the inn."

"There's no way I can keep her out, given what my guests pay. And can I say something off the record, Peter?"

"Trust me," said McGarr, wryly.

"Where's the harm? Great form, that girl, and a bit of a fling away from home can do a marriage a world of good, I'm told. Rumor has it, some of my guests come back just for her, not the fishing."

Which makes you . . . ? McGarr kept himself from asking. Instead he removed a slip of paper from his jacket and reached it to Tallon. "Recognize this number?"

"Of course—it's one of the numbers here."

"It's also the number from which Ellen Finn was paged three times, shortly before she was murdered. She left her work on the river to find a phone to answer it."

Like a large grizzled bird turning an ear to the ground— the hooded brow, pugged nose, and sunken cheeks, Tallon canted his head. "Impossible."

McGarr only waited.

Tallon's dark eyes rose and caromed off McGarr's, fixing on a point on the vaulted ceiling. "Of course, we have phones in every room, several in the dining room, the bar, the kitchen, the maid's closets, here." He pointed to the phone on his desk. "The calls could have been made from any one of them, if what you say is true. But—"

"All dial out?"

Tallon nodded. "Those not in the rooms are restricted to local calls. Electronically."

"No charge."

"Not locally."

"Who was about Friday afternoon?"

As though plainly disturbed by the news, Tallon wagged his head. "Perhaps several of the inn staff, surely the chef and his crew were in the kitchen preparing, since we have a good amount of transit trade Friday nights, in addition to the guests. And we were booked solid."

"Was Grace O'Rourke about?"

Tallon had to think. "I think she might have been, although I couldn't say for sure. If some of the guests are late rising, she hangs about to do up the rooms, when they leave or come down for a bite to eat."

"Were you here?"

His bushy eyebrows knitted. "I don't understand. What's the purpose of that question? Surely, you don't—"

Tired of his carry-on, McGarr asked again in a stronger voice. "Were. You. Here?"

"Not for most of the afternoon. I was fishing with the lads, I was."

"What time did you return?"

"Oh—fourish, I'd say. To help with the setups, don't you know."

"Here in the inn."

Tallon nodded.

"What about the pub? Did you go into the pub?"

Again, he had to think. "No, I don't think so. Not that I can remember, although I do from time to time. To show the flag, so to speak." Tallon twined his fingers across his chest and smiled woodenly, McGarr noticing for the first time that Tallon's teeth were not good. "I hope you don't think me a suspect in this?"

"You went nowhere near the pub?"

He shook his head. "Not that I can remember."

"Not upstairs either?"

Tallon sat up suddenly. "Ach, sure—now that I remember—I was. Didn't I check the work in the room we're renovating over the pub."

"The room where Manus Frakes and Quintan Finn laid the carpet that afternoon?"

"Aye."

"What time was that?"

"Oh, I'd say it was teatime. Six or thereabouts. Peter, I hope you—"

"Were Frakes and Finn there?"

Tallon shook his head. "Long gone. Or, at least they weren't in that room. I can remember speaking with a Dutchman—is that where you got this?—about the work, since they'd made a balls of the job and the whole thing would have to be torn up and begun again. Or trashed. It wasn't right at all, you can see for yourself. It's still there."

"And where was your wife?"

"Sylvie? Why do you ask?"

"Please—just answer my questions."

"In the inn, I suppose. Most Fridays she naps in the afternoon—to be fresh the night long, don't you know. The first I saw her, I think, was in the dining room . . . no, she was behind the reception desk, I recall."

"You don't share the same quarters?"

"No—but don't get the wrong idea. Like yourself, I smoke, and Sylvie gets headaches. The allergies, her doctor has told us. Otherwise, everything is . . ." Tallon winked. "No complaints, not a one."

Apart from her own, McGarr recalled from his interview with the woman. "Is she about?"

"Who?"

McGarr stood. "The wife."

Tallon was now leaning back in his chair with his hands around his head. "She's not here."

"When will she be back?"

"I'm not sure. Her mother took sick, and she's over in Bruges."

*What?*, McGarr was tempted to ask. Instead he waited.

"It's serious, she was told, and she left this morning. Only child—they're very close."

And was it a kind of glee that McGarr now read in Tallon's eyes? He thought so. "Take me to her quarters."

"Why?"

"Because I'd like to look around."

"Why?"

McGarr's hands shot out. Seizing Tallon by the front of his shirt, he pulled him across the desk. Buttons popped; the phone, a desk lamp, and a credenza crashed to the floor. They were face-to-face.

"Because I'm thinking of filing charges against you and your would-be wife."

"Charges of what?" Tallon managed.

"Complicity in murder."

"But they would be false charges. Now, take your hands off me, please."

McGarr only stared into the man's dark eyes. False or not, Tallon and his inn would be branded. And in a country where sin could be forgiven but was never forgotten, at the very least he would lose his Irish trade.

Dropping Tallon on the desk, he turned to the door.

Sylvie Zeebruge's apartment was on the second floor. "So she can be close to the guests," Tallon explained, using a key to let McGarr in. "She tells them, 'You need anything at any hour, knock on my door.' She caters to their least little whim."

The apartment was even more completely furnished than

the inn proper, if that was possible. In regard to walls or any flat surface, it was as if the woman exercised a form of horror vacui.

She had left in a hurry, it appeared, when McGarr stepped into her boudoir. Drawers in the chifforobe were ajar, and clothes lay on the bed. Her dresser was a chaos of cosmetics, the top, the drawers; it was a fragrant mess.

McGarr moved directly to the bathroom and the cabinets by the sink, which were filled out with more vials, jars, spray bottles of cold cream, deodorants, perfumes, and hair preparations than a well-stocked *perfumerie*.

He opened several of the drawers.

"What are you looking for?" Tallon asked. "Perhaps I can help you."

"This." McGarr held up a hairbrush with more than a few hairs snagged in the bristles. "I'm going to take this."

"Why?"

McGarr only slid the object in a pocket. "Who was Tony Moran?"

It took Tallon a moment or two to speak, as though he was framing his response. "A local fella, older, a bachelor poof. He passed away a year ago . . . no, two, I believe."

"Friend of your wife?"

Tallon shrugged. "She's been known to have friends, and he could afford to come in here. He was into computers, and helped us with ours."

"She cook for him?"

"Perhaps—I don't know. She cooks every Thursday on the chef's day off."

"And Moran came in on Thursdays?"

"Could be. It's usually slow, and he could speak a bit of Flemish. He'd studied for the priesthood with some Belgian order, don't you know."

"Were your wife and he linked, romantically?"

"What? Are you daft, man? Sylvie's a big, full woman—you saw her yourself—and Moran was a wee fella and rather . . . effeminate and bookish, if you know what I mean. Never married and not a tale heard tell about him and a woman. You know, sexually."

"What about his involvement with Gertie McGurk—she had to sue his estate for the twenty-four thousand quid he left her?"

"That may be true. It was in all the papers, and certainly they went places together. But I'll tell you this—I'll bet my last farthing that Tony Moran never so much as kissed any of the women he looked after. Pubs weren't his style, nor the company of men. He was just . . . a nancy boy who preferred nancies, not boys."

A quaint term, McGarr thought, but he had known men who had enjoyed the company of women without having to know them sexually. At the same time, he knew rather effeminate men who were very much interested in women and women in them.

"Let's ring up your wife in Belgium."

"Well—I'm not sure she'll be home. The mother's in hospital, as I said."

"Then, we'll reach her there."

"But—"

"You don't know the name of the hospital?"

Tallon shook his head.

"Then, we'll just have to phone the police and have them find her."

When Tallon opened his mouth to object, McGarr added, "Not to worry—I speak the language."

"Flemish?"

"French. Your wife speaks that, too, I trust. Was she ever a blond?"

Glumly, his head lowered, Tallon passed out the door in front of McGarr. "Not to my knowledge."

"Why don't we use the phone in your quarters?"

Tallon stopped and turned to McGarr. "Why?"

"Well, having seen how the 'wife' lives, I'm curious to see where you hang your hat."

Which was in the attic on what amounted to a fourth floor. But, given the steeply sloping roof of the building, it was a vast space that Tallon had furnished in a field-and-stream motif, with paintings and drawings of shooting and fishing scenes.

There were also photographs of him and his "missus" with a number of fishing and hunting parties, the fish and game spread out at their feet, shotguns slung over their forearms.

"The wife hunts?"

"Of course—she prefers cooking game. It's what we're noted for."

Overhead in one room Tallon had arrayed in racks perhaps ten dozen fishing rods of various sizes and weights for different sorts of lakes and streams.

In another room that had no ceiling apart from the towering roof of the inn, stuffed and mounted heads of wild animals had been hung from the beams as trophies.

A large double-fronted gun case built of butter-colored deal stood in the center of that room. The inventory of shotguns was impressive; many were by Purdy—handmade with engraved plates, checkered stocks, and hefty price tags. "These your guns?"

"Some of them. The rest are Sylvie's, whose father was hunt master to the King of Belgium."

Other guns included high-caliber big-game rifles, some with sighting scopes.

Along the walls were cataloged wading boots, rubberized macs, Wellies, and wide-brimmed rain hats with chin straps.

"We tell first-time guests—just bring yourselves—we'll supply the rest."

"This phone the same number as the inn?"

"One of them."

"The number that paged Ellen Finn?"

Tallon nodded.

McGarr let the phone ring at the number in Belgium for the longest time, but there was no answer. Calling the police in Bruge, he was told that Sylvie Zeebruge's mother, Sophie, could be at any one of a number of hospitals in the large metropolitan area.

"Fact is," the desk officer there went on, "nowadays people go to any hospital they choose, anywhere in the country."

"Would it be possible to obtain a list of all Belgian hospitals?"

"I have one right here."

"Could you fax it to me?"

"Of course."

McGarr gave the fax number of his office in Dublin, then rang up and told the desk man there to begin checking for a Sophie Zeebruge.

"Begin in the Bruges area, but I want you to locate this woman and see if her daughter, Sylvie, is at her side. And if you reach Sylvie, ask her to contact my cell phone immediately."

When McGarr rang off, he glanced up to find Tallon staring out a window at the darkened street, as though lost in thought.

# 17

# Rubber, Duck!

Hugh Ward wondered if every country chemist shop had bells on its doors.

Certainly, the one-man operations at crossroads towns and country villages did, and he had been listening to the jangle of bells all morning and much of the afternoon, when he hadn't been driving. Chemist shops were few and far between in rural Ireland.

The impetus of Ward's quest was singular: Thunderbolt condoms. In all his twenty-plus years as a combatant in the "War-d"—was his metaphor—between the sexes, he had never happened upon Thunderbolt condoms, and he imagined that they were an off brand not sold in Ireland.

Further—given their point of origin in the States—the items had probably been brought back by some enterprising chemist or a relative, because of the difference in price or the evocative name that Bernie McKeon so enjoyed.

In any case, the Thunderbolt condoms found in Ellen Finn's purse had been—like the photos she had taken of the Frakes and the two thousand quid—an afterthought by the murderer or murderers, he was certain.

And over the top, which was always the case with those who felt their own guilt so thoroughly that no simple remedy could do. They had to cover up the crime totally.

So, between the 3:00 P.M. probable death of Pascal Burke and the 6:00 P.M. shooting of Ellen Finn, one of them had driven out to a chemist and purchased condoms to "salt" in Ellen Finn's purse and flat. As Noreen and Ruth had pointed out, a pregnant woman—who was not promiscuous—had no real need for condoms.

"Hello—anybody about?" Ward had to call out. In spite of the bell, nobody had appeared, and he could smell the evening tea being prepared beyond a curtained passageway at the back of the shop. There was a decidedly spicy edge to the odor.

Finding yet another bell on the counter, he rang that insistently, and at length a dark-skinned man appeared, wearing a cardigan jumper over a white shirt and tie and octagon eyeglasses with wire bows. A name tag said, "S. Gupta, M.S., Chemist."

"How may I help you, sir?"

Ward produced his photo ID and the packet of Thunderbolt condoms, explaining, "I'm with the Serious Crimes Unit, and I'm here on a matter of utmost importance. Do you sell these?"

Gupta reached for Ward's ID, rather than the packet. After studying it closely, he glanced up, "You're sure you're not a tax man?" His voice, while cultivated, carried a slight East Indian inflection.

Ward shook his head. "Murder Squad. We're investigating the three deaths in Leixleap. And this piece of evidence could prove crucial."

The chemist's eyes flashed on the packet of condoms, before he bent at the waist and said, "If you'll step around here, Superintendent."

A large drawer was filled with different brands of condoms. "I keep them here because, after all, this *is* Ireland."

Where old attitudes linger, went unsaid; and yet, only two decades earlier an East Indian chemist would probably not have been able to make a go of a small shop in rural Ireland, because of Irish attitudes. Credit the recent prosperity that was changing the country.

"One of my relatives brought me a gross of Thunderbolt condoms from the States when he visited on holiday last summer," Gupta continued. "He mistakenly thought Ireland still banned birth-control devices, and selling condoms would give me an edge, so to speak.

"So, being that they're truly superior condoms—finely textured but strong, I'm told, and the profit margin cannot be beaten—we sell them as brand X, whenever somebody comes into the shop asking for condoms and not naming a brand."

"And when last did you sell some?"

"Me?" He had to think. "About two weeks ago, I believe."

"What about Friday between three and six in the afternoon?"

"I'm afraid I was golfing. My daughter was tending the shop."

"Can I speak to her? As I said, it's quite important."

"Surely." Gupta stepped behind the curtains and opened a door.

Ward could hear the telly and the sounds of dishes being washed.

"Shila!" he called out. "Could you come out here for a moment?"

After a while a girl appeared who could not be more than fourteen or fifteen, but graceful in her movements and pretty, with bright dark eyes and well-formed mouth.

A flurry of Punjabi was spoken by her father, which caused her to look down, as though embarrassed.

"Shila is bashful. Especially about such matters, and I can't tell you how many times I've explained to her that all such functions are human functions and part of the purview of our activity here in this shop," her father explained didactically, one finger raised in front of his nose.

The girl then said something and walked back behind the curtains.

"Pardon me, Superintendent. But—"

More talk transpired in the shadows there, before Gupta emerged. "Shila speaks English better than me—I mean, I— but I think it has something to do with her age.

"Anyhow—she sold two packets of Thunderbolt condoms to a man on Friday afternoon just before teatime. He also wanted a lubricant and was in such a hurry that he left without his change, which was four pounds fifty-three pence. Shila put the money in an envelope, which is in the register, she says."

Tapping a key, Gupta opened the machine, removed the coin tray and produced an envelope that said in precise script, " 'Change of customer, Friday afternoon, 5:15.' We try to do everything legally here."

"Can she describe this customer? What did he look like? Big, tall, small, short, fat? Distinguishing marks? What was he wearing?"

Again Gupta stepped behind the curtain, and what sounded like a debate ensued, with the father's tone becoming stern.

Back out, Gupta raised his palms, "Alas—she didn't look at him. She says, she couldn't. She was alone in the shop, he was a man, and it's the one item that she has trouble . . . dealing with, if you can understand . . . ?"

Ward nodded. "But anything—the way he spoke, the way he walked, an item of clothing—could be helpful." An idea occurred to him. "What if I were to bring her a photo? Could she identify him from that?"

Yet again, the exchange occurred between daughter and father, who again appeared apologetically. "Maybe the photos will help her remember. She says she . . . blocked it out. It seemed to be to her a bad experience for both of them. He asked for them, she gave them to him, he slapped the money down and just left."

"Did she go after him with the change?"

Gupta called over his shoulder. "Shila?"

"No—I was alone! I told you that!" The door to the living quarters was wrenched open and slammed shut.

"She's that age," Gupta tried to explain.

Ward nodded. "Do you have one of those disposable cameras? You know the type that you use once—"

"This way." Gupta led Ward to his camera and film inventory.

Ruth Bresnahan was in the bedroom that Quintan and Ellen Finn had shared for the seven months of their short marriage, and she felt about as sad as she ever had in her life.

The bigger problem was: Ruth was not sure that the sadness, which weighed on her like a millstone, was caused by what had happened to a poor young married couple. Or what was happening to herself. And the very selfishness of the latter scenario, if true, would be enough to make Ruth rethink her life.

She had never been self-absorbed; she would not allow herself to become so now.

But all about her, on nearly every surface that she could see, were pictures of the two handsome young people together: before, during, and after marriage. Baby pictures, kid pictures, it even looked as though they had been playmates together before school and friends after they had left and become young adults.

In other words, they had been soul mates in addition to becoming love mates, and for the year that Ward and she had been apart, Ruth had been denied her soul mate.

Why? Because she had decided that she should forestall marriage and motherhood, which she had looked upon as a trap. What was it some German writer had said? "When your child is born, you are the dead one."

And hadn't her own mother confided, "You get married, you give birth, and it's wonderful, having your own child. What we're meant for. But taking care of others makes the years race by. Suddenly you're old, your body is broken, and then you die.

"Ruthie—it's the wise woman who puts that off as long as possible."

But then, her mother—who was still very much alive—had married a much older man. Yet after her father had died, her mother suddenly had nobody but Ruth, who was 140 miles away in Dublin, pursuing her career. In other words, she had nobody but a distant daughter.

Ruth sat on the bed and scanned all the undergarments she had assembled. On one side were the brassieres, thongs, merry widows, and other contraptions that she had taken from Gertrude McGurk's room in the safe house that she shared with the brothers Frakes.

On the other side were similar items that she had found in the dresser in the Finns' bedroom. And all were similar in most regards from size—38D cup, twenty-eight-inch waist, and "Long" in any of the wear that hung past the hips to where they were made, which was almost exclusively the UK or Ireland. The only difference was, two of the brassieres had underwire cups to lift the breasts in the tawdry way that so attracted men's eyes.

Sex—Bresnahan decided—picking up a garter belt clustered with spikes and equipped with other straps for who-knew-what purpose—was so effing depressing. The problems it got people into. And yet sex couldn't be denied. That much she knew.

Dropping the item back into the pile, Bresnahan rose from the bed and entered the toilet, where earlier she had dumped the dead couple's laundry on the floor.

And among the collection was Ellen Finn's choice in undergarments. Most were plain and made of cotton. Her bra size? It had varied, as her pregnancy wore on, but she had begun at 34C. In other words, petite. Small. When compared to Ruth herself or, say, Gertrude McGurk.

Ellen Finn's knickers were small as well, and many of them were clean and bore regular creases from having been folded after being washed. In haste, the murderer or murderers had simply stuffed the clothes that they had pulled from the drawers of the dresser into the hamper, Ruth was convinced, before adding the more provocative items. They had assumed that the police would not think to look there.

Still in a funk, Bresnahan moved through the apartment to the door that separated it from Carson's flat at the front of the building. It had been open when she arrived, as though Carson was now living in both areas.

Spartan was the term that sprang to mind, as Ruth scanned the table in the kitchen with its single chair, the bedroom with a cot, and the few changes of Leixleap Inn uniform clothes and one dress suit with its pair of plain black brogues grouped neatly under the hanger.

Everything spick-and-span. The two plates that he owned had been washed, dried, and put away. In the fridge was a bottle of milk, a butter dish, and a packet of tea. Nothing else, since Carson probably ate at the pub. If he ate.

The entire flat smacked of his solitary life spent largely in penal institutions. The one decoration was a framed snapshot of a young woman holding a baby. It sat in the middle of the kitchen table across from the chair.

But what it said to Bresnahan was plain—that even this hard man who had endured years of hardship and deprivation had a priority. His deceased daughter and his granddaughter.

And perhaps it was time for her to consider children for herself. With whom? Why, with her soul mate, of course.

But didn't he already have a child and a half by another woman with whom he was also living?, she could hear her friends asking incredulously when time came to announce her condition.

Yes, but that was his decision, she would reply. Mine was to have his baby.

And who knew—she only now realized closing the door to the mews apartment and turning to look out at the Shannon that was streaming mightily below her—she might already be pregnant.

Not feeling much like sex over the past year, she had abandoned taking the pill. And far be it from Hugh Ward—Daddy-O ex caliber—to wear a condom.

Nor would he tonight, she decided, trying to remember if it was today or yesterday that she was ovulating.

Either or, she would make sure she was covered.

Bernie McKeon decided that this assignment—the double murder and possibly three here in Leixleap—was his reward for having been dutiful over the years.

The office guy. The inside man. The interviewer (or "in-terror-gator," as one barrister continually referred to McKeon in court).

Because, here in late afternoon he sat for the second day in a row at a crowded friendly noisy bar—which in his considered opinion was civilization at its best—shepherding a pleasant glow with no end of festivity in sight. Add to that, his sumptuous room in the inn was only a short . . . er, canter away.

The refrain: *"If that's all there is . . . let's keep on dancing,"* kept playing over in his head, and several times in the last few minutes he gave it voice.

"Did you hear the one about the man who asked his wife of fifty years if she would get married again, were he to die?" Benny Carson now asked the end of the bar where he was holding forth, cigarette in one hand, glass in the other.

Peering over his spectacles, his pale blue eyes—the very color of the uniform jacket—were bright and gay. " 'Well, ducky,' says her nibs, 'I might feel the need for companionship, and you would want me to be happy, wouldn't you?'

" 'Surely, certainly, most assuredly I'd want you to be happy,' says he, 'but would you let this person sleep in our bed?'

" 'Now, the bed's brand spanking new and you know how much we paid for it. It would be a waste not to put it to good use.'

"A bit miffed, your man says, 'So, if you'd get married after I died and you'd let your new husband sleep in our new bed, answer me this—would you let him use my golf clubs?' "

Carson paused to pull from the cigarette. " 'No, categorically not—I wouldn't let him do that.'

"Cheered, your man asks, 'And why, dear heart, would you not let him use me golf clubs?'

"Says she, 'Because he's left-handed.' "

The joke was easily the tenth that Carson had told in the last half hour, and in the two days that McKeon had been listening to him, not one had been repeated.

"You've a great memory and a knack for telling a story, Benny," McKeon said a few minutes later, when Carson moved near. "But, answer me this—how many are your own?"

"*All* of them, of course. Duly copyrighted and lodged in the British Museum."

"Go on now, you heard most of them in the drum, where there's little else to do."

His smile cracking, Carson shot McKeon a sidelong glance that was anything but pleasant. "Not a one. You know the riff about laughing through your tears? Or, you have to look at the bright side? Or, the glass is half-full not half-empty? Well, it's all bullshit, which is what the drum teaches. The truth."

McKeon waited for Carson to continue, not knowing what he was hearing. A strange sort of whining? Self-pity? The common jailhouse theme of, "I am what I am because of what I've been through? What you made me"?

"There's no bright side, no glass—the sharp edge of which could provide you with a solution to your problems—and you wouldn't dare let yourself shed a tear."

McKeon let that pass, and when it was apparent that Carson would say no more, he asked, "So—how did you spend your days there? Or was it all wasted?"

"Not a bit of it. When we got a chance to converse, we spoke—as most people do—about what we know best."

"Which is?"

"Crime." Carson smiled and reached for the tea that he kept in the Powers bottle. "May I freshen that for you, Bernie?"

McKeon pushed his collection of wet banknotes forward. "As long as it's not a crime."


While Maddie was at tea with Ruth Bresnahan and Hugh Ward, Noreen only just managed to nip in the front door of the greengrocer's shop before Moira O'Rourke locked the door.

"Phew," she said, nearly out of breath. "I nearly didn't make it."

"Pity you did, Mrs. McGarr. Can your husband be far behind?" The O'Rourke woman scanned the street before closing the door and drawing the blind.

"So?" she demanded of Noreen.

Who debated being cagey and asking her about this-and-that before getting to the point. But to what purpose? Moira O'Rourke had already "made" her, Noreen believed the police term for being discovered was, and indirection was now impossible. But not common courtesy, since what she had come to say was nothing that one person should spring on another, no matter the purpose.

Which caused her to decide that she would not have made a good cop, in spite of how much she was attracted to the profession.

"I think I know something that you don't."

"Little wonder—you the Dub' art expert with your well-connected parents and husband, the cop." Moira O'Rourke had crossed her arms, and the bib apron presented a formidable front. And yet the apron was also belted, which showed her to have a narrow waist and contained hips.

How old could she be? Noreen wondered. No older than thirty-eight or forty. And with a little care to her appearance, she could be a handsome woman whom Pascal Burke might have found attractive, considering how glowingly she had spoken of him.

Question was—had the glow been imparted by Grace O'Rourke's say-so? Or by Burke himself?

"What is it that you know that I don't?"

"It's about Grace, your niece," Noreen replied, probing to see if she did know.

"What about Grace?"

"About her health."

"What about her health? Grace is as strong as a horse. I've never known her to have a sick day in her life."

She didn't know, Noreen decided. And, summoning her courage, she blurted out, "She's carrying Pascal Burke's child. By her own admission."

There was a pause in which Moira O'Rourke seemed to assess the information. Then she bowed her head for a moment, raised it, and presented Noreen with a visage of rage that she had only ever seen onstage.

"You!" she seethed. "You're out of here!"

Grasping Noreen by the arm, Moira O'Rourke nearly picked her off her feet, and in one smooth and powerful motion had her out the door.

"And never come back!"

# 18

# Working Girls

As the crow flies, only about a hundred miles separates Leix-leap from Newry.

But unfortunately crows did not build the roads in Ireland, and McGarr spent the better part of three hours driving to the Northern Ireland city at the head of the Newry River.

Arriving just as darkness was falling, he soon found 8 Canal Lane, named for the eighteenth-century man-made waterway, the banks of which had many fine shops in its old commercial buildings and fashionable private houses nearby.

Gertrude McGurk's mother's abode was anything but. An aged brick row house, it had narrow windows and a low door, and there was a slate missing at the peak of the roof.

McGarr did not stop there. Instead, he parked by the nearest pub and went in.

The bar was milling with locals and workers from the shops that had only just closed, and a short, older man dressed in khakis with a windbreaker and cap to match was scarcely noticed.

It was the costume that Maddie had dubbed his "somebody's da'" clothes. "Yes, yours," had been McGarr's reply.

"How can you stand to wear those things? They're so . . . out of it."

When the second drink was placed before McGarr, he motioned the barman closer and showed him one of the photos Ward had taken from the Frakes's safe house near Leixleap. "Know her?"

"Gertie? Of course."

"She come in here often?"

"Regular, like—when she's in town, which is seldom these days. But she was here last night, as a matter of fact."

"What time would you say she comes in?"

The young man glanced at the clock. "Soon, I'd say. Unless she's otherwise employed." Which was accompanied by a slight but telling grin.

McGarr could wait, the chief of the Garda analysis lab in Dublin having assured him that a chemist would remain on duty throughout the night, if necessary—waiting for the three samples of hair that McGarr would deliver.

And it was pleasant just sitting there, musing over several glasses of malt that eased down into his soreness and made him feel almost normal for a while.

About an hour later, Gertrude McGurk made her entrance, carrying her coat so all might view the tight wrap of red spandex that made two buff-colored mounds of her breasts. She was a tall woman with a wide mouth and good teeth that black lipstick made seem all the more brilliant.

Glossy as though wet, it complemented whatever she had done to make her eyes look sunken and deep; she was also wearing knee-high black patent-leather boots and elbow-length black gloves.

The color of corn silk, her hair had been shocked or permed in such a way that it stood straight out from her head like a pale sunburst. In all, she looked wraithlike or, as McGarr suspicioned she preferred, like a fallen angel.

He waited while she greeted this one and that and then
had a short animated conversation with a large man to whom
she handed an envelope. McGarr asked the barman to get her
a drink. Delivering it, the young man lit her cigarette and
pointed to McGarr.

Who raised his glass and beckoned her to him. When she
hesitated—glancing first at the door and then behind her at
the man she had spoken with—McGarr moved his fingers and
thumb together in a gesture that said, Let's chat.

Reluctantly, she began moving toward him, having to
pause for a word or a laugh here and there.

"You broke into my room. You read my letters," she said,
sliding onto the stool beside him and forking her fingers
through her strange hair in the manner of a film star. "It's
how you found me. I should've burnt them fookin' letters
from me fookin' mother. Imagine her writing shit like that."

Crossing her legs, she pulled on the cigarette and looked
off dramatically.

"Does she know your secret?"

"What secret?"

"The one under those chic gloves."

She gave McGarr a sidelong glance; in the dark circles, her
eyes seemed very blue. "You didn't come here to talk about
my habit."

"You left a hair on the pillow beside Pascal Burke's corpse.
Tell me the hours you were with him."

"You're fookin' lyin'. I didn't know Pascal Burke, and I
was never with him."

From his jacket McGarr removed the photograph of her
wearing Burke's uniform jacket and cap. Her arm was around
his shoulders, her knee in his crotch.

"We found this in your trophy room. Or is it your
morgue? Let's try again—Burke called you Thursday night

from Dublin but you weren't home. Where and when did he meet up with you in Leixleap?"

She only shook her head and looked down into her drink.

"Where did you spend Thursday night?"

"Can I tell you something?" Her eyes flashed up at him. "I'm not going to say a thing. I've been here before with arseholes like you, and it's none of your fookin' business where I was or with who. You've no jurisdiction here, and there's the end to it."

She reached for her jacket, but McGarr put a hand on it. "Listen to me for a moment—one phone call, just one, and I could have you in a jail cell for longer than you could tolerate, given your predilection.

"Remember, it was two cops who were shot, and the cops here—cops anywhere—take that personally. And I bet some of them already think you should be in jail. For your own good." McGarr took his hand off the coat and pulled his cell phone from a jacket pocket. "Your choice."

Looking defeated, she glanced over at the man she'd passed the envelope to, then back down at her drink.

"Now—you spent Thursday night in the Leixleap Inn, right?"

She blinked but said nothing.

"And Burke, who arrived Friday morning, got in touch with you there and asked you to come to his room Friday morning." McGarr was guessing, but she blinked again, which he took as an affirmation.

"And you did."

She wagged her head. "Let's get something straight—you're not here to bust me for drugs."

"No."

"Or prostitution."

He shook his head.

"So, ask yourself this, Mr. Guard, Mr. Policeman—why

would I whack a poor harmless sod like Pascal fookin' Burke, who was going through a mid-life crisis or some fookin' thing and was tired of the old bags he was shagging in Leixleap and just wanted what I could give him—a bit of young, a bit of talent.

"Where's my advantage in murdering him? Where's my edge? Compared to the action I was getting at the inn where not a man-jack among them blinked at a hundred quid a throw or two hundred for the night, Pascal Burke was like a charity case. A mercy hump.

"Twenty quid, thirty quid. Once when he had me meet him on the job by the river, he managed to cough up fifty quid. But once only. And I had to put up with his shite about loving me, marrying me, wanting to leave everything he had to me.

"But"—she turned and looked McGarr in the eyes—"I hadn't got it on with Pascal Burke in a month."

"Then how did your hair get on his pillow?"

"You don't know it's my hair. You're just guessing."

McGarr's eyes bored into hers, until she wagged her head at her glass. "Around noon, when I was between jobs, like, that I'd already set up in the inn, I went down to pub for a drink and to check my calls back at the house. And there was Pascal on the machine, begging me to see him. So, I had a quick one or two, and I went up to him.

"*But,* like I said, we didn't get it on. And even if I'd had the time, I wouldn't have. Pascal was the type of man to keep putting off, to keep begging. If he could have you anytime he wanted, he lost interest, which is why he dropped so many of the others, after he'd shagged them silly.

"I think"—she picked up her drink and looked down into the ice cubes—"I think it was the mother thing. I think he loved her more than he knew, but, her being his mother, he couldn't do anything about that.

"So, there he was all the years that she was alive *in* her life, so to speak—seeing her daily, waiting on her hand and foot; a good-looking pleasant woman, I met her—but with no possibility of getting *in* her. Physically, sexually.

"And if he was attracted to you, and you showed him how good you could be, then put him off. Well—" McGurk opened the palm of one of her black gloves, as though to say that's where she'd had him.

"Rather like Antony Moran," McGarr suggested.

Her eyes rose to his, and she smiled slightly. "Yah. *Just* like Antony Moran. The very same, although two different types altogether. Antony was an angel."

Whose relatives were rather different, McGarr mused, and had to be taken to court. "Up in the room with Pascal Friday," McGarr prompted.

She closed her eyes and shook her head. "The door was open and there he was between the sheets, expecting me. I told him to fookin' forget it, I had a real paying client to attend to, and he'd get no freebees from me.

"But I did lie down with him, teasin' like, there in the bed but me in my clothes. And I let him kiss me and feel me up and say all the stupid fookin' things he always said."

McGarr waited.

"About wanting to marry me, set me up in a house, get me away from hooking which"—she glanced up at McGarr—"you won't believe I chose. But I did and do, and it's not the drugs, like you think. It's the . . . freedom."

McGarr held her gaze, not wishing to debate her. It wasn't the first time he'd heard an addict in deep denial describe a drug habit as freedom. "How long were you with him?"

"Ten minutes. Fifteen, tops. When I went into the loo to redo my face, I heard him on the phone, calling somebody else. Beggin', pleadin'." McGurk shook her head. "He was a sad case, any way you look at him. But I'm sorry he's dead, nonetheless. At least he was gentle, and he could be fun.

"Other than that, Mr. Policeman, the only other mention I heard of Pascal that afternoon was when I was moving on to my second appointment, I heard the owner at the end of the hall near the stairs giving out to some other woman and Pascal's name was mentioned."

"By the owner, you mean Tallon?"

"No—his hag, the French woman."

"Sylvie Zeebruge? She's Belgian."

"Whatever. They were into it, they were, and loud."

"Who was the other woman?"

"I couldn't see that far. My eyes aren't all that good, and glasses in my profession . . ." McGurk shook her head.

"Then, how did you know it was Madame Sylvie?"

"Her shape—it's one big droop. And her voice with the accent and all."

"What time did you get through with your work there?"

She hunched her shoulders. "It was quick. A little after one, I'd say."

"And then where'd you go?"

"To the pub for another drink."

"Which way—through the arch or . . ."

"Or. How could I get through the arch? It's locked."

"But you have a key."

"Me? Christ—don't be stupid. How would I get a key?"

It was McGarr's turn to hunch his shoulders.

"Well, I don't. And that's the truth."

"If it is, then you won't mind my taking a hair from your head."

"What?"

"The hair on the pillow next to Burke? If it matches your hair and also matches the DNA on the condom Burke was wearing when he got shot, then you're likely his murderer."

She had to think for a moment, stubbing out the cigarette and reaching for her drink. "What if it doesn't?"

"Then, you're not."

She lowered her head toward him. "Be gentle, now. Maybe you'd like a real hair, one I could charge you for. Ever get the yen for some young yourself, Chief Superintendent? I could make you very happy."

Which McGarr rather doubted. "I already bought you a drink."

"Well, now you can buy me another."

McGarr plucked a hair and then another that seemed more lifelike.

"Ow—that's two."

"We'll make it a double, if you tell me something else."

"I'll do anything for a double."

"Yous okay over here?" the barman asked. The other man was now only a step away.

"Are those yours, or are they enhanced?" McGarr pointed to her breasts.

"Kinky wanker," she said to the barman, raising her chin to mean McGarr. "Has a hair fetish. Takes them down to Dublin and sticks them on the wall." She slid off the barstool.

"And, of course, they're mine. Bought and paid for with a lifetime guarantee. Those who know don't mind, and those who don't keep coming back.

"You through with me, or . . . were you asking for yourself?"

McGarr smiled. "One last thing—what about the Frakes? Where do they fit?"

"The questions he asks," she said to the barman and the man who was now standing behind McGarr. "They *were* my buddies down there. Friends. Associates. But you saw them yourself—they're really just boys, when what every working girl needs is a strong man. At least one."

Meaning a pimp. "Where are they now?"

"What—me tell you? I'm not that low, yet." Glass in hand, she turned and walked away.

But before McGarr could settle up and leave, her pimp eased into the bar beside him—a powerfully built man maybe thirty-five with a scarred face and a string of diamond studs running up the edge of one ear. "Who are you?"

McGarr took a card from his billfold and slid it toward him. "*The* McGarr?"

Who finished his drink and wished he could stay for another.

"Who're you looking for?"

"Manus and Donal Frakes—know where they are?"

"What will it buy me?"

McGarr glanced at McGurk. "A bottom woman, I should imagine. And then, maybe you venture south from time to time. Who knows when you might need a favor."

"You won't forget?"

McGarr shook his head. "How far would I have got if I did?"

The pimp flipped over the card and wrote down an address in Bray, south of Dublin. "It's a scrap yard in front, with living quarters in an old cottage out back. At night there's a dog. But during the day people come and go."

McGarr slipped the card back in his pocket. "Why are you doing this?"

"Payback." He pointed to his scarred face. "With any luck, you'll take no prisoners. If they're dying—and only if they're dying—tell them that Dessie from Newry sent you. The one who got the acid in the face."

The forty-mile run to Dublin was quick along the N-1.

And after dropping off the hair samples from Grace O'Rourke, Sylvie Zeebruge, and Gertrude McGurk at the police lab, McGarr looked up Pascal Burke's home address and drove out to Ranelagh, an older suburb of the city.

The house was Edwardian in design, a brick structure with tall chimneys and multipaned windows. McGarr could see from the plethora of mailboxes by the front door that it had been converted into flats.

Burke had lived in the attic, the landlady saying, "It's so much like Jekyll and Hyde, the stories we're reading about poor Mr. Burke in the papers. Shot in bed naked with a married naked woman who worked for him.

"Why, I kept thinking, it must be a different Pascal Burke than the one we know. Our Mr. Pascal Burke was forever the gentleman. And how he took care of his widowed mother until the day she died three years ago come Christmas. Hand and foot, I tell you. He never went anywhere without her. He was the most devoted son a mother could ever want.

"That's when he moved up here," she continued, opening the door to the apartment. "From the big flat on the second floor. He said it was time to start saving money, don't you know. And then, the aerie here has a separate entrance—up the fire escape from the car park out back."

McGarr stepped into an apartment that bore all the signs of a suddenly downsized life—too much big furniture in too small a space, most of it so out-of-date as to be near antique. Little wonder that Burke preferred the spacious and Spartan room over the pub in Leixleap.

Doilies decorated the arms of wing chairs, throw rugs lay on top of carpets, and even the telly was ancient. Black-and-white only, McGarr bet. In short, the flat looked like a time warp or a museum honoring the mother.

Pictures of her—young, old, pregnant, in formal wear with a décolletage that would make a stripper blush—were everywhere. She had been a beautiful natural blond with an angular body, when young. And when older and fuller, the look that she presented the camera was still fetching and seductive.

"Thank you," McGarr said to the landlady, who seemed loath to leave. "I'll have a quick look round and show myself out."

Once the door was shut, McGarr conducted a thorough search of the flat, which was not difficult, given the paucity of detail concerning Pascal Burke's personal life. It was as though the man did not have a history, and everything that had been saved from his past referred to his mother in some way or another.

As for his father—who had been named Edmund, like the Dublin-born, British politician and statesman—he was pictured only once on their wedding day. He had died when Burke was seven.

Sandwiched between a heap of bills and junk mail that Burke had kept in a wicker basket on his kitchen table were three recent letters postmarked Leixleap with no return address. They were all unsigned.

Each said, in effect, what one passage stated in the third and final letter:

> *Pascal, you have to stop your philandering immediately. When you come down here to Leixleap, it takes you days to come see me or even ring me up, and I hear tell that you are also seeing other women.*
>
> *You know it's just a reaction to your age and to the loss of your mother. But I won't have my health and reputation brought into question.*
>
> *You and I are the same age. We enjoy the same things and have great good times when we're together. WE ARE MEANT FOR EACH OTHER, Pascal, and the sooner you realize it, the better.*

*I won't wait forever, and you'd be a fool if you
did. What is more, I won't let you.*

In yet another letter with a Leixleap postmark, were several photographs picturing the bearded Burke with a handsome but sizable woman around his age, which was forty. In one, he was seen laughing fully while the woman, who had wrapped an arm around his waist, lifted him off the ground on one hip.

There was a green plastic derby on his head and green beer in a glass on the table. On the back was printed, "NEW ORLEANS, MARCH 17. DIDN'T WE SHOW THE YANKS HOW IT WAS DONE." Because of the printing, it was impossible to tell if the handwriting was the same as in the letters.

The date was St. Patrick's Day, of course. What struck McGarr was how much the woman looked like Burke's mother did in middle age, apart from hairstyle and dress.

Pocketing the photo and the letters, he continued with his search, which yielded only one other item of interest: a bill from a solicitor for, "The preparation and filing of last will and testament, Mr. P. Burke."

Reaching for the phone, McGarr dialed his own office and asked John Swords, the night-desk sergeant, to find the home phone number for Terence Maher. "He's a solicitor with the firm of Maher, O'Connell, Fallon and Fitzgerald in Mount Street."

McGarr hung up and moved to Burke's closet, where he began going through the pockets of his clothes, looking for whatever turned up. Some people removed everything from their pockets every night, and all that remained was lint and shards of this and that. While others forgot things—ticket stubs, receipts, credit-card sales-slip duplicates.

Burke was the latter. Nearly every pocket turned up something, the most notable item of which was an envelope from the Leixleap Inn. Folded in half as though used as paper for the note, "Sylvie in Belgium." The phone number followed.

In the telephone directory, McGarr looked up the country code for Belgium and was about to dial the number when the phone rang. It was Swords with the phone number of the solicitor, Terence Maher.

"It's late," a voice grumbled when the phone was answered.

McGarr explained to Maher who he was and why he was calling. "Perhaps you read about the double murder down in Leixleap?"

"Double murder and suicide, wasn't it? A lovers' triangle."

"Me to you?" McGarr seldom conveyed information about a case to any third party, but you had to give in order to get. "It was no suicide."

"Your coddin' me." Maher no longer sounded sleepy, and McGarr could imagine the man saying to his colleagues on the morrow, "I heard it from the Chief himself." Or, worse, ringing up some friend in the press.

"The young couple were murdered to cover up the first murder of Pascal Burke, which is why I'm calling. I'm in his apartment now looking at a bill for your services for the preparation and filing of a will. It would be helpful were I to know the beneficiaries and if you know the size of the estate."

There was a pause. "Ah-ha. This is extraordinary, it is. But . . . in this case, given the nature of Mr. Burke's death . . . let me see—can you hold on a minute? I have all that stuff on disk, and I'll have to fire up the machine."

McGarr then heard a woman's voice and some muffled conversation with only, ". . . a hell of an hour . . . nerve of the man," plain from her, and ". . . the Chief Superintendent, McGarr himself" from him.

After a while, Maher came back on, "Chief—all his earthly possessions, of which I believe he had few—a car, the flat there in Ranelagh, which he owns, and the family seat which is a small cottage in West Cork—go to a certain Gertrude McGurk of Newry.

"Burke came to my office six or seven months ago and gave me the particulars."

"Is that a change of beneficiary?"

"No, I don't think so. I can remember him telling me that he didn't have a will when he first walked in.

"Tell me, Chief—do you have a suspect?"

"Three. All women. But that's the most I can say."

"Would this Gertrude McGurk be one?"

"I can't say, Solicitor Maher—libel, defamation of character. You know those waters better than I, I'm sure. Did Burke say anything to you about who she was to him and why she was his beneficiary?"

"As I remember, something to the effect of a fine broth of a woman who might need a hand up someday. But when I saw her age, which he listed here as twenty-six, well . . . I suspected she might be a daughter or some relation." Maher waited for another scrap of information, but McGarr only thanked him and rang off.

Finding the country code for Belgium in the phone directory, McGarr dialed the number for Sylvie Zeebruge that he had found in Burke's clothes. After a long series of rings, it was answered.

"*Oui?*" It was a woman's voice.

"May I speak to Sylvie Zeebruge, please?" McGarr said in his best French.

"Speaking."

"Sylvie, this is Peter McGarr," he continued in English. "How is your mother?"

There was a pause, as though she was debating whether to speak to him. "Ill."

"I'm sorry to hear that. Are you planning to return to Ireland?"

"Perhaps."

"May I ask you a few questions?" When only silence followed, McGarr continued. "Your husband has told me that you and he are very close. And yet I didn't get that impression when we spoke. Are you still a couple?"

Again, she did not reply.

"Hello, Miss Zeebruge—are you there?"

"Yes."

"Antony Moran—what was he to you?"

"A friend."

"Nothing more?"

"Do you mean—did we have good times, enjoy the same things, and have sex?"

It was McGarr's turn to be silent.

"Yes, all of that. Many times. I miss him."

"And Mr. Burke, did you have sex with him as well?"

There was a hesitation before, "I've had sex with many men, and I'm proud of it."

"Did you have sex with Mr. Burke?"

Yet again, she did not answer.

After a while, McGarr continued. "It appears from my investigation that Mr. Burke was like you and bedded any number of women, including Gertrude McGurk."

When yet more silence ensued, McGarr added, "In fact, it appears he preferred her."

"What do you mean?"

"I just got off the phone with his solicitor. There's a will, and she's his inheritor. The house here in Dublin, where I'm sitting, whatever money he had, and the family seat down in Cork. It all goes to her."

"What? I don't believe you."

"Shall I give you the number of his solicitor? You can ring him up if you like."

"You lie."

"I don't. I think you know that."

"Say it again."

McGarr did, and he then heard what sounded like a quiet sob before a hand was placed over the speaker of the phone.

After a while, he added, "But maybe she won't get any of it."

"What? What did you say?"

"I said, maybe she won't get all of it."

"Why not?"

"Because it seems that Mr. Burke might have left a child. Or, at least, there's the possibility that he has." Again, McGarr waited.

"Go on, damn you," she fairly cried. "What is it you have to tell me?"

"Only that a woman claims to be pregnant by Pascal Burke, and I was calling in part to ask you—as owner of the property where his body was found and where he often stayed—if you know if he had relations with the woman."

"Who? What woman?"

"Why, one of your employees." Playing it out, like this, was cruel, McGarr well understood. But Sylvie Zeebruge had chosen to leave the country, and he was interested in her reaction.

"I can't think of an employee of mine that Pascal might have fancied. Now I know you're lying."

"Why would I lie?"

"To catch me up."

"I could only catch you up, were *you* lying to *me*." Or were you Burke's murderer, McGarr thought. "Have you been lying to me?"

"This woman's name, please. The one who is my employee and who is pregnant by Pascal. Then, I'll know if you're lying."

"Grace O'Rourke."

"You must be joking."

"I'm not."

"You have to be. *Grace?*"

"The very one."

Sylvie Zeebruge began to laugh the deep, wet laugh of a long-term smoker. Finally, she said, "I hope you don't expect me to believe you. This . . . ploy. What is it you expect me to say?"

"Nothing more than you have, and I'm thankful for your candor. Would you like Grace's phone number? You might ring her up and verify her condition for yourself. What I just said."

McGarr waited while it sounded as though she was lighting a cigarette. "Don't bother, I have her number."

"Do you have any idea when you'll be returning to Ireland?"

"None."

"Well then, I thank you for your cooperation. I hope I won't have to disturb you again. I'll ring off now."

"Wait!" she fairly shouted. "Now you have my interest up—what makes you think Grace is pregnant by Pascal?"

"She told me so."

"A young woman's fantasy. Women think, women *hope* they're pregnant, all the time."

McGarr wondered if she were speaking for herself. "You must know Grace after all this time. I know liars, I know people who speak the truth. Grace doesn't lie. In fact, Grace O'Rourke is also loyal. Can I tell you how she protected you? No matter how I tried, no matter what I said, she wouldn't give you up."

"Give me up, how?"

"Being yet another of Mr. Burke's lovers."

"Can I tell you something?"

McGarr was hoping she would.

"I was his only *real* lover, he told me so. And as soon as I could get rid of Tim—my husband, as you call him—he and I were going to make a match. It was the cause of my sorrow when you spoke to me earlier. The other women in Leixleap who Pascal knew? They were . . . diversions to him, he told me. What is the phrase? Casual sex which, from time to time, we all need.

"But the very idea of Pascal and Grace being together is . . . ludicrous, to say the least. Either she fantasized the entire liaison, or she lied to you."

"She did not lie."

"Then, you're a fool."

"Sometimes, but not now. Do you have her phone number? Why don't you give her a call? Judge for yourself."

"I have it, and I will."

"Promise?"

"You can be sure."

"Incidentally, what hospital is your mother in?"

After an execration in French, the phone went dead.

Leaving the attic flat by the fire escape, he wondered if Burke had secreted women up the narrow passageway, after his mother's death. Or had he saved his carousing for Leixleap and the banks of the Shannon?

It was just after midnight by the time McGarr got back to the analysis lab. The chemist was waiting for him in the lobby, hat and coat on, ready to go home.

"There's but the one match—the hair on the pillow matches the hair taken from Gertrude McGurk. But she wasn't the party who had sex with Pascal Burke. In fact, none of the three samples of hair you gave me—McGurk's, Grace O'Rourke's or Sylvie Zeebruge's—matches the DNA samples taken from the exterior of the condom."

Which meant that none of the three women—Gertie

McGurk, Grace O'Rourke, or Sylvie Zeebruge—had been in bed with Burke prior to his being shot through the temple.

Stumped by the news, McGarr climbed back into Noreen's Rover and headed back to Leixleap, where he arrived at the inn nearly two hours later.

In the darkness of his room, McGarr placed the contents of his jacket and pockets on the dresser, as he did at home, and sat in the reading chair in order to untie his shoes. . . .

# 19

# War Stories

Which was where Noreen found him the next morning.

"Peter," she shook him gently, since he sometimes awoke with a start. "Where'd you get this?"

McGarr had been dreaming about New Orleans in such detail that he did indeed come to suddenly.

Although he'd never been to the American city, he dreamt he'd gorged on gumbo and jambalaya, listened to hours of great jazz in smoky cafés, danced to Cajun music, and even kissed some gorgeous woman who was dressed in a Mardi Gras costume that included the most bewitching mask . . .

And suddenly, there was Noreen.

"You look like you've seen a ghost. Or you've had a guilty dream," she remarked.

Bingo, without the *had* part.

"Do you know who this woman is?"

McGarr thought for a moment that she could read his mind. Until she showed him the snapshot that he'd found among Pascal Burke's correspondence.

McGarr shook his head.

"It's Moira O'Rourke, the greengrocer. She chucked me out of her shop bodily yesterday evening when I told her about Grace being pregnant by Burke. With murder in her eyes."

Which brought McGarr up from the chair. "We better get over there."

"Why—do you think she might do something to Grace?"

"This Moira is probably the one who was sleeping with Burke when he was shot."

"Hah! I knew it."

McGarr made his way to the bathroom. "How did you know it?" he asked while applying shave cream to his face.

"Well—I wouldn't call it a woman's intuition in this day and age. It's something more like—"

"Beginner's luck."

"Tut-tut—jealousy is unbecoming. And just think of the time you could have saved and the labor it took for you to reach the same conclusion."

"Well, now we need proof." McGarr reached for a towel. "May I come along?"

"As an observer only—promise? Where's Maddie?"

"More homework, sent by fax."

"And the rest of the crew?"

"Downstairs, I should imagine. It's nearly nine."

Stopping at the door to the dining room, McGarr looked in and signaled the others to follow him.

It was a typical winter day, McGarr could see, as he stepped outside. Masses of dense clouds were racing across the country from the west, and the air carried a sea tang that hinted at more rain. Or snow.

"Fresh day," Noreen remarked, as a burst of chill wind nearly stopped them; ahead was the quaint-looking shop with "O'Rourke" in green Irish letters across the front. Stacked bins of fruit and vegetables lined the footpath. The door was standing open.

"It looks normal," Noreen went on, having to run a bit to keep up with McGarr.

Bresnahan, Ward, and McKeon joined them at the door, and McGarr entered first to find the woman from the photo standing behind the counter. But it was a Moira O'Rourke far different from the person Noreen had encountered there twice before.

Gone was the bib apron and bandanna tied round her head. Today her hair was permed, her face made up, and she was wearing a plain navy blue suit that fit her snugly and made the most of her angular figure. Her hands were behind her back.

McGarr reached toward his belt, where he was carrying a handgun.

Through a dry laugh Moira O'Rourke said, "So, today you brought government reinforcements, Mrs. McGarr—the husband and his entourage. How like a Dub' altogether."

"Where's Grace, your niece?" McGarr asked.

"She got a phone call from Belgium last night, and lit out for parts unknown, taking her love child with her, since she had no option."

Surveying the blush in O'Rourke's cheeks and her eyes that seemed overbright, McGarr suspected that the woman had been drinking.

"Here—she left a note." It was what O'Rourke had been concealing behind her back.

*Moira,*
> *I know you'll never understand, so I'm leaving.*
> *But what I do understand, that you don't, is how brilliant and lovable Pascal could be when he was on to you, but how bad, horrible, the worst he was at*

*other times and to other women. For your own sake
you should realize this.*
    *At least I have his baby.*

                                  *Grace*

    "You must know where she went," McGarr said, folding the document and putting it into a pocket.

    "Nary a clue. To hell, for all I care."

    McGarr swept a hand, and the other staffers moved into the shop to search the premises. "I'd like to pluck a few hairs from your head with your permission."

    "Excuse me?"

    McGarr pointed to her head. "Your hair—I need some."

    "Why?"

    "To compare it to other evidence found beside Burke and on his person."

    "You mean, like fingerprints?"

    "But more accurate. Did you murder Pascal Burke?"

    The question caught O'Rourke, as McGarr had intended, off guard. "Of course not, you . . . But there's no need for taking any hair."

    Drawing in a breath, she glanced over McGarr's head, then back down at him. "It was me in bed with Pascal before he got shot. He"—she shook her head and clasped her hands before her—"rang me up that morning, telling me he was desperate to see me.

    " 'You've got to come over now,' says he. 'I need you more than anytime in my life,' he goes on. Can you imagine how long I had wanted to hear that from him? If I could cry now, I would. But that's not like me. I got all my crying in when I saw him dead.

    "So, that morning when Grace got back from her work in the inn, I asked her to take over here in the shop, telling her I had to put my car into the garage because it needed some attention.

"But," Moira O'Rourke shook her head, "I never dreamed that Grace was being . . . serviced by the blighter as well. How could I? Janie—hadn't I raised the calf myself, after my sister passed away? The ingratitude! It's shocking.

"And him! When I got up to his room, didn't he whisper every class of thing to me—how, when he got the rise in pay for having completed twenty years with the Fisheries Service and sold the flat in Dublin, then we'd elope and later find ourselves our own wee place somewhere here around Leixleap.

"And after it"—her eyes flashed up at McGarr—"the sex was over didn't he promptly fall asleep as usual, snoring away like milord by the fire. So, not being sleepy, I thought I'd return here to the shop, since it wasn't fair"—she shook her head—"to Grace to make her work both jobs in one day. Shame on me."

Arms now folded, Moira O'Rourke looked down at her shoes and shifted from foot to foot. "And then, when I got into the loo, didn't I discover that I was having my period, and I was bloody after all our . . . activity. It was even on the tiles.

"But I had only reached for the washcloth, when there was a terrific explosion in the bedroom that nearly stopped my heart, it was so loud. I was gripped with fear and didn't know what to do. And I can only believe that it was a fair piece of luck, considering what happened to poor Ellen Finn, that I didn't go out there.

"I don't know how much time passed with me just standing there frozen, like. But I heard the door open and close, and somehow I got the courage to look out. And I found what had been done to him. Ruined, he was, dead even then.

"I can't remember everything that happened after, but I know I was worried about the blood—my blood—on the floor and about the scandal that I'd never live down, if it was found out that I'd been in bed with him when he'd been killed. Sure"—her eyes caromed off McGarr's once again—"I'd be ruined. I'd never get a man.

"And in my haste, didn't I drop the blessed bottle of cleanser that I'd found beneath the sink. It broke in a million pieces and took me forever to clean up.

"Somehow, I got it done, got my clothes back on and me to the door, thinking rapid-like, Shit—if I'm seen and anybody puts me together with him . . . Then the other worry was whoever had done it. Maybe they were out in the hall waiting for me. And which way should I go—down through the pub or cross over through the arch into the inn, which I could do since I'd copied Grace's passkey . . . you know, without her knowledge, so I could visit Pascal.

"The pub, I decided. It was quicker, and if I kept my back to the bar, maybe nobody would notice. But the minute I got to the stairwell, I heard the door below open, and in steps Benny Carson, the barman.

"I don't think he saw me—at least, he didn't look up—so I ran down the hall to the archway door and just nipped behind it when Carson appeared around the corner.

"But when I got into the inn proper, I heard loud voices coming from Madame Sylvie's room, and before I could get through the hall and onto the main stairs, Mr. Tallon came out looking madder than a bear with a sore head. 'What are you doing here?' he asked me.

"Not knowing how to reply, I said I was looking for Grace.

" 'She was just here looking for you,' says he, which I thought strange since Grace should have been at the shop." Yet again, O'Rourke glanced up at McGarr. "It was closed, when I got back. Locked tight.

"Later in the evening, when Grace got home, she said her

doctor had a cancellation and could fit her in. And she had come to the inn to tell me she had closed up the shop. But she was crying at one moment and laughing at the next, not like her usual self, which is fierce quiet.

"So," O'Rourke raised her hands and let them fall to her thighs, "that's it. That's what I know."

"Why didn't you come forward with this information earlier?"

"I told you—face is everything here, and I'd like to have a husband and family, just like every other woman. Also, I didn't want to be blamed. And finally"—her eyes shied—"I thought Grace did it. Killed Pascal."

"And you do now."

She only stared at him.

"Why?"

"Because when Pascal first began staying at the inn after his mother died, Grace was always coming back home with stories of how he was such a 'whore,' she called him. A 'slut' was another word she used. And I thought maybe she'd found out about us, and it pushed her over the edge. She can be violent, you know.

"Later, after your wife here told me about her being pregnant, I thought—and still do—she did it for that. That he made her pregnant, and, of course, he wouldn't marry her. Never in a million years."

"Why not?"

"Why marry a crazy woman, who could pass that on to the children, when you had the pick of the crop all along?"

"And would he marry you?" The pick of the crop, McGarr nearly added.

"Like I said, he told me he would that very afternoon."

"Could you give me some idea of the time Burke was shot?"

She shook her head. "But by the time I got back to the shop it was nearly four."

"Was the door locked, when the two of you were in bed?"

She had to think. "I think so. I had to let myself in with the key, and when the door closed, it must have locked itself."

"I want you to think, now—can you remember any little detail, any one at all, about what went on in the bedroom while you were in the toilet? Or about the bedroom before you."

O'Rourke thought for a moment, then glanced at McGarr and rolled her eyes, almost as though ashamed. "Well—it's funny how the mind works. I can remember stepping out of the toilet and seeing that Pascal had been shot and—with eyes wide-open and no breath coming from him—was surely dead. And me thinking, I never smelled the perfume that's hanging in the air. And then, you know, feeling guilty about having a thought like that at a time like that."

"You're sure it was Carson coming up the stairs?"

She nodded. "He buys all the pub greens for salads and sandwiches from me, not a wholesaler. He's a fine man entirely."

"Where in the inn did you meet Tallon?"

"Coming out of Madame Sylvie's quarters, like I said. And leaving her in tears, he was. I could hear her crying, sobbing even—until the door closed."

Bresnahan, Ward, and McKeon had reappeared, not having found Grace O'Rourke or anything else, he could see from their expressions.

"How did you get up to Burke's room, and what time was that?"

"Around one, I'd say. I came through the inn. That time of day there's a lunch crowd in the dining room, but scarcely anybody in the halls."

"But you met Madame Sylvie."

"How do you know that?" she asked, before closing her eyes and nodding. "Oh—the bitch, of course. McGurk. Didn't I see her slipping out of a room at the end of the hall when Sylvie and me were having it out."

"Having it out about what?"

"Pascal, of course. Or, at least, my using the archway to be with him."

"She and Pascal were . . . ?"

Moira O'Rourke shook her head. "No more than nodding acquaintances, I'm sure, her being . . . fifty, if she's a day. And—ask anyone—the woman's a harridan at best."

"How did she confront you? What did she say?"

"The key. She demanded I give back the key. Says I, 'How can you take it back when it wasn't yours in the first place? I had it made myself.' 'From Grace's key no doubt,' says she. Says I, 'None of your bloody business from whose key, it's my key and those blasted doors shouldn't be locked anyhow. It's against the fire code,' And I left her."

"Did you lock the doors after yourself?"

"Always."

"Why *always?*"

"Don't they provide a measure of privacy? You wouldn't want every foreign yoke in search of the pub walking by your door, would you?"

"What about the fire code?"

"Ah, shit—I made that up. What do I know about fire codes?"

McGarr, who had interviewed literally thousands of suspects over the years, had an ear for the truth, and Moira O'Rourke's tale sounded truthful. All the details about the bathroom were spot on, literally.

Yet it was also plain that she was a self-seeking woman who could think on her feet, and her having admitted to being with Burke when he was murdered certainly put her in the mix of suspects. And McGarr had been wrong before.

"Where did Gertie McGurk go after leaving the room?"

O'Rourke shook her head. "Sylvie dared to put a hand on my arm, and when I pulled it away, I must have moved. But she didn't pass us by, I know that."

Said McGarr, "I'd still like to take a bit of your hair." Given Pascal Burke's sexual proclivities, he could rule nothing out.

"Well then, back here where it won't show. The perm is new." Moira O'Rourke turned around and lifted the back of her hair so McGarr could pluck a few hairs on the nape of her neck.

"And I'm afraid you'll have to repeat everything you just told us to Detective Superintendent McKeon here. In a formal statement," McGarr added, slipping the hairs into an envelope.

"How long will that be?" Turning back around, she seemed put out.

McGarr canted his head inquiringly.

"I mean, I have produce in the bins on the footpath, and no Grace to mind the shop."

"And perhaps an engagement?" McGarr motioned to her costume.

"What if I do? I've done nothing wrong here, nothing to be ashamed of."

"Then you won't mind speaking with Detective McKeon." McGarr turned for the door.

"Aren't you going after her?" Moira O'Rourke demanded.

"After whom?"

"After the bitch, Gertie McGurk. She was there. Without a doubt she had a key. And if I know anything about her, there was something for her to gain by Pascal's death."

McGarr turned to Ward and Bresnahan. "You two come with me."

And to Noreen, "I'll try to be back by tea."

"Where're you going?"

"Bray." It was time to interview the only other party who was still alive and had been near the scene of Pascal Burke's murder. Apart from Moira O'Rourke.

The town in County Wicklow about a dozen miles south of Dublin had been a fashionable seaside resort early in the nineteenth century, with a long esplanade tracing the shore, wide streets, and the eminence of Bray Head, which rises out of the Irish Sea to nearly eight hundred feet.

As a child, McGarr had spent many Sundays in Bray, since his mother's brother, John, had owned a house on the seafront. Back then, the uncle and his neighbors never thought it necessary or wise to visit Dublin, which was viewed as a distant and squalid metropolis.

Now Bray was either yet another suburb of Dublin or a small city in its own right, McGarr mused, as Bresnahan turned the car off the highway and wheeled slowly past a shopping center, office buildings, and row after row of businesses that had been the sites of houses or woods when McGarr was a child.

"It's the laneway up ahead on the left," Ward said. He had a computer on his lap with a map on the screen.

Sitting in the back, McGarr removed his Walther from its holster and checked the action. After its bath in the Shannon, he had cleaned and lubricated the usually dependable weapon. But it was older than he, and he knew of handguns that had failed because of metal fatigue.

"I want you two to remember that we're here to make two arrests and conduct an interview," he remarked, slipping the Walther into the pocket of his mac and reaching for the

Street-Sweeper, a highly portable, 12-gauge, automatic shotgun. "Not for revenge."

Yet he saw Bresnahan's eyes meet Ward's; they were still
smarting from the incident with the eels.

"Just a couple of IRA thugs poking a bit of fun," said
Bresnahan, under her breath.

"A big person could overlook that," Ward chimed in. "Let
it go. Sure, it's their warped background, what they know of
society and the police, that made them do it. Otherwise, they'd
be jokin' at the bar, like everyone else."

"And mind the child," McGarr advised further, sliding
shells into the weapon. "She'll be about someplace."

They had already discussed strategy. Bresnahan now pulled
the car in and only McGarr got out, adding, "And if later
they complain—and you know them, they will with the whole
anti-Republican thing—you two could be in trouble."

"Yes, Father," said Bresnahan. "We'll just have to will
them into the car."

"By the power of suggestion," Ward put in.

"No touchy, no feely—sounds boring, doesn't it?"

McGarr closed the door. Years ago, he would have burst
into the scrap yard and beaten every bit of information out
of the Frakes *before* they were ever formally interviewed,
which would occur after their hospital stay.

But all that had changed after several court rulings that
had disposed large sums of money on career criminals, several
with IRA backgrounds.

Suddenly chilled after the warm car, McGarr tightened his
fedora on his brow and stuffed his hands into the pockets of
his mac. In one, he had placed the Walther; in the other, the
Street-Sweeper.

Driving toward Bray they had debated who should make
the first approach, Bresnahan and Ward being eager to make
the collar. But McGarr was certain that the night of the attack

on the car, the two had been watched by the Frakes probably through the night-seeing scope of the Kalashnikov, whereas he was almost certain neither of the brothers had got a good look at him, during the altercation at the old mill.

It was night, they had been in pain, and costume and setting were everything. Here McGarr looked like some little old man, which, of course, was what he was. And he doubted the Frakes's egos would allow them to believe that a bald, pudgy codger had kicked their arses.

The large wooden gates to the scrap yard were closed, but a small door was open a crack. Pushing it back, McGarr stepped in.

Vast clutter greeted him. There were heaps of various metals rusting and corroding in piles that seemed to have been placed randomly around the large yard; avenues of crushed cars lined the walls.

Catching sight of McGarr, a Rottweiler in a tight pen began a chorus of hoarse barks, and a bearded man popped his head out of the open door of a battered caravan of the sort placed at building sites.

"Be right with you," he called out. "Don't come any farther. I'll be right there."

McGarr kept advancing.

"You! I told you to stay there," the man roared when he reappeared, jumping down from the caravan.

Maybe forty, he was large and round. Reddish hair sprouted from the open front of his grease-stained coveralls that were so tight-fitting he could not possibly be armed. A ginger beard made his lips seem very red and wet.

"You deaf?" There was an Ulster burr to his speech.

McGarr stopped. The man's anger could mean only one thing—either one or both of the Frakes were in the caravan with him. Or there was something in there that he did not want the public to see. Like a gun.

"What's your problem?" he asked when he reached McGarr.

His stomach was now nearly touching McGarr; but the closer, the better. "It's with my car. There's a part missing, and I think you might have it."

"Which part?"

"The injector, but there's also a strange sleeve that Mercedes put on their diesels back in the sixties. Maybe if you see it. . . ." The strategy being to get as many out of the yard as possible before going in after the Frakes.

"I don't know what made you think I sell parts. This is a commercial operation."

"But I see you've got the very same car—the diesel Merc over there. And I've come all the way from Monaghan Town. If you'd just have a look. Jaysus—I've been everywhere."

The large man let out a sigh. "If I have it, you'll have to take it out yourself. I never heard of a sleeve on a Mercedes injector."

"A factory modification," said McGarr, letting the man step by. "Makes the car all the more valuable. As a collector's item."

"Really? You know about these things?"

"In detail."

McGarr followed him through the yard and out the narrow door into the street.

"Where's the car?"

McGarr pulled the Walther from his pocket and slammed it into the man's temple. "Get down on your knees and slide onto your belly."

"What? Fook off. You're not going to use—" When the man's hand jumped for the gun, in one motion McGarr chopped the butt down on his wrist and kicked his legs out from under him. "That's not quite the knees, but it'll do."

Bresnahan and Ward were now beside him.

"You have a name? Some ID?" McGarr asked, slipping the gun back into his mac.

"Fook you, arsehole—that's me name. And who're you to ask?"

"FYI, FY Arsehole," Ward put in, "we're the police."

"You stupid shit," Bresnahan said through a laugh.

"Where are they?" McGarr asked.

"Where are who?"

"See?" said Bresnahan. "The proof is in the pudding."

McGarr scanned the street to make sure there would be no witnesses, before lashing out with his foot. It caught the man in the lower back. Howling in pain, he rolled over, his face coming down hard on the slate of the footpath.

"So much for the power of suggestion," said Ward.

McGarr hunkered down. "Let's start again. You have a name?"

"Muldoon."

"The Frakes in there?"

"Yah."

"Where?"

"Donal is in the caravan."

"And Manus?"

"Last I knew he was in the cottage in back with his little girl. Bad wrist and all."

"Are they armed?"

"Of course."

"With what?"

"That I've seen? Handguns, and Donal has a Bull Pup."

Said Bresnahan, "Now, there's news." The Steyr AUG Bull Pup was a rapid-fire military assault rifle that was also equipped with a sniper scope.

"They go out at all?"

"They don't dare." For good reason, his tone seemed to imply.

"Phone in the caravan?"

"Yah—but he won't answer it."

"Answering machine on it that he can hear?"

"Answering *service*—for security."

"Phone in the house?"

"Same deal."

So asking Donal to come out to lock the door in the gate was not possible either. And Donal was the problem, McGarr believed, after his experience with the Frakes in the old mill on the Shannon. Manus—with his injury and his daughter— might be reasoned with.

But knowing that Donal was armed with an automatic weapon changed everything; now virtually any tactic could be justified.

"What's their pull with you?"

"Old mates."

"You own this place?"

"After a fashion."

Which probably meant that in some way Muldoon had extorted the yard from its rightful owner.

But McGarr knew what had to happen. "Muldoon—we need your cooperation."

"For?"

"A bit of consideration, when it comes to sentencing."

"Sentencing for what?"

"Harboring fugitives, for openers. Then there's the place itself and how, after your fashion, you happen to be ensconced here. And even if you do own it, there's the Bull Pup. Added to your past, I'm sure you'll be wanting consideration. Who knows, you might even get some today."

Muldoon thought for a moment, then, "How long will they be going away for?"

"A long, long time."

He raised his body off the slates. "I never wanted them here in the first place. They forced themselves upon me."

Force obviously being the language of currency among them.

Muldoon shook his head. "Donal. He's bent, Donal is."

Who, looking out from the caravan a few minutes later, saw Muldoon step into the yard and unlock and open the large doors that permitted cars and lorries to enter the yard.

Leaving again, Muldoon returned with Bresnahan and Ward in front of him, their hands raised. In his right hand, Muldoon held McGarr's Walther, unloaded, of course.

Donal appeared in the doorway, looking like a larger, better-built version of Muldoon, coveralls included. The assault rifle was in his hands.

"Big Red! We meet again. How'd you fancy them eels? And is this the wee fella you were about to throw a leg over there in the car? I'm happy you saved yourself for me."

"And you," she shot back. "I see you hired yourself out."

The large man's brow furrowed; it was the only part of his swollen face that seemed unbruised.

"As a punching bag."

Ward began chuckling.

"Tell me—was it a wee old man about so high who kicked your unlovely arse from pillar to post? My bet? He can do it again. In fact, I think I can hear him coming. I'd run, were I you."

Which was when the unmarked Garda car burst through the open passageway and bolted toward them, Bresnahan, Ward, and Muldoon throwing themselves to the side as McGarr bore down on the old caravan.

Frakes did not know what to do, how to react. But the assault rifle was in his hands. Snapping it up, he squeezed off a clip at McGarr, who threw himself across the seat.

Before the car slammed into the caravan, sending it hurtling back into the yard where it toppled over and struck a stack of crushed cars. That teetered, the metal whining, before toppling over and burying the caravan.

Already, Ward had sprinted toward the cottage in back, while Bresnahan had followed the car and caravan with her weapon raised.

Her immediate concern was for the assault rifle; if Frakes still had the Steyr AUG, he could dominate them with its firepower.

But she had watched as Frakes had been jettisoned from the doorway of the caravan by the force of the crash, and she found him on his hands and knees, struggling to get up.

The assault rifle was a few feet away; Bresnahan walked over and picked it up. "Donal?" she asked. "Say, 'Big Red— I'm so sorry for the eels.' "

He raised his head to her, and she repeated her request. "Say it!" A sharp stomp bowled him over.

"Big Red," he began, and she led him through the contrition.

After the crash, McGarr had snatched up the Street-Sweeper from the floor of the car and scrambled out to join Ward, one on each side of the cottage door.

It was an ancient stone structure with tiny windows and a low door, and the formerly thatched roof had been replaced by corrugated metal that had rusted out in places.

"Do we wait for Rut'ie and the rifle?" Ward asked.

McGarr shook his head; the Street-Sweeper was an ideal close-quarters weapon. "I'm sure she has her hands full."

"And all the fun."

"Ready?" Raising the shotgun, McGarr rapped the butt against the door. "Police! Throw out your weapons and come out with your hands on your head."

"I've only one good hand, and it's holding my child. I'm coming out."

Stepping well away from the door, McGarr and Ward kept their weapons before them, as Manus Frakes ducked out the low door, his daughter in his arms. His other hand lay limp by his side, no sling, no cast.

"D'ya have me beeper?" the little girl asked McGarr.

"I do—and you'll have it back to you in no time." Or one very much like it. And to Frakes. "Put your daughter down and turn around. Do you need medical attention?"

"I need something. My arm is useless, like this."

At the car, McGarr called for an ambulance and backup.

"Where's Muldoon?" Ward asked.

"Gone," said Bresnahan, the Bull Pup trained on Donal Frakes who was sitting on the ground. "He used the crash to split."

Said McGarr, "Call it consideration."

Ward tapped Manus Frakes on the shoulder. "No need to smile," he said, snapping Frakes's picture when he turned around.

"That the last of them?" McGarr asked, as they heard the wail of sirens coming up the street.

"Yup—I've got Tallon, Carson, and Mr. Frakes here in this." Ward pointed to the disposable camera in his hands. "And I've also got the pics of Quintan Finn that you removed from his flat and of Burke from his place."

"You better get going, then."

"What about me?" Bresnahan asked.

McGarr pretended to have to think. "Well, if the chemist's daughter is as shy as Hughie reported, you better lend him a hand."

Or any other little thing, thought Bresnahan.

Several hours later in the special-care room of a nearby hospital, McGarr took Manus Frakes aside while a nurse looked after his daughter.

Frakes's wrist was in a cast, while his brother, Donal, would be held overnight for observation. A Guard was posted at the door of his room.

"Listen to me closely, Manus—can we agree that the worst part of the situation you're facing is the loss of your daughter?"

Frakes nodded.

"Benny Carson may be a convicted felon, but he's a rehabilitated convicted felon with a verifiable source of income and a permanent address.

"And at the very least you'll be brought up on two counts of grievous bodily assault on Guards, weapons possession, and the destruction of property." The three cars, McGarr meant— his own and two unmarked Garda vehicles.

"You know how this goes. You cooperate with me, and I'll see what I can do."

Frakes nodded again. "You have a smoke?"

"This is a hospital."

"That's right. Well—there's not much to tell. In the morning, Friday morning, I picked up the carpet for the room from a Traveler fella I know and brought it back to the inn."

"What time was that?"

"Let me think."

Neither as tall nor as broad as his brother, Manus Frakes was a dark man in his early thirties with a trimmed beard and mustache and longish hair that curled at the nape of his neck. His eyes were hazel.

Wearing a leather bomber jacket and with a gold Celtic cross on a gold chain around his neck, he looked more like a musician or artist than a thug. But thug he was, in trouble with the law since an early age, mainly in the North.

"About one, I'd say. It's a two-man job, but when I woke up that morning, Donal was still drinking, and I know Tallon—if the carpet didn't get put down right, I'd not get paid.

"So, I looked for somebody in the bar to help me up with it, and there was Quintan Finn talking to his fookin' uncle."

"Benny Carson."

Frakes nodded.

"Who's your father-in-law."

"*Was* my father-in-law, who just wants my child any way he can get her."

"But at the bar—" McGarr prompted.

"Well, Quin' was a helpful sort, and he knows . . . knew something about laying carpet, since he'd put down all of it in his flat. Gertie held the door, and we got it upstairs."

"She follow you up?"

Frakes nodded. "To get the door in the room for us."

"She have a key?"

He closed his eyes and nodded. "If there's a lock, Gertie has a key for it, and I'd hazard she's been in all of the rooms of the inn and pub more than once.

"Anyhow, she let us in, I thanked her, and she told me I owed her a drink. And we set about the job."

"Did Gertie go back down to the bar?"

Frakes hunched his thin shoulders. "I imagine so. It's where she was . . . you know, working. Unless she had something already set up.

"So we carried on, and I was glad to have Quin' along, because we finished the entire thing with the edging and everything in a little under two hours, I'd say. Quin' was a great man with a hammer."

"What about Tallon—didn't he inspect the job and pay you?"

Frakes shook his head. "After we finished up, I went down to the bar and phoned him to say I'd finished, rather than walk into the inn dressed for work. He's very particular about that."

"What time was that?"

"Oh—I had a pint or two. And I had to wait because Benny was on the phone for the longest time, there in his little office in back of the bar. I had to wait for him to get off. So, I'd say—three-thirty or quarter to four.

"When I finally got hold of him, he said he'd view it later, and not to worry, 'You'll get your goddamned money.' His words."

"Did you see anybody else up there, while you were laying the carpet?"

Frakes had to ponder some more. "I think I saw a woman out of the corner of my eye when I passed by the door, which we left open for ventilation. You know how new carpet stinks."

"Who was she?"

"No idea."

"Where was she?"

"I think . . . either in the hall or looking out the door of a room. Or maybe I saw two women. We spent most of the time on our hands and knees, looking down."

"Did you hear anything that sounded like a shot?"

"Now that you mention it—when I was down in the bar. Some one of the lads actually got up and looked out in the street."

"Why'd you try to kill Carson?"

Frakes regarded McGarr. "I don't know what you mean."

"Somebody tried to murder Carson Saturday evening using a high-powered rifle with a nightscope."

Frakes shook his head. "I haven't fired our gun like that in . . . a month of Sundays, nor has Donal to my knowledge. It was something we were trying to sell. You know, at the right price.

"And, look—I don't like Benny Carson. I never really cared for the man, and he blames me maybe rightly for his daughter's death. But I didn't try to kill him."

"What about Donal?"

"He was with me, right by my side at the mill all night long. He never left."

"So, who do you think murdered Pascal Burke and later the two Finns?"

Frakes tilted his head and eyed McGarr. "I can't prove it, and I don't know why he's involved. But I've thought about this, and I can tell you one thing. Where there's trouble and Benny Carson is around, he's behind it in some way or other. And he's behind this."

"Could he have got by you when you were laying the carpet?"

"Like I said, sure."

"Could one of the women who you saw or passed by have been Ellen Finn?"

"Maybe, but Ellen would have stopped in and said hello. The two of them had just been married and were happy as larks."

"I'm going to share something with you, and maybe you can help me out—right up until this morning we thought it was a woman who murdered Burke. The other murders were certainly orchestrated to cover up the first.

"You know the players. What women were involved with Burke enough to be in bed with him, enough to have a reason to kill him? Also, why would Carson involve himself in a cover-up? What did he have to gain? I'm trying to understand this."

"I wish we could smoke."

McGarr gestured with his head, and they walked out of the hospital and sat on the wall by the entrance.

"It could only have been Gertie. She'd do a deal with the devil. Or Carson. Didn't she bilk poor Tony Moran who—if he fancied anybody—it was Madame Sylvie."

"Zeebruge?"

Frakes nodded. "The inn lady. They were like brother and sister, the way they got on. But who ended up with all he had? Gertie."

"Tallon says Tony Moran was gay."

"What?" Frakes dropped his cigarette and ground it out under foot. "He wasn't Hulk Hogan, if that's what Tallon means, but Moran had the other approach—he was nice to them, bought presents, took them places and, I bet, suddenly he had them in bed before they even realized their knickers were off."

"Like Moira O'Rourke, the greengrocer?"

"Rumor had it a year or two ago that she went to England and aborted Moran's child. And that's what broke them up, not Madame Sylvie or Gertie McGurk. Up until then, everybody in Leixleap thought for sure Moran and she would get married."

"Moran and Moira O'Rourke."

Frakes nodded and accepted a second cigarette from McGarr.

"But after she came home he wouldn't even speak to her on the street."

"How'd he die?"

"Heart attack. Gertie's a great cook, and she had made him a big meal, but he couldn't eat it. He went into the next room, sat down, and signed off.

"Sylvie Zeebruge thought Gertie had poisoned him and demanded an autopsy, which was performed." Frakes shook his head. "Natural causes."

"A few months ago Pascal Burke had a will drawn up—"

"Don't tell me—naming Gertie."

McGarr waited.

Frakes tilted his head back and laughed. "She worked on that for at least a year, telling Burke that the only way she would ever consider moving in with him was if he put her in his will. But if he did, and he could prove it, she would. In her own way, she's . . . like, admirable, don't you think?"

Or, pernicious, thought McGarr. "What about Burke himself? I have it he was probably bedding Sylvie Zeebruge and certainly Moira O'Rourke. He was paying Gertie McGurk, and Grace O'Rourke tells me she's carrying his child."

"Really?" Frakes shook his head. "Now, that's a shocker. Grace O'Rourke? One thing about Pascal Burke—he was in no way a coward. Grace O'Rourke is bent, you know. She was in and out of the bin, I'm told, before Madame Sylvie gave her the maid job and as much as took her under her wing. Kept her even.

"As for Burke, Gertie and he would have made an excellent pair, birds of a feather. Both schemers and liars, with the difference that Burke never expected anything more than the sex.

"But he'd say and do anything, even spend more than he should to get that. Later, he'd have to deal with the problem of what he said, and I don't know how many times in the pub he entertained us with a tale of how he wriggled out of a promise to some widow or spinster.

"On a few occasions, women actually came in looking for him to have it out, like." Frakes again bent back his head and laughed. "He'd say, 'I know, dear. I'm wrong, darling. I've been so distracted, lately. Let me do thus and so. Here, have a drink. How can I make this up to you?'

"Then something like, 'Can't we go out to your car or up to my room and discuss it? This is no place for . . . intimacy.' All the while nodding or winking to us at the bar. Once, when the woman consented to go up to his room, we applauded the moment the door was closed."

McGarr considered that for a moment—Burke who had lived with his widowed mother all his life and without a doubt understood the needs, wants, fears, and fantasies of the middle-aged women he preyed upon.

"So, let me get this straight. In your scenario, Gertie does Burke for Carson, and Carson covers it up with the murder of the Finns to make it look like a double murder by an enraged husband, followed by his suicide?"

"Something like that."

"What does Gertie get?"

"What does the will say?"

"Twenty something thousand pounds, the flat in Dublin, and a cottage in West Cork."

"I'd say that's a decent pay packet for a millisecond of work."

"Yes, but what does Carson get?"

"Beyond my daughter?" Frakes shrugged.

# 20

# Check, Matey

"Do you think the Chief knows?" Bresnahan asked Ward, as they were leaving the Garda motor pool, where they picked up another car.

"Knows what?"

"Knows that we're back together."

Sitting in the passenger's seat, Ward's head swung to the window. "Rut'ie—I want you, I need you, I think I love you, but how can we possibly get back together? You know, permanently. I have a family."

"What about tonight? Tonight you don't have a family." As yet, she kept herself from adding, while feeling very much the part of a Jezebel.

"Ah, Rut'ie—it's wrong, and you know it, too."

"I know, I know"—she reached over and patted his thigh—"but you're weak." Which is why you're in this . . . pickle. "And you can't resist me." Which is why you'll have a family with me, too. And why we'll be yoked for life in the same way that you're yoked to the other woman, now being a *family* man. "And you shouldn't try.

"So, sit back, relax, enjoy the ride."

And the look of . . . was it, acceptance? Or terror. Was cheering. He even seemed to nod a bit, as Bresnahan swung out onto the N-4 and put the pedal to the metal.

McGarr also had to pick up another car, and it was dark by the time he pulled the Cortina through the archway that separated the two halves of Tim Tallon and Sylvie Zee-bruge's business.

The Leixleap Inn and Pub, half of which would soon be owned by Benny Carson.

And it occurred to McGarr that he did not know enough about their relationship in that regard. Who owned what?

Perhaps the information was contained in Tallon's safe, which Tallon had shut—out of habit, he had explained—when McGarr had entered Tallon's office the day before.

The public rooms of the inn were crowded with diners, and even the small bar was ringed by an angling party who were speaking animatedly about a large pike that one of them had landed.

And there Tim Tallon stood among them. "No, no— there's no question about the catch whatsoever," he was saying in a voice that carried out into the reception area. "It was a 'gaf,' " meaning a guide-assisted-fish. "And I want it mounted right there." Tallon pointed to a spot over the bar.

"What are y'talkin' about, man?" an obviously Scottish fisherman said back. "Ye were nowhere to be seen, when we pulled that leviathan into our boat ourselves."

"Yes, but who told you to fish there, and who told you what to fish with, and who came through with the net, I ask you."

McGarr stopped at the reception desk. "My wife and child come down yet?"

"Hours ago. They've eaten and returned to your rooms.

And you'd better hurry yourself. Full dinner service closes in a half hour."

But McGarr didn't feel like a big meal; in fact, he wasn't hungry at all, which was unusual for him in the evening. It was the case, of course, that was throwing him off his feed. He was missing the key element, what would put the tangled picture of Burke's relationships and motive for the three deaths together.

And so instead of going up to his rooms to see Noreen and Maddy, he got a drink at the bar—nodding to Tallon, who was still holding forth—and took it back to a seat in the foyer where he could see the stairwell up to the guest rooms and, in the other direction, down to the basement.

There he waited for a while, nursing the large drink and listening to the sounds coming to him from the dining and game rooms, the bar and reception area.

And it struck him that the rooms of the inn were much more accessible than the rooms of the pub, since anybody with a passkey could come and go at will and not be seen. The key could be had for the price of a room, and, like all keys, it was duplicable.

But once the pub was closed at—what? Officially at half eleven—but actually probably closer to 1:00 A.M. after cleanup and the totaling of receipts—then any guests, McGarr assumed, were out of luck. Nobody in his right mind would hand out keys to the front door of a pub. Not in Ireland.

But access to the rooms over the pub could be had through the archway. And both Sylvie Zeebruge and Grace O'Rourke had official keys, while Moira O'Rourke and Gertie McGurk had provided themselves with duplicates, the latter working the building as she did, with Tallon's acquiescence.

As for motives, for McGurk there was Burke's will, if she had known about it. For Grace O'Rourke it might have been pique that she was pregnant with his child yet he had just bedded her aunt and had been bedding—she knew from her position as maid—a raft of other women.

Moira O'Rourke, on the other hand, admitted to being on the scene and was desperate to land a husband, that much was plain. Could Burke have told her that he had no intention of marrying her and instead planned to move in with the younger McGurk?

And finally there was Sylvie Zeebruge, who—like Moira O'Rourke—had already lost a probable lover, Antony Moran, to McGurk. McGarr was willing to bet that Burke had bedded her, too; and during his interview with her, she had seemed truly saddened and dismissive of her "husband," Tallon. And who could blame her? Imagine being yoked to that piece of work, McGarr thought with a shudder. Tallon, he could see, was now at a table in the dining room, testing the patience of some other guests.

But McGarr did not think any one of the four women could have achieved the attempted cover-up of Burke's murder alone. Whoever had slain Burke had to have had help.

When the phone rang and the receptionist stepped into the dining room to fetch a guest, McGarr stood and moved to the stairwell, as though finally going up to his rooms. Instead, he stole down the stairs to the cellar.

It was almost hot there with the boilers and water heaters perking away, now that night had fallen. And, after jimmying the door to Tallon's office, McGarr switched on the lights and removed his jacket, before placing his ear against the cold cast iron of the old safe.

Perhaps twenty minutes later, the last of the tumblers clicked over, and McGarr, wrenching down the handle, swung the heavy door open.

In it, he found a raft of computer-generated data about the business: "Profits from Operating Revenues," "Profits Before Taxes," "Profits After Taxes," "Net Profits" all having separate accounting sheets that were stored neatly on shelves within the safe, Tallon being—to McGarr's surprise—very much the bean counter.

So much for local lore that had him a do-nothing gobshite while the wife ran the inn and Carson the pub. All the while Tallon had kept his eye on profits.

There were two strongboxes, the first of which took another few minutes to open. In it, McGarr found the several food-and-beverage licenses necessary to run both inn and pub, and each had been made out to, "S. Zeebruge, owner and permittee," six years earlier, as was the deed of the year before. Meaning Tallon, like Carson, had merely been a kind of manager.

And yet, when McGarr examined the back of the deed, there were two assignees named: "Benjamin J. Carson and Timothy P.J. Tallon in equal shares, for the consideration of 1,000,000 pounds." And the date of the assignment, was two—no, now three—days earlier, the date of the first two and possibly the third murder.

A contract, which was in the same folder as the deed, said that the payment of the sum, "owing to Sylvie Zeebruge in the amounts of 500,000 Irish pound apiece for Benjamin J. Carson and Timothy P.J. Tallon, will be paid as later arranged."

Sylvie Zeebruge had also signed that document, and McGarr checked the signature against her handwriting on the earlier licenses. They matched. None of the other documents had any bearing on the murders.

Replacing the documents, McGarr picked up the first of the two strongboxes in order to lock it again, when he felt something on the bottom. He turned it over and found a flat key secured by a length of strapping tape. A label on the flange said, "Gun case."

McGarr was about to peel the tape off, when he heard,

"You! Get out of that, I tell you!" And two strong hands fell upon his throat and wrenched him to his feet.

McGarr dropped the box and tried to peel the fingers away. But the hands were large and the grip strong, and he was driven, stumbling, into the desk, the chairs, the worktable with all its documents, lamps, and fax machine. The computer crashed to the floor, before McGarr—managing to gain his feet—doubled over and pulled his attacker onto his back.

Kicking a foot straight up with all he had, McGarr sank a heel deep into the man's groin, and with only the other foot holding both their weights, they began to fall.

Twisting his body as they tumbled forward, McGarr brought the force of his weight onto the other man's back, knocking the wind out of him. Suddenly, the hands were gone, and with everything he had, McGarr threw back an elbow, catching the side of the face and slamming the head into the floor.

Rolling over, McGarr got to his feet. It was Tallon.

"I'll have your job for this," Tallon managed to say, still sprawled by the overturned table.

McGarr's first attempt at speech failed. But finally in a hoarse whisper, he managed, "Not before you show me your gun case."

Taking the cell phone from his jacket, McGarr punched in Dublin and asked them to connect him to McKeon. "You with Carson?"

"Of course. He's standing right here on the other side of the bar."

"Meet me at Tallon's quarters on the fourth floor of the inn and bring Carson along."

McGarr had scarcely rung off, when the phone bleated. It was Ward, who had something to tell him.

\*        \*        \*

The chemist shop had just closed, when Ward and Bresnahan arrived. And they had to walk around to the living quarters in the rear.

Again, the Guptas were at tea, and, although invited to take seats at a large kitchen table where sat the family of five, they declined, Bresnahan saying, "Thank you, no—we'd just like to have Shila look at these pictures. Perhaps she could step outside with us for a moment."

Her father came, too, and in the light over the back door Bresnahan showed the girl first the photograph of Pascal Burke, then Quintan Finn, Manus and Donal Frakes, Benny Carson, and finally Tim Tallon.

"That's the man," said the girl.

"This could be very important. You're sure?"

"He has a belt with a large blue stone in it. Turquoise. The biggest stone of that sort I've ever seen."

"Shila has an interest in petrology," her father explained.

"And this woman," Ward showed the father a picture of Ellen Finn. "Do you recognize her? Has she ever been in your shop?"

The father shook his head; so, too, the daughter.

"What about this other woman?" Ward showed the father the picture of Gertie McGurk with Pascal Burke, the one where she had Burke's uniform cap on her head.

"No," said Gupta, smiling. "And I'd remember her, I'm sure."

The daughter had never seen McGurk either.

"Don't think this will go unreported," Tallon said at the door of his attic apartment on the fourth floor of the inn.

"I want all here to note that I'm opening this door only under duress. Only after I was beaten by this man."

"Stuff the blather, Tallon, and open the door," said Carson. "I'd like to see what these yokes have on you that's so important they've called me away from my tea."

But when Tallon inserted the key in the lock, he found that the door was open. "Ah, so—you've been in here, too, I take it, and bringing me here is just a ruse. Your way of covering another illegal entry."

The top drawer on one side of the large double-fronted gun case had been opened as well, and a stainless-steel rod that had been inserted through the trigger guards of the near dozen handguns stored there had been drawn back. A small key was still in its lock.

"Anything missing?" McGarr asked.

"You should know, because 'twas you who took it—a SIG-Sauer 225."

Which was a costly lightweight 9mm handgun.

"How many illegal searches did it take to find *that* key?" Tallon pointed to the key in the gun lock.

McGarr ignored him, pushing shut the top drawer and unlocking and searching the successive drawers on both sides of the case. In the bottom of the last, he found what he was looking for—a short-barrel target rifle equipped with a nightscope.

"It's Remington National Match," said McKeon, who had been a firearms instructor for part of his stint with the Irish Army. "A fine weapon that you can fit in the boot of your car. It must have set you back a few bob, Tallon."

Bending, McKeon picked up the rifle, holding it by the barrel and the very end of the butt. He sniffed the area around the bolt. "And fired recently, as well."

"Why do you need me for this foolishness?" Carson asked. "I've got a crowded bar downstairs."

"Who will miss you over the next few decades, I'm sure," said McGarr.

The small man only laughed slightly, his eyes bright. "You've got nothing on me."

McGarr pointed at the target rifle. "Of course, you know your *partner* here"—he swung his finger to Tallon—"tried to kill you the other night. It wasn't Frakes, was it, Tallon? It was you."

"Don't be absurd. I fired that gun at targets the other day out at the range in Athlone and just haven't had a chance to clean it, is all.

"And why ever would I want to shoot at Benny?"

"Because you're greedy, and you weren't satisfied with the half of this business that you and Carson extorted from your wife. *After* Carson bailed her and you out of the problem that would have lost your soft spot here as chief mouth and bull thrower."

The sparkle had gone from Carson's eyes, and he was now regarding Tallon with a look of assessment.

"And brilliantly, I must say," McGarr went on. "Since Carson's cover-up—had it been successful—would have put you two in the catbird's seat, and turned the tables for you, Tallon, with the 'wife' here at the inn.

"From cuckold and gobshite 'manager' to owner with a hold over your 'wife' that she wouldn't dare break."

Carson drew a packet of cigarettes from his pocket. "I'm paying five hundred thousand quid for my half of the business, and I have a contract to prove it."

"I saw it—to be paid 'as later arranged.' But there would be no arrangement, unless it was you arranging to turn her in if she demanded so much as a penny for the place."

"He's no proof—" Tallon began to say, before Carson spoke over him.

"The woman signed the bill of sale, the deed, and the transfer has been filed, my solicitor assures me."

"Didn't I explain it all to him yesterday?" Tallon put in.

"And whatever little problem Tom and I have can be worked out later." Lighting a fresh cigarette, Carson glanced up at Tallon, who avoided his stare.

"But your imaginative line of reasoning intrigues me, Chief Superintendent," Carson continued, blowing out the smoke. "And, Tim—it's always helpful to know where your attackers are coming from. So as not to be sniped at from afar, don't you know."

"Sounds like a veiled threat to me, Tallon," McKeon observed.

"Not at all, not at all. I'd never think of such a thing—me, a frail old man with only former jailbirds and loonies for friends.

"And Tim, boy, did you not hear what the Chief implied? That the 'wife,' our benefactress, plugged poor Pascal Burke. Bingo, right through the nut. Now, why ever would she do such a thing?" Carson gestured with the cigarette, pointing to McGarr's chest. "You to play, sir."

"Because she was enraged that Pascal Burke had returned from Dublin and sought out the company of another woman, and that other woman was Moira O'Rourke, who had taken Antony Moran away from her. Also, she knew that the O'Rourke woman was with Burke, having bumped into O'Rourke, who used the archway for access to Burke's room."

"You have proof of that?"

"They were seen arguing in the inn, early Friday afternoon." McGarr was guessing here; but who else could it have been?

"By whom, may I ask?"

"Your own Gertie McGurk."

"A witness who can be made to swear. Or perform in any way that you choose, for a price. Continue, please."

"After their 'session' was over, Burke fell asleep, and O'Rourke picked up her clothes and went into the toilet to dress and leave. That's when Sylvie Zeebruge entered the room with her passkey.

"Any noise she made wouldn't have awakened Burke, who would have thought it was Moira O'Rourke perhaps leaving or coming back for something that she'd left behind. Anyhow, he was through with her for the moment. And who else did he possibly have to fear with so many of the women in town virtually worshiping at his feet?

"Sylvie Zeebruge knew where his uniform and gun were, of course, having been in bed with him herself doubtless on numerous occasions. Also, she knew guns from an early age, her father having been a huntsman, and she a hunter herself.

"Taking the Glock from its holster, she moved to the bed and performed a kind of coup de grace on Burke—putting the philanderer out of the misery of his mid-life crisis. And ending her . . . pique, I'll call it, with him, men, and trying to find somebody special in her life different from you, Tallon."

Who had nothing to say for once.

"Why didn't she shoot Moira O'Rourke?" Carson asked.

"Because there was no sign of her, and the report of the unsilenced gun was loud. The killer panicked."

"I can't fathom how you concluded it's Madame Sylvie, who's the gentlest person. A veritable lamb."

"Because she left the scent of her perfume in the room, O'Rourke reported. Something she had never smelled before."

Carson began chuckling. "It could be she never smelled horseshit before either, 'stupor-intendent.' But I do at the present moment."

He turned to Tallon. "Tim, boy—you're the expert on fishing here. You should show this poor man how to do it properly."

"Sylvie returned to her room," McGarr continued, "and phoned you, Tallon. And when you got up to her room and were informed about what had happened, the two of you argued."

Said Carson, "Surely, that's another report from Gertie."

"No, Moira O'Rourke."

"Your ear-and-nose witness." Carson turned to Tallon. "Tim, this whole ball of wax gets better and better. We'll laugh about it in years to come, so we will."

"And you, Tallon—in a panic you rang up Carson here, who would know about such things as getting rid of bodies or covering up crimes, being experienced. You spoke at length and then met at the murder scene."

"To marvel at Pascal Burke's capacious mickey, which at last we got to see, don't you know."

"And you, Carson—having the knack—devised a plan so much in your self-interest that you would at once rid yourself of your hated son-in-law, gain custody of your granddaughter, and enrich yourself beyond the ken of any recently released professional convict. Suddenly, you'd have family, place, status, and steady money.

"Tallon, here, would also benefit immediately. He'd have the whip hand over the wife. And the purse. Convincing her must not have been hard for you either, Carson, with all your tales of life in the drum.

"And look at the alternative. If she goes up for Burke's murder, both of you are two old unemployed men, but at least you, Carson, wouldn't have been thrown out on the street."

Carson had lit yet another cigarette. With his thumb he picked at the filter. "Academically, now, with not an admission of the slightest bit of guilt, I ask you why didn't whoever tried to cover up Burke's murder simply go get Moira O'Rourke and have her death look like a suicide? Distraught, like, after having banged her banger?"

"Anybody even remotely acquainted with Moira O'Rourke would find that impossible to believe."

"Ah, now, Chief—you must know better than I—it happens. Women of that age with unrequited marital ambitions, why, nothing's beyond them. And Moira would probably have made note of that in a departing statement."

Said McKeon, "The question would have been how you could have managed her death at that moment with time running out. First, you would have had to find Moira O'Rourke. Second, you'd have had to get her into the room. Alive? Not after what she'd witnessed. And killing her someplace else would be messy at best.

"But Ellen Finn would surely come to the room, after being paged. She worked for Burke. And weren't Manus Frakes and her husband, Quintan, right there on the scene. And it all came to you, Benny—how you could put it together."

McGarr cut in. "You and Tallon, here, got her up to the room, and you knocked her out with a blow to the side of the head right when she was coming in the door, I bet. So it was you, Carson, who struck her, not his nibs here." McGarr's eyes swung to Tallon.

"Then the both of you stripped her, put the item of lingerie on her, and it took your combined strength to place her on top of him.

"Tallon—who couldn't watch and you wouldn't have wanted him to watch, since a graphic eyewitness in court whenever he cracked would damn you—was dispatched for the condoms and lubricant. And even that he bungled, selecting an out-of-the-way country chemist who's lucky to sell a packet a month.

"And we have a positive ID that it was you, Tallon, who bought them. The girl behind the counter will swear to that."

"Girl?" Carson asked. "How old a girl?"

"Fourteen."

"Another expert witness, Tim. Unimpugnable."

"She described you to a double B, Tim." McKeon pointed to Tallon's waist. "As in belt buckle. I wonder how many men in Ireland, who've been positively identified in a photograph, possess one of those?"

"And while Tallon was away," McGarr went on, "you completed the ugly business, Carson. You lined her head up with the wound in Burke's chest as well as you were able, and fired down. But it was a messy business nonetheless, and you had to get rid of a shirt and take the bold step, for a man used to years of living with only one change of clothes, of buying another."

"Isn't it amazing, Tim, how thorough the man is? Only three days in town, and he's been into everybody's closets."

Said McKeon, "There was your skill as a forger and raconteur with your tales to Peter and me of a long-term affair between Ellen and Burke.

"Being light on your feet, you even offered us Gertie McGurk, when informed that it was probably a woman who had murdered Burke. Didn't she live with the Frakes?"

As though tiring of the chat, Carson shook his head. "And I suppose you're going to throw Quintan's suicide into the mix?"

McGarr only waited.

"Why would anybody murder his nephew? The son of the sister whose husband had been so good to him?"

"To deflect suspicion, since only a total surd—the term you used when speaking of Donal Frakes, if you remember—would murder his sister's son. But who else could more easily have got him drunk and suggested a reconnaissance of the Shannon than you, his uncle?

"Did you get more blood on that shirt, holding Quintan's hand on the gun and pulling the trigger? Or those spiffy bar jackets?" McGarr pointed to the Prussian blue uniform coat that Carson was wearing. "I bet if we were to conduct an inventory we'd find one shy."

"Aren't they shy altogether, Tim?" Carson asked. "Always walking out of here whenever your back is turned. Didn't you stop in for a wet at a bar in Athlone the other day, and find a barman wearing one and bragging about having ripped it off?"

Without raising his eyes from the floor, Tallon nodded. "That's true."

"What's also true," McGarr went on, "is that murderers, like you two, always try too hard. In addition to the condoms, there was all the nightwear stuffed into the drawers of Ellen Finn's dresser. She was a small woman.

"The items you added had been purchased by a tall, big-chested woman, somebody about the size of Gertie McGurk. Which worked for you, as long as McGurk was a suspect. It was more of the clever touch, wasn't it Carson? In case the thick Guards sent down from Dublin got that far.

"But Gertie McGurk has no need for underwire cups, not with implants."

"Come, Tom—we don't have to listen to his salacious suppositions regarding women's breasts, artificial or otherwise. Trust me—they don't have enough evidence to charge a soul, and they should be after the Frakes and their whore, what done the crime." Carson stepped toward the door.

But Tallon did not move.

"Curiously, Mr. Tallon doesn't seem to want your company, Benny," said McKeon.

"And then, his rifle and he are coming to Dublin with us. For openers we'd like to discuss why he tried to kill you and fired at me. One bullet that passed through the shattered windscreen struck the cushion of a seat and is still intact. Also, there's the matter of the condoms.

"Know what, Tallon? I'll bet anything what I said earlier

is right—you didn't fire the shot that killed Ellen Finn, and you had no part either in Burke's death or Quintan Finn's supposed suicide.

"All you did was try to help out your wife, and Carson here took the ball from you and ran with it. Murdering Ellen and Quintan Finn was his idea from square one, and he carried out both murders.

"The condoms, the underwear—all his," McKeon added. "As only an accessory, who willingly cooperates with the police, there might still be a few good years left for fishing on the river."

"Don't listen to them, Tim. Come with me," Carson insisted. "We'll ring up that solicitor of ours. They're reaching. They can't pull us in for a packet of condoms and a spent bullet."

Carson now had a hand on the doorknob, and the three other men watched as Tallon's eyes searched the carpet on the floor, trying to decide.

Finally, his head came up with his jaw squared. "Right you are, Benny. Imagine these gobshites trying to drive a wedge between me and the wife, and now me and you. There's nothing they won't do.

"McGarr—as I observed the other day—you were a bastard then, and you're a bastard now. I'm done with you. That's the end of our friendship."

"Good lad," Carson cheered, opening the door.

In it stood Sylvie Zeebruge with arms raised and something in her hands. A gun.

"No!" McGarr roared, reaching for his weapon.

But the first shot struck Tallon, like a punch, driving him back into the room, and a second and a third slammed him down into the carpet.

And as she swung the gun at Carson, McGarr and McKeon fired simultaneously again and again, virtually pinning the woman to the wall of the hallway behind her. As she slumped down, the gun fell from her hands.

Quickly, McGarr was by her side, while McKeon tended to Tallon. But if she wasn't already dead, she would be, McGarr could see. She would not survive the many wounds clustered on her chest.

"Ah, Christ," said McKeon, kneeling over Tallon. "Right between the eyes."

Carson's plain black brogues—prison issue, McGarr decided, and much like the shoes of Guards and priests—now appeared where McGarr was squatting beside Sylvie Zeebruge.

"Looks like check and mate to me, Chief Superintendent, and I hope you're a good loser. I also commend you for your marksmanship. They train you well. In that."

Carson turned toward the stairs. "You know where to find me. I promise I won't go anywhere. And you can ask me any class of thing here, down in the bar, in Dublin, if you like. Polygraph. Affidavits. I'm always available. I'll answer your call."

McGarr rose from Sylvie Zeebruge's corpse and followed Carson toward the stairs. "It's not my call you'll be answering. I'm washing my hands of you."

Stopping at the top of the stairs, Carson turned to him.

Cell phone in hand, McGarr punched in his Dublin office. "Put me through to a Dermot Finn, who has a Leixleap phone number."

"My brother-in-law? You wouldn't. I'll go to the barracks and demand protection." For the first time, Carson looked worried; his face was drawn, his eyes narrowed.

"On second thought, while you're looking for Finn's number get me Declan Riley at the Leixleap barracks."

"I'll go to your Commissioner."

McGarr covered the speaker of the phone, "Who'll be certain to listen to you, a convicted cop killer twice over. Count on me to tell him."

"But I have the child to take care of. Think of her."

"She has her father."

"Who'll be in jail."

It was McGarr's turn to smile. "Perhaps. But, as I remember, Manus never fired a weapon, and the most I'll see him charged with is the destruction of public property. Given the promise of restitution and a good word from me, he might not have to do any time whatsoever.

"And speaking of restitution—could your sister Honora Finn be your closest relative? One of them, I should imagine. Wouldn't it be poetic justice if she ended up with this place?

"Granted, it's no substitute for a son, a daughter-in-law, and a grandchild, whom you stole from her. But it's better than nothing."

"You may as well shoot me now." Carson's hand moved to the placket of his pale blue barman's coat.

"Gladly," said McGarr, pulling his Walther from its holster. "But you're not stupid. You have no gun. And this will be the better way for everyone involved, especially the Finns. It will give them greater . . . closure, I think the word is."

"Declan," McGarr said into the phone, "would you know where Dermot Finn is at the moment?" McGarr listened for a while, then, "Why don't you swing by and pick me up. I'd like a word with Finn, in private."

Carson started down the stairs. "Don't expect me to roll over on this, McGarr. Forewarned is forearmed. And I'll not die because of your illegality." He disappeared around the newel post.

# Epilogue

Several months later, McGarr, McKeon, Ward, and Bresnahan were returning to Dublin along the N-6 that passes over the Shannon at Athlone, and McGarr suggested they drop downriver to Leixleap for dinner. "My treat. As I remember, the food was quite good."

"And sights better, we hear," McKeon put in. Earlier in the week, McGarr had received a phone call—one of several recent updates—from Sergeant Declan Riley concerning the status of what amounted to the Benny Carson-Dermot Finn standoff.

It seemed that every night since Tim Tallon and Sylvie Zeebruge had died and McGarr had spoken to Dermot Finn in private, Finn had appeared in the pub or inn—the control of which Carson had assumed until the estates of the deceased could be settled—and purchased a drink.

Nursing it the night long, Finn only stared at Carson, his eye following the man wherever he went. Carson complained first to Riley, who said he could do nothing. "It's a public place, and you're open for custom."

Later, Carson had gone to court. But with Finn being a

blameless citizen, who had neither said nor done anything injurious to Carson—Riley himself had testified—the suit was dismissed.

And Carson kept languishing under Finn's "Gorgon gaze," Riley called it, relishing every passing moment. "The son of a bitch was always gaunt, but now he's a rail—sunken eyes and his bones mere hanging points for the blue jacket, don't you know.

"Sure, it's slow torture, but I only hope he doesn't die in his sleep."

McGarr, who was sitting in the back of the car with McKeon, tapped Ward on the shoulder. "Ring up Riley and ask him to join us at the inn."

It was spring now, and the days were growing longer. At twilight they crossed over the Shannon with Leixleap before them on the other bank, looking like a storybook village.

Perched on a bluff, its riverfront wall and neat rows of shops—dominated by the spire of the church and the eminence of the great stone inn, every window of which was lighted—were cast in a soft mauve light. Below, the Shannon rolled toward the sea, black and slick as obsidian.

But no Carson was in sight either in the pub where the four Dubliners stopped for a jar, or in the inn where McGarr gave his name to the receptionist for the first available table. "There'll be five of us."

"And how have you been keeping, Chief Superintendent?"

"Respectably."

"Which is all that can be asked these days, please God," said the woman with some feeling.

"And your new boss, how's he?"

The woman's eyes told the story.

"I don't see him. Is he about?"

"Down in the office, I suspect. He doesn't spend much time up here." Her head swung toward the small bar, where sat Dermot Finn apart from the group of obvious anglers who were regaling themselves there.

Riley joined McGarr and the others for a drink, saying, "I can't imagine how it happened, but now the whole county knows. And Carson is a pariah. People see him coming, and they cross the street. The shopkeepers, even—they hang up if he calls. If he stops in, they treat him as though he wasn't there.

"All this stuff"—Riley raised his glass—"the food in the kitchen, the sheets on the beds Carson has to order in from outside. And if Finn himself doesn't put him down, sooner or later somebody else will and properly." Riley's eyes met McGarr's for a brief but telling moment.

With that, the aging sergeant finished his drink and excused himself. "The missus would never understand how I could eat here with him in charge. But don't let that ruin your meal. The chef stayed on, and the fare is the same."

And excellent, when it arrived.

McGarr began with smoked eel and rambled on to spring trout poached in white wine with apples Charlotte for desert, an espresso, and a snifter of piquant Calvados, since he was not driving.

And it was only when the digestifs arrived that he noticed that Bresnahan was not having one. In fact, he now realized that he had not seen her take a drink in some time.

Perhaps she was on a diet, he reasoned, since her face seemed fuller, and she had taken to wearing rather loose clothing of late. "Aren't you having anything, Rut'ie?"

There was a pause in which Bresnahan seemed to have to gather herself. "No, thank you, Chief, and there's something I have to tell you."

"Let me," said Ward. "Ruth is pregnant and will have our baby in August."

McGarr glanced at Bresnahan, who nodded and attempted a smile of happy guilt.

"But, Hughie," McKeon blurted out, "didn't you just have a baby by"—but thought better of it and instead reached for his glass.

"And Hughie and I were wondering if you think it's a . . . deal-breaker."

The deal having been don't-ask-don't-tell, during the years in which Bresnahan and Ward had been a couple, "fraternizing" being strictly forbidden by Garda policy.

"We were thinking that, after I had the baby, I'd come back to the Squad, since whose business is it anyhow, as long as Hughie and I are agreed."

McKeon, who was as conservative in matters domestic as criminal, couldn't help himself. "What about Leah? I hope you're not going to abandon your kids by her. What does she have to say about this?"

"She's all right with it as well," said Ward.

"You've spoken to her?"

Ward nodded. "She's happy for us."

"You're coddin' me. That's bigamy."

"No, Bernie. Hughie and Leah aren't married," Bresnahan advised.

"But, then, aren't you two going to get married?"

Bresnahan and Ward both shook their heads.

"Where will you live?"

"I'll move into Hughie's place. It's big, and my mother will come up from the country to baby-sit, when I come back to work. *If* I come back to work." Her eyes drifted to McGarr.

"But where will you live?" McKeon asked Ward.

"Both places. The three of us will work it out."

McKeon had to think about that. Finally, he said, "Well— times certainly have changed. Waiter!"

All eyes then turned to McGarr, who had decided years before that he would hate to lose either of his two able junior staffers and had turned a blind eye to their former liaison.

And then—he thought—wasn't it said that Brian Boru, Ireland's legendary chieftain, had twenty-eight children by a number of women including his official wife, and when it came time to name a successor, he chose one of his bastards and not a legitimate son.

Also, Bresnahan and Ward had chosen the proper moment to drop their bombshell, since the excellent meal and brandy had imparted a glow to McGarr. And now the sight of Carson, who had appeared in the door of the dining room, warmed him further. "We'll see by and by."

Which cheered Bresnahan and Ward, who clenched hands beneath the table. It was the most they could expect from the man who could not acknowledge or be seen to be complicit in their arrangement.

Said McKeon, rising to go out to the bar, "I'm going to pretend that I didn't hear any of this." But he, too, now noticed Carson, and he sat back down. "My God, don't he look like death warmed over."

Not having seen them and studiously avoiding looking into the bar, Carson was moving from one table to another, nodding to his guests and inquiring after the state of meals and drinks. And when, finally, he caught sight of McGarr and company, he called over a waiter and said something, before disappearing back downstairs.

Shortly thereafter, a bottle of Calvados and four glasses were delivered to the table. Where they were left.

More than a half year later on a brilliant day in fall with high bright skies and warm winds from the south, McGarr had only arrived in his office in Dublin Castle when he received a phone call from Declan Riley.

"It's about our man, Benny Carson. Wasn't he found this morning newly dead, drowned in a pit of slurry."

McGarr turned and looked out the open window into Dame Street that was crowded with commuters and tourists at the early hour. "At one of Dermot Finn's fertilizer operations?"

"Aye. But the lucky part is, Finn and Honora have been in Spain a fortnight now, and in their absence Carson had closed the inn and was selling off everything not nailed down to some Dublin furniture broker. But I guess that's off now."

"Who found him?"

"Wasn't it meself who did—out for a bit of a walk with the dog early in the morning."

"Down by a slurry pit."

"The vapors are good for the chest, I'm told. And strange how he was situated when I came upon him.

"Those big rakes that they use to spread the excrement around? Carson must have grabbed for it when he lost his footing and fell. He had it pressed tight to his chest, mouth and eyes open like in shock that he had come to such an end. A few inches under the surface of a pool of shit. Pity he couldn't swim."

"Is it anything that might call for my attention?" McGarr asked.

"Ach, no—don't trouble yourself. He was foolish to be wandering out there in the middle of the night."

"Then, I take it it's a death by misadventure."

"Precisely. I'll mark that down in my report, and my best to the missus and your gang. I'll tell you one thing—it's a grand day down here entirely."

"Brilliant altogether," McGarr echoed, ringing off.

"Rut'ie," he called out from his cubicle, "get Noreen on the phone, I have some news."

Without any of the difficulty that she had experienced throughout the summer, Bresnahan popped up from her desk and appeared in the doorway of the cubicle.

"I will, of course, Chief. But first, the news."